The Stepney Feud

Carol Hellier

This is a work of fiction. Names, characters, places, and incidents are either the product of the author's imagination or are used factiously, and any resemblance to actual persons, living or dead, business establishments, events or locales is entirely coincidental.

Cover Design
Francessca Wingfield @ Wingfield Designs

Formatting
TBR Editing & Design

For my beautiful grandchildren. Each one a gift from above. There is nothing so precious as family.

And to my niece, Lauren Ashley Rose Hellier, who sadly took her own life on the 15/09/2022 ....
We all miss you angel.

SAMARITANS HELP LINE: 116 123

CAMPAIGN AGAINST LIVING MISERABLY (CALM): 0800585858

PAPYRUS – PREVENTION OF YOUNG SUICIDE: 0800 068 41 41

SOS SILENCE OF SUICIDE: 0300 1020 505

DON'T LET SOMEONE WHO DOESN'T
KNOW YOUR VALUE
TELL YOU HOW MUCH YOU ARE WORTH.

Prologue

19 November 1951

The woman carried the new-born baby girl tightly in her arms, as she headed towards her destination. The night air was colder than usual. The weatherman on the radio had said to expect snow. Would the baby freeze to death? Maybe that would be best for all concerned, she decided. Without hesitation she climbed the three steps to the children's home and laid the tiny bundle at the door. Her heart rate had increased at the thought of being caught and her hands trembled slightly, she told herself it was because of the cold. She watched as the baby wriggled, ashamed that she felt nothing. After tucking a white rabbit into the blanket, she left a note with the baby's first name. Why, she wasn't sure. Maybe it was to soften the guilt she felt, the guilt that would only worsen over the years. She shook the thoughts from her mind as she banged loudly on the door. Immediately a light came on. The woman then turned on her toes and ran away without looking back.

Chapter One

September 1975

Millie's knuckles turned white as she gripped the edge of the seat. "Levi the light's red!" She turned towards her husband and was greeted with a sneer.

"Levi the light's red!" He mimicked in a whiny voice. "Stop fucking moaning, you always ruin a good night out. Next time...."

"LOOK OUT!" Millie screamed cutting him off. The impact shunted her towards Levi. Her hair whipped around her face as she was tossed around like a rag doll, despite the seat belt holding her in place. The sound of crunching metal filled her head and then the windows exploded. Glass shards flew around the pickup truck, hitting Millie's hands and face. Her head collided with the passenger door and then everything went black.

Millie slowly opened her eyes to the sound of screaming. She moved her hand over towards the driver's seat, as she felt around for Levi. "Levi?" She called through the pain. "Levi. I can smell petrol. We need to get out." Millie pulled at the seat belt that was digging into her chest. "Levi.... Levi I'm stuck.... Help. Someone help me." Millie's heart pounded in her chest as though it was trying to escape her body. "Someone help me.... Please." Millie faded into darkness once again.

* * *

Millie could hear the distant sound of sirens, they were getting closer, but everything was still black, she slowly began to open her eyes and tried to focus but everything was hazy. The noise around her was building, screams mixed with sirens. Tyres screeching to a halt. She could hear people running. The noise cut threw her head like a chainsaw. She squeezed her eyes shut to blot it out.

"Over here." She heard the male voice shout. "Check the driver while I check the passenger."

Millie opened her eyes and turned towards the voice. She stared at two legs; it was then she realised she was hanging upside down. Her chest tightened as she fought for air. She clawed at the seatbelt as her eyes grew wide. "Help me." She mumbled through the pain.

"Shhh, stay calm. We are going to get you out, but first I need to check you over.... Now miss, what's your name?" Millie watched as the man pulled at the twisted door, but it wouldn't open.

The tightness in Millie's chest worsened as she struggled to breath. "I don't feel right, I'm...." Millie went silent.

* * *

Millie woke to the sound of beeping. She could hear someone speaking, but she couldn't understand what they were saying. She groaned as she lifted her head up, inches from the pillow and then flopped back down. Her head hurt. She closed her eyes for a moment, trying to remember where she was. The smell of disinfectant hit her, making her feel sick. She could taste the bile in her mouth, so she swallowed it down. She raised a shaky hand to her head to soothe the pain and felt a bandage. As she moved her hand further, she discovered the bandage was wrapped around her head.

"Millie?" A gentle voice questioned.

Millie opened her eyes and turned her head to where it had come from. A man in a white coat was standing beside her, smiling. "I need to get home." Attempting to lift her head again she let out a pained sigh. She realised it wasn't only her head that hurt but in fact her whole body.

"You're not going anywhere just yet Millie. You are in hospital.... Do you remember what happened?"

Millie followed the doctors' eyes to a monitor, immediately her chest tightened, and her breathing became faster.

"It's okay, take a couple of long slow breaths, like this." The doctor told her as he checked her pulse.

Millie watched the doctor breath in through his nose and then out through his mouth. She attempted to do the same and relaxed a little.

"It's okay Millie, you're going to be okay.... Now can you tell me how old you are?"

"I'm twenty-three." Millie replied as she watched the doctor nod, like he was giving her his approval.

"Can you remember what happened to you?"

Millie fought the foggy haze clouding her mind, willing herself to remember. "Pub. I was.... We were.... Where's Levi?" Millie watched as the doctor looked over to a nurse, who was standing at the end of the bed. Neither answered. "Where is he. Where's my husband?" Millie noticed the doctor freeze for a second before he seemed to compose himself. "What aren't you telling me?"

"Millie, we need to concentrate on you first, you've been drifting in and out of consciousness since you arrived here. Most likely because of the nasty cut on your head. Its caused a concussion however all your vital signs have remained good throughout and I'm pleased with your recovery. Now I need you to stay calm. Are you hungry?"

"I don't know.... My throats dry." Millie shifted slightly in the bed. "Ouch. I feel like I've been hit by a bus, everything hurts."

"You did take quite a battering, but most of it is superficial. God was certainly smiling down on you that night... Nurse can you get Millie some water please.... There's two police officers here that need to speak to you. I just need to check you over before I can allow them in. We can discuss your husband after." Holding Millie's left eye open, he shone a tiny light into it and then did the same to the right one. "Your reflex actions are good. Do you remember what happened to you?"

"I already told you, we were in the pub." Millie turned her head and looked at the window, the sky looked dark and stormy. "How long have I been here?"

"Three days Millie."

Millie frowned. "Three days.... How did I get from the pub to here, and why isn't my husband here?" Millie noticed the doctor breathe a sigh of relief as the nurse came back.

"Ahh here we are, take small sips of water, otherwise you may feel sick." The doctor advised her.

Millie sipped the cold water as the nurse held the cup to her mouth, when done she pushed the cup away. "So, what happened to me, was I attacked?"

"We can discuss everything later. I'm going to see the police officers now; they will be in shortly. I will accompany them, so I don't want you to worry. If at any point I feel you can't continue, I will ask them to leave. Okay?"

Millie nodded to the doctor and watched him walk out of the room with the nurse following him. She could hear their voices as they rose in anger and listened intently in the hope that she might learn what had happened to herself. The doctor seemed to be sticking up for her. She suddenly heard the word Inspector. Millie thought they were just normal old bill. Something big must have happened. She held her breath as the doctor entered the room with the two suited police Inspectors then pulled the covers up, in a feeble attempt to protect herself. From what, she wasn't quite sure.

"Millie. This is Inspector Lodge, and this is Inspector Rhymes. They are going to ask you a few questions, while I observe."

Millie's eyes darted between the two men. They didn't look friendly to her, but then she had never got on with the old bill. Levi was always getting into trouble, so the police were regular visitors at home.

"Millie. It is okay if we call you Millie?" Lodge asked.

Millie nodded slowly before replying. "Yes of course. Am I in trouble?" Millie noticed Lodge had a twitch in his right eye, every so often it would blink while the other remained open.

"No, not at all. We just need a little help to figure out what happened. Now what do you remember from the night of the 3rd of September?"

"When.... I don't know when that was." Millie looked at the doctor as the tears formed in her eyes.

"It's fine Millie. What the Inspector meant to ask was, what are your last memories before waking up here?"

Millie felt the doctors hand grip hers and felt grateful for the small comfort it gave her.

"No one can hurt you here Millie. Remember that." The doctor told her.

Millie turned back towards Lodge; she would address him as he did all the talking. "I.... We were in the pub."

Before Millie could continue, Lodge cut in. "Who's we?"

"My husband and myself. It was his cousin's birthday, so everyone was celebrating. The pub was packed.... I spilt my drink and Levi got mad at me." Millie shook her head. "I'm clumsy." Millie thought back to the way Levi had grabbed her arm and yanked her up out of her seat.

"Then what happened?" This time Rhymes asked impatiently.

"Levi took me home."

"Were you drunk Millie?" Lodge looked at the doctor before continuing. "Was Levi drunk?"

"I don't drink, inspector. Levi doesn't like it…, As for him, I really couldn't say. You would have to ask him. In fact, I want to see my husband now and I'll ask him. Where is he?" Millie watched as Lodge and Rhymes looked at each other, both raising their eyebrows. "What's going on, where is he. Tell me!"

"Millie calm down." The doctor replied. "I'm sorry inspectors, can we do this later?"

"Doctor not only did three people die in that car crash. In the dashboard of Levi's pickup truck, we found a large amount of Cocaine. So, no. We can't do this later."

Rhymes stood and lent over Millie. "You will tell us everything you know, and you will tell us now."

Millie's eyes went wide. "Dead. Cocaine?" She repeated through shallow breaths. As she tried to move away from the Inspector the doctor bellowed, causing her to jump.

"SIT DOWN INSPECTOR." Once Rhymes had taken his seat the doctor continued. "Millie's memory has not fully recovered from the crash, it may take days, even months before she can remember everything, and this little charade isn't helpful to her recovery. Just look at her. Surely you can see she's scared and confused. Now I must ask you to leave."

The noise of Rhymes' chair as it scraped back caused Millie to flinch. She noticed all three men were staring at her. Millie closed her eyes, her body started to shake. The Inspectors words played over in her mind. *Three dead in the crash. Cocaine in Levi's pickup.* Millie opened her eyes as she listened to the raised voices outside her door.

"So, you have no idea when her memory will be restored?" Millie heard Lodge ask.

"I feel there's far more going on than what we know. Millie is malnourished, she also has a lot of old injuries to her body. When we x-rayed her there showed old fractures. Two to her left wrist and one to her pelvis. Also, she has some nasty bruises on her abdomen. These are most definitely pre-accident."

Millie covered her ears with her hands and closed her eyes to blot out the doctors' words, but it was too late, she was there.

Millie was suddenly back in her mothers-in-laws kitchen; she was curled up in a ball on the floor, as she tried desperately to protect herself from the punches Levi was raining down on her. She let out a scream as she felt her wrist crack.... That was the first fracture.

Millie opened her eyes and let out a sob. It never worked when she tried to blot the past out. She knew that. Every night in her dreams, she relived the horrors. Millie refocused on the doctors' voice; he was still talking.

"All I'm saying is the evidence speaks for itself. It could have been her husband; the old bruises would point to him or another family member. However, the old fractures could have been years ago. She grew up in a children's home. Unfortunately, it's easy for accidents to happen in places like that and never be reported. Now I really must get on with my rounds Inspectors. I will contact you if there's a breakthrough with her memory."

Millie watched the door. Her heart rate had increased as she had listened to the list of her injuries. The flash backs danced in her mind as if they were happening now. She felt the perspiration cover her body as the blows rained down on her. "NO!" She cried out. Millie rolled up into a ball, covering her head with her arms. Through her tears she saw the doctor run in.

"Millie.... Millie look at me. Christ child, who did this to you?"

Chapter Two

Millie sat, propped up, in the hospital bed, while her best friend Rosie, sat perched on the edge. The smell of cabbage had replaced the smell of disinfectant and Millie couldn't decide which she hated the most. She listened to the busy footsteps of the nurses and the continual hum of voices. She wished she could blot them all out. Her head still hurt even though she had taken painkillers an hour before.

"It's good to see you awake Mil, I came in this morning, but they wouldn't let me see you. They said you were too upset after the Police visit yesterday, "said Rosie..

Millie looked up as a nurse walked by. It was the same nurse that had comforted her yesterday after the Police visit. Millie smiled as the nurse waved, before she continued on her way. "Don't remind me.... They said three people died in the car crash. I remember leaving the pub, but I don't remember getting into Levi's pickup.... And where is Levi? Why hasn't he been in to see me?"

"Maybe he's here, as a patient?" Rosie shrugged. "Do you really care? I know I don't."

"He's my husband Rose." Millie sighed. "Maybe you could ask at the front desk?"

Before Rosie replied the doctor walked in. "Millie. You're looking much better this afternoon. Did you manage to eat something?" He grabbed the chart from the end of her bed and studied it for a moment.

"Yes, thank you." Millie watched the doctor's face closely as he nodded.

"Jolly good." The doctor then replaced the notes at the end of the bed and turned to walk away.

"Get some rest, I'll go and see if I can find anything out. I'll be back in a bit." Rosie jumped up and pecked Millie on the cheek then marched out of the room.

Millie smiled to herself. Rosie was on a mission. She rested her head back against the pillow and closed her eyes. She tried to focus back on that night. They had left the pub because she had spilt her drink. Levi was angry, he had pushed her into the pickup after calling her a useless.... Millie shook her head; she hated the c word. He often called her that, amongst other things. So, they were in the pickup. Levi pulled away fast, causing the wheels to spin. Millie could remember gripping the seat.

"Millie. I've got dinner for you. Look, beef stew and dumplings and then for dessert we have jam roly-poly and custard. We'll have you built up in no time. Now how do you like your tea?" The woman placed the tray onto the table and pushed it over the bed.

"One sugar please." Millie smiled, despite not being hungry. "I did have some toast a little while ago."

"That was three hours ago. You need to eat, build your strength up so you can go home." The woman placed the cup of tea down onto the table and smiled. "I'll come back and collect the plates in a little while."

Millie picked the knife and fork up and looked down at the plate. There was a heap of cabbage piled up, taking up almost a third of it. She pushed it to the side and then started to eat. The beef was a bit chewy, so Millie left most of that, however the dumplings were mouthwatering with the gravy covering them. It had been a long time since she had eaten a hot meal. Mainly she lived on the odd sandwich or piece of toast. That was the trouble when you lived with your in-laws. The kitchen wasn't yours, it was your mother-in-laws, and her mother-in-law, the great Flo Cooper, didn't like to share, and that included her son.

A short while later Millie placed the knife and fork down onto the plate and rubbed her tummy. She had eaten too much. As she reached for the jam roly-poly the door opened again, but instead of seeing the dinner lady she saw Rosie and the doctor enter. "What are you doing back so soon?"

"The doctor wants to talk to you." Rosie replied.

Millie felt the bed move, as Rosie sat on the edge of it, and grabbed her hand. Her body immediately tensed, and she felt her eyes water. She knew she wasn't going to like this.

The doctor pulled over a chair and then sat down, clearing his throat as he did so. "Millie.... We need to talk about the accident and your husband."

"Can we talk about my husband first. Like where is he?" Millie watched as the doctor glanced at Rosie.

"Can you look at me please and I'd like an answer." Agitated, Millie pushed the table away as she looked down at the swirling strawberry jam in the middle of the suet pudding. It reminded her of something. "Red."

"What?" Rosie asked.

"Red.... The light was red. Oh My God! Levi went through a red light. He killed those people." Millie saw the flashback. The way she was shunted to the side of the car, the glass splintering. She started to cry. "Levi killed those people. Is that where he is, in prison?"

"Millie, Levi isn't in prison.... He was one of the three, he's dead." The doctor answered.

All the colour drained from Millie's face. "No. No people like him don't die." Millie felt the bile hit the back of her throat. Leaning over the side of the bed, she brought up all her dinner.. The wave of sickness continued until the retching subsided and there was nothing left for her to bring up. She wiped her mouth on the back of her hand and looked at Rosie.

Rosie's face looked sombre as she shook her head from side to side. "I'm sorry Millie."

Breaking down, Millie started to cry. Her high-pitched screams filled the room. "What.... Am. Am I.... going to do without him." She managed between sobs.

"You are going to live a long and happy life. Look at me.... Millie, I said, look at me!" Millie felt Rosie's hands on her shoulders. "No more injuries Millie. No more being scared of saying the wrong thing. No more lying to people about the black eyes.... Millie, your life starts today."

"You don't understand." Millie looked at Rosie with pleading eyes before collapsing into her arms.

"I do, I really do. I know you loved him. Sshhh, it's going to be okay." Rosie whispered.

The doctor rested his hand on Millie's shoulder. "I'll prescribe a sedative."

"Thank you doctor." Rosie replied.

Millie sobbed louder; how could she tell her friend the truth? She knew Flo would never let her go, after all, with Levi gone Millie was now her meal ticket.

Chapter Three

Paul Kelly stood up as he wiped the blood splatter from his cheek. He turned to face Jamie Carter, his business partner. Paul's temper was starting to boil over. "Are you at any point gonna get your fucking hands dirty, or are you just gonna stand there looking all pretty?" Picking up a foot, Paul threw it into the plastic bag, along with the rest of the dismembered body parts. He glared at Jamie, as he slid down his blood-soaked overalls and stepped out of them. As he threw them into the bag, Paul rolled his eyes as he looked down and saw his latest victim's eyes looking back at him. "Fucking druggies." He mumbled under his breath. Focusing back on Jamie he waited for a reply even though he already knew the answer. Jamie Carter never got his hands dirty.

Paul gritted his teeth as he heard Jamie laugh. "You don't need to get your hands dirty, we've got enough men on the payroll." Jamie replied cockily.

Paul grinned when he noticed Jamie looking down at his shoes.

"You've got blood on my shoes. You do know how much these cost me?" Jamie moaned.

Paul ignored his whining voice and continued. "Certain jobs call for discretion James, or is that too hard for you to comprehend? We've got some toerag druggie on our turf, thinking they can get away with robbing my premises which is costing us both money, and you're okay with that? Well, I'm not and to be honest, I find it strange that you are."

"I didn't say I was okay with it...." Jamie mumbled.

Paul sighed and took one last look around his warehouse, and in particular, the plastic sheeting that was now bloodstained, he picked up the bag and threw it over his shoulder with a grunt at the weight. As he walked towards the exit, he called over his shoulder to Jamie. "You can clean this mess up; I'll get rid of him." Ignoring Jamie's protest, Paul Kelly left the building, laughing to himself. He kicked the door shut behind him as he made his way outside into the fresh air. He took a deep breath to clear his nose of the metallic smell, which was the only bit he didn't like. The smell, you could even taste it at times when there was a lot of blood splatter.

It was now daylight and the rain had finally stopped, but there was still a nip in the air. Paul attempted to unlock the boot while struggling to hold the bag over his shoulder, he struggled until the key slipped from his grasp and fell to the floor. He let out a loud sigh and looked around, briefly checking he was still alone. Satisfied he dropped the bag and picked up the key. Once he had opened the boot, Paul placed the dismembered body parts into his old beat-up bottle green Vauxhall. He cursed as he tried to close the lid. He had to smash it down three times before it stayed shut. As he walked to the driver's side, he took a closer look at the tired bodywork. It had seen better days, the car looked more fitting for the scrapyard than the road. Jamie wouldn't even sit in it. He often moaned that the motor was beneath both of their social standing. That was the difference between them. Paul knew the motors' real worth, the bodies it had moved without detection from the old bill was priceless.

The drive only took thirty minutes, which was just enough time for him to calm down. Paul was a grafter, unlike Jamie, always had been. He wanted to make something of his life. He wanted respect, which was something lacking as he grew up. His Mum and dad had come over from Ireland as newlyweds. There was a stigma to the Irish back then. So Paul worked hard to make something of himself. All that was lacking in his life now was the love of a good woman, kids, and a lovely home. Paul smiled at the thought, one day, he decided.

Paul turned into Ronnie Taylor's scrapyard. Ready to dispose of the corpse. Ronnie was a good friend of his because they had served time together in Belmarsh. This was where Ronnie, being older, had taken Paul under his wing and taught him the ropes.

As the tall metal gates closed behind him, he jumped out of the motor and walked towards Ronnie. The familiar smell of burnt rubber and engine oil hitting his nostrils. There were cars stacked up five or six high all around him and he could hear the grab crunching metal in its claws. "Ron, good to see ya mate, you're looking well." Paul grabbed the other man's hand and gave it a firm shake.

"Good to see you too son, and likewise, smelters fired up, where is it?" Ronnie asked.

Paul walked to the back of his car and opened the boot. He pulled out the bag of body parts and once again threw it over his shoulder. "Jesus, it weighs a fucking ton." Paul remarked before he followed Ronnie to the smelter. The heat hit him instantly. Paul placed the bag down and then pulled the protective gloves and face shield on.

"Throw the lot in." Ronnie motioned. "Looks better than a workout that." Ron laughed.

"Think I'd rather lift weights." Paul replied as he pulled the gloves and face shield off. He reached into the back of his jeans, and pulled out a wad of notes then handed them to Ronnie. "It's all there unless you wanna count it.'

"I trust you, and besides, I know where you live." Ronnie laughed as he placed the money into the inside pocket of his jacket. "I'm glad you're here, I was gonna phone ya. Scotch?"

"Yeah, why not." Paul followed Ronnie into the portacabin and took a seat on the three-seater sofa, facing the door. He watched Ronnie pull a bottle of scotch from the bottom drawer of the filing cabinet along with two glasses. He poured them both a large measure. "I can't stay too long; I need to get to the hospital for visiting time."

"How is that dear old gran of yours, making a speedy recovery, I hope?" Ronnie asked as he handed Paul his glass.

"She'll be the death of me. Seventy-six and still thinks she can do what she did when she was twenty." Paul rolled his eyes and took a sip of the scotch, savouring the flavour. "Anyway, what did you want to talk about?"

"I've got a business proposition for you. It's gonna need a bit of capital, but it's gonna make us a lot of money." Ronnie smiled broadly, showing a set of perfect white teeth.

"I'm all ears." Paul could almost see the pound note signs in Ronnie's eyes. He sat forward and downed his drink before he returned Ronnie's smile. "Tell me more."

Chapter Four

Millie rolled over in the bed and faced the door. She was bored. She had been here for two weeks now and longed to go home. Well not home, she didn't have a home. Not now Levi was gone. She missed him. She knew she shouldn't, but she did. He was her husband. What was the old saying? 'You've made your bed now lie in it.'

Millie closed her eyes; she could see Levi's handsome face. The face that she had fallen in love with. Millie sighed, and then there was his mum, which was one hurt too many, one hurt she would never tell. Millie felt the tears trickle from her eyes, unable to stop them. She rubbed viciously at them, she had to be strong. Millie opened her eyes as a strange feeling hit her and she looked at the door. Her vision was blurry, but she was certain a woman was staring at her from the doorway. "Can I help you?" Millie asked, a little concerned.

The woman turned and walked off before Millie could get a good look at her. She listened as her footsteps faded into the distance. Millie climbed out of bed and made her way to the bathroom. It was just down the corridor, and passed the nurses' desk. Millie turned on the tap, cupping her hands so that they filled with cold water. She then held her breath as she splashed it over her face. She felt a little shaky after the encounter with the woman. Could she be one of Levi's relatives keeping an eye on her, or was she imaging things? Millie shook her head and turned her thoughts to Levi; it was his funeral later that day. Her doctor had advised her not to go, stating it would have a detrimental effect on her health. But Millie knew why he had said it. It was because of her old injuries. She had refused to answer the doctor when he had tried to question her. It was no one's business but hers and she refused to talk about it. Millie looked at the window, the sky looked blue, a nice day for a funeral, she thought. She was glad the doctor had advised her not to go, it was the excuse she needed, but what would the travelling community think? A wife not attending her husband's funeral, it was unheard of. Heading back to her room Millie smiled to the nurse at the desk.

"You're looking a lot better. How are you feeling now?" The nurse asked as Millie stopped.

"Much better thanks. Do you think I will be able to go home soon?" Again, Millie thought, what home?

"That's down to the doctor. Why don't you ask him when he does his rounds this morning?"

"Yes. I will. Thank you." Millie started to walk away but then paused and turned back. "Nurse, about 15 minutes ago I saw a woman standing in my doorway. She was wearing a hat and scarf; do you know who she was?"

"No, I'm sorry, I didn't see. Don't worry though, it would have been someone who works in the hospital as it's not visiting time, they would have been noticed otherwise."

Millie smiled and walked away. *You didn't notice them though, did you?* she thought. As she climbed back into bed Millie looked at the clock. It was already 10.30am. The two Inspectors were coming to see her again today. They were bringing Levi's possessions with them. They were hers now. Including his wallet. He always carried cash and she would need that now to escape Flo. They were due at

11am. The funeral was at 1pm. She needed to get her clothes from Flo's, she needed her white stuffed bunny. There was no way she would leave that behind and she wouldn't be able to get it when Flo was there. If she went back, Flo would never let her leave. The funeral was the only opportunity she would have to collect her stuff and run. Millie turned onto her side and kept her eyes on the door, all she could do now was wait.

The Inspectors didn't turn up, instead two Police officers came. Millie felt annoyed, obviously this part of the job was beneath them. The two officers handed everything over and made Millie sign to say she had received the items that were once her husband's. Once they had left Millie held Levi's wallet to her chest and closed her eyes. Her heart hurt, it was a physical pain that she hadn't expected. Would she ever get over this? She wondered. She wiped away a lone tear. She should be with him today, to say her final farewell, but she couldn't. Her thoughts turned to Flo; it was her fault.

"Hey Mil, how are you feeling today?" Rosie called over.

Millie watched as Rosie made her way towards her bed. "I'm fine. Rose, I need you to help me with something." Millie explained her plan and watched as Rosie's eye's bulged, she wasn't sure if it was shock or fear.

"You want what?" Rosie gasped.

Millie watched Rosie shake her head violently, her dreadlocks whipped around her face. Millie thought she may get whiplash.

"Please Rose." Millie placed her hands together in a praying motion. She dropped her hands when Rosie nodded.

"I can't believe I agreed to this. It's madness. What if we get caught?" Rosie argued.

"You stay here then. Get in the bed and make out your asleep." Millie watched the door to see if anyone was coming.

"Great idea Einstein. You've got blonde hair and I've got black dreadlocks. And let's not talk about the skin colour difference." Rosie held out her hand and shoved it into Millie's face.

Millie stifled her giggles as a nurse approached. "Shhh. Now go and get a wheelchair. Tell them you are taking me into the gardens for some fresh air, and hurry."

Millie laughed as Rosie stuck her tongue out and walked past her. "If we get caught, I'm telling them it was your idea."

"Just go and be quick. The funeral starts in 45 minutes. We need to watch them leave the house." Millie pulled her bag out of the bedside cabinet. She placed Levi's wallet into it along with his house keys. She never had her own keys, she wasn't allowed. Flo said family only. What she really meant was no gorgers. And Millie, despite marrying Levi and having his surname, was most definitely a gorger. Millie felt it was a derogatory word used by the Romany community to describe non-Romany's, but then pikey is probably much the same.

"Here you are, madame. Your chariot awaits." Rosie announced.

Millie smiled as Rosie curtsied and pointed to the dilapidated piece of junk she had just wheeled in.

"For Christ's sake Rose, it's got a flat tyre!" Millie sat on the rigid plastic seat and winced. Despite the bruising healing, it was still tender to touch and as the wheelchair was pushed along, the puncture caused a lopsided movement. Millie grabbed the arms and smiled at the nurses as she was wheeled past.

"This is bloody hard to push." Rosie moaned.

"It's harder to sit in with a bruised arse.... Look, stop at those toilets and I'll get changed. Where's the clothes?" She hopped out of the wheelchair and grabbed the bag as Rosie held it out. "I won't be long" Millie called over her shoulder as she walked into the toilets. Minutes later she returned. "There, what do ya think?"

"I think my clothes are a bit big for you, roll the trousers up at the bottom or you'll end up going arse over tit." Rosie ordered. "Come on then, the quicker we get there the quicker we get caught."

"We are not going to get caught. Keep an eye out for the taxi." Millie burst through the exit and breathed in the fresh air. "I feel like I've been released from prison." Millie stopped when Rosie pulled her back.

"Are you sure you want to do this, it's gonna bring back memories, and not necessarily good ones?" Rosie asked.

"That family has taken everything from me, Rose. It stops today. Now if you don't want to be there that's fine, I'll understand, but this is something I need to do." Millie walked towards the taxi and smiled when Rosie joined her. As she reached for the door, she noticed her hand was shaking. Was this something she really needed to do? She wondered.

"It's okay Mil, I'm here. Canning Town please sir. You can drop us off at the park on Dover street." Rose called. "See, you're getting stronger already. Now you're out from under his control you can think for yourself again. I knew you were in there somewhere."

Millie smiled. One day she would tell her the truth. "Yeah. Things can only get better, right?"

"Right....and on that note, I want you to move in with me and Bobby." Rosie told her.

"I'm not moving in with you and your man. Rose you need your own space and besides what does Bobby say about this?" Millie asked.

"He cool man." Rosie mimicked a Caribbean accent.

Millie laughed despite the sick feeling that was building in her stomach. She focused on the hustle and bustle of the streets as the taxi made its way nearer to her old home. She wrapped her arms around herself as the feeling of dread worsened.

"We're here." Rosie informed her. Millie was pulled from her thoughts and nodded, while Rosie grabbed the door and climbed out.

After Millie had paid the cab driver she walked slowly across the park. "We can sneak through the bushes over there. Keep down though, they mustn't see us." Millie ducked down and made her way to a hole in the hedgerow. "Sit here and keep an eye out."

Millie watched as Flo and Elijah exited the house, as Millie stared at Flo a cold sweat covered her body. Her eyes darted to the parade of cars that seemed endless, and as for the flat bed ford trucks that drove past carrying the wreaths, there must have been ten of them, all carrying the flowery tributes. Levi wasn't particularly well thought of in the travelling community, but he was one of them and he would be seen off as they always saw their dead off. With a lavish funeral and a big piss up afterwards. The men would tell their stories of Levi while the women sat sharing their own. It was one of the things she respected about them, their loyalty to their own kind. "I should be there." Millie said, followed by a sob.

"What.... Millie Levi's gone and if you were there that woman would punish you for the rest of your life. I know it's hard, but you was the one that thought up this plan, you need to go through with it." Rosie whispered.

Millie thought for a moment and then nodded. "It doesn't make it any easier though." She held her breath as she listened to the car doors slam and then waited until the last vehicle drove away.

Rosie nodded. "I know, but it will get easier Mil, I promise.... Come on, it's all clear."

Chapter Five

Millie followed Rosie up the garden path and then stopped and stared at the green front door. "I can't do this."

"Well stay out here and keep guard, I'll go and get your stuff." Rosie replied. "Give me the key."

Millie handed Rosie the key and stepped back. "Be careful."

Millie watched Rosie as she slipped the key into the lock and let herself in.

"I won't be long."

With her heart racing Millie turned and looked around the front garden, there was a pile of rubbish with car tyres and an old mattress dumped in the middle. The place looked a mess. Millie jumped as a car tooted its horn somewhere down the street. Scared of being seen she pushed the front door open and stepped inside. "Rose?" She called out, surprised when Rosie walked out of the lounge. "What are you doing, we need to be quick."

"I thought you said they'll be out for hours?" Rosie replied.

"Yes, but just in case. Come on." Millie climbed the stairs and then watched in horror as Rosie wandered into Flo's bedroom. "Rosie, we haven't got time for sightseeing."

"Chill, get your stuff, I just wanna see what the witch's lair is like.... Oh my god, it's all lace and lavender." Rosie called out as Millie watched her disappear into the room.

Millie entered her own bedroom and looked at the stripped bed. The blankets were neatly folded on top, and the room looked like it had been cleaned. She opened the wardrobe and felt relieved when she spotted her white bunny. She grabbed it and held it firmly to her chest, closing her eyes as she did so. It was the one possession she'd had since birth. The children's home staff had told her it was found with her when she had been discovered as a baby. That was the only information she had been given. Millie opened her eyes when she heard the click of the front door.

"I won't be a minute mate." Elijah called out.

Millie heard the front door slam, followed by footsteps coming up the stairs. She placed the bunny into her bag and stood behind the bedroom door. She could hear the footsteps getting closer and closed her eyes as she swallowed down the fear that was overtaking her body.

"Hello. Who's there?" Elijah asked.

Millie yelped as the door pushed her back into the wall unable to move. As the door was pulled away from her, Elijah's face came into view. She noticed the shock in his eyes, but that was soon replaced with anger as he grabbed her by the arm and dragged her onto the landing. Millie struggled against his grip, but it was too firm.

"Why you little bitch. Thinking of robbing us are ya, while my son's being buried. Time someone taught you a lesson."

Elijah slapped Millie around the face. The stinging sensation stunned her as she flew sideways and then crumpled onto the floor. Elijah stood over her and undid his belt, followed by his zip while Millie watched wide eyed. His trousers dropped as he grabbed her legs and pulled her body underneath him. Millie felt the burn from the carpet along her lower back and winced at the pain. The sneer on his face was identical to Levi's and in an instant Millie felt more disgust and hatred for him than she ever had.

"Get off me!" Millie twisted around as she struggled to get away from him. "I only want my stuff.... Please. Get off!" Her breathing was fast, and she could feel herself hyperventilating. The next voice she heard was Rosie's.

"She said get off." Rosie had picked up an ornament and it was aimed at Elijah's face.

Elijah scrambled to his feet. His face looked flustered. He stood there with his trousers around his ankles, as Millie watched him watching Rosie. Millie's eyes darted to Rosie as she approached with the raised ornament.

While Elijah was focused on Rosie, Millie took her chance and kicked out with her legs and knocked him off balance. As he swayed at the top of the stairs, she brought her legs back one more time and kicked out, sending him backwards down the stairs. Millie stood up, pulling her trousers back up as she did so. Her eyes rested on Elijah. "He's not moving." She panted. Her whole body started to shake, and a film of sweat gathered on her brow. Millie made her way steadily down the stairs as she held the bannister for support. Her legs had turned to jelly, and she didn't think they would support her. As she approached Elijah she crumpled onto the bottom step as she stared at the bent-up figure. "He's in a funny position. Oh no, Rose I've killed him!" Millie placed her hand to her mouth. "I've killed Levi's dad." Millie covered her face with her hands and started rocking backwards and forwards. "I've killed him." She repeated. "I've killed him."

"Millie, we haven't got time for this. Grab what you need before whoever he was with comes looking for him." Rosie ordered. "Millie?"

Millie removed her hands and stared into Elijah's lifeless eyes. "He's dead." She whispered. "I killed him.

"Yeah, and he deserved it. Mil he was going to rape you. Now get your stuff, we need to go." Rosie ordered.

Millie felt Rosie tug at her arm, she slowly stood and allowed Rosie to lead her back to the bedroom.

"Millie concentrate. We need to be quick."

"I...." Millie turned and looked at Rosie. "We need to call the Police."

"Are you stupid? Do you really wanna go to prison for something that was an accident.... Look, you didn't mean to kill him. He was gonna rape you. Now get your stuff. We'll need to go out the back way and hop the fence."

"Ouch, what was that for?" Millie rubbed at her cheek where Rosie had just slapped her. "Don't you think I've suffered enough?"

"Exactly Millie. You've suffered enough at the hands of this family. Now get your stuff. We need to go now." Rosie opened her bag and held it out. "Put your bits in here."

"I can't take anything now; they will know we were here." Millie replied.

"What about your birth certificate?" Rosie asked. "You may need that."

Rifling through the bedside cabinet Millie pulled out a tin. "All my stuff is in here." She opened it, grabbed her birth certificate and shoved it into her bag. "That will have to do. Come on." As she made her way down the stairs Millie froze. Elijah's eyes seemed to be following her. "Rose I..."

"Millie. Yes, you can. Now move."

As they made their way to the back door, Millie watched Rosie as she wiped anywhere that they may have touched.

"Right, let's go. We need to get out of here and back to the hospital before we're home and dry."

Millie reached the fence at the end of the garden. "It's too high, I don't think, what the fuck Rose?"

Rosie grabbed Millie before she had finished speaking and picked her up.

"Put your legs over, hurry up, Christ girl, your heavier than you look!" Rosie panted.

Straddling the fence, Millie managed to drop to the other side and watched as Rosie flung herself over. "I don't believe you just did that." Millie rubbed her ribs, as pain shot through them. "Just as well we're going back to the hospital, reckon I'll need patching up again."

"Stop moaning and start walking. We ain't out of the woods yet.... Look, there's a phone box. I'll bell us a cab.

*****

Twenty minutes later Millie was running into the hospital when she collided with a man.

"WATCH IT!" Paul Kelly bellowed.

Millie's eyes went wide as she shrank back against the wall. He was built like a mountain. "I'm sorry." She said quietly. "I didn't see you." She watched as he looked at her clothes, and noticed the grin spread across his face.

"Did you get dressed in the dark?" He asked.

Millie ignored the comment and turned to Rosie. "I'll get changed; you find a wheelchair." As she reached the toilets Millie peeked back at the stranger to find he was still staring at her. She threw him a dirty look before she entered the safety of the women's toilets. Once Millie had changed back into her hospital gown, she took a seat on the toilet and placed her head in her hands and started to sob. Things were going from bad to worse and now she was a murderer.

"Millie. You in there?" Rosie called. "We need to get you back; it's nearly visiting time."

"Yeah, I'm just coming." Millie wiped her eyes and flushed the toilet.

"You been crying?" Rosie asked.

Millie noticed the sympathetic look on Rosie's face. "I don't need sympathy, Rose. Come on, before they send out a search party."

Millie sat in the wheelchair and grimaced as the stranger

continued to stare at her. She put her head down and avoided eye contact until she heard his voice again.

"You been out on day release then?" Paul grinned.

"Don't think that's any of your business, do you?" Millie snapped. What was it with these men that liked to intimidate women, make fun of them, make them feel inadequate. Millie sighed. Just as she was about to throw an insult at him, she felt the same tingling in her body as before, like she was being watched. Millie shivered. "Rose."

"What Mil?"

"Someone's watching me."

"Yeah. His name is Paul Kelly." Rosie replied.

"What?" Millie screwed her face up in confusion.

"Paul Kelly, you know the one you nearly flattened when we run in." Rosie laughed. "You should have seen his face, he looked like he was gonna explode until he looked at you."

"No. Not him.... Some woman, I caught her watching me this morning and I just got the same feeling."

"Mil, I think you need to take things easy, now you're seeing things."

Millie noticed Rosie's voice soften, it was like she was speaking to a child. This annoyed her. She wasn't a child. She didn't need to be told what she should or shouldn't do. Wasn't that what she had just lived through. "No, I'm not. What I need is to get out of here. It could be one of Levi's family. I don't need the gipsies after me."

"Why would they come after you? You've been in hospital, after Levi got pissed and crashed his truck. If anyone were stalking you it would be one of the relatives of the other people he killed."

"Thanks Rose." Millie replied dryly.

"What for?"

"You have a knack for making things better." Millie rolled her eyes. Now she had something else to worry about.

Chapter Six

Millie stood and watched Rosie as she unlocked the front door to her flat and motioned with her head for Millie to go in. "Make yourself at home, I'll pop your stuff in the spare room. Then I'll make us a cuppa."

Millie looked around the flat. It was tiny but homely. There was a tiny two-seater sofa with an armchair arranged around a coffee table. Millie could smell furniture polish and guessed Bobby had been ordered to clean before they got there. Millie made her way to the bathroom. Again it was small but spotless. Rosie was lucky, she had her own home and a man that loved her. Millie's thoughts drifted to Levi. Had he ever loved her? She looked down at her wrist and gave it a gentle rub. Every winter it would hurt, the doctor had said it was worse because of the two fractures. Before she could stop herself she was there again.

Millie lay on the bed with a drunken Levi holding her down. He had a cigarette hanging from his mouth. Again he was accusing her of flirting with other men. As she lay there pleading and begging, he took the cigarette and held it on her arm. She screamed so loud that Flo came rushing in. 'Stop Levi' Flo had shouted. It was then Levi grabbed Millie's wrist and twisted it causing the second fracture.

Millie sobbed, bringing herself back to the present, her hands gripping the basin to keep herself upright. Her legs felt shaky._She took a couple of deep breaths before turning on the tap, and cupped her hands, so they filled with the cold water, and then splashed it over her face. She looked up at herself in the mirror. "You're weak." She told herself.

"Mil, tea's ready."

"I'm just coming." Millie called back. She walked into the hall and popped her head into the spareroom. Even that was nice. She hadn't been here before. Whenever she had met Rosie, it had been in Canning Town. She could never afford to be out too long for fear of getting accused of having an affair which would lead to another slap. "It's lovely in here Rose, homely." She walked over to the window and looked at the photos all lined up on the sill, when she spotted an old black and white pic of Scot, Rosie, and herself she smiled. They were pictured in the garden of the children's home. All smiling. "It seems strange being back in Stepney." She called to Rosie. "Strange but good."

"It's where you belong girl, and like I said, it's a fresh start." Rosie placed two cups on a small coffee table and sat down. "It's good to take the weight of my feet."

"Aren't you worried about Elijah?" Millie asked.

"We'll cross that bridge if it comes to it, my main concern is you. That family have done so much evil, we've done the world a favour."

"But if Flo finds out, I'm as good as dead." Millie sat down and reached for her cup. "Do you know Stepney is the last place I felt any true happiness."

"And now you're back you can experience it again. You should never have left, let alone marry a Traveller." Rosie replied then sipped at her tea.

"Rose, no lectures, please." Millie placed her cup down and sank back into the seat. "I need to find a job."

"You've just been discharged from hospital, you know what the doctor said, you need to take things easy and build yourself back up."

"I also need money; I'm not staying here rent free." Millie noticed the flicker of annoyance in Rosie's eyes.

"You've given me fifteen quid, that more than covers everything. So just relax and make yourself at home.... Guess what?" She smiled.

"What?"

"Scot's coming for dinner tonight, we can chat about old times and have a laugh like we used to. It'll be fun." Rosie replied.

"Have you told him?" Millie asked.

"Told him what?" Rosie looked at Millie with a frown. "What are you going on about?"

"Have you told him about Elijah?" Millie's hands started to tremble, so she clasped them together tightly.

"Of course I haven't. And I haven't told Bobby either. Millie, I said we bury that memory. It can't be that hard for you to do, you did it enough when you were with Levi." Rosie shook her head. "I'm sorry Mil, I didn't mean that. No, I haven't told anyone and never will."

"All the bad memories with Levi are all in my head. Just because I don't talk about them doesn't mean I've buried them. I live with them every day and relive them every night when I close my eyes.... That also now includes Elijah." Millie wiped at her cheeks with the back of her hand as a stray tear fell.

"Hey. We are in that one together. No-one will ever know.... You know you need to start replacing those bad memories with new happy ones."

Millie nodded. "I know what you're saying is right.... But I think I should go to the Police and tell them what happened, that way they may go easier on me."

"No Mil, definitely not." Rosie snapped.

"But..."

"But nothing. If they ever come looking, we can deal with it then. It's been a week Mil, what are you going to say, oh I didn't have time to report it then, I was too busy.... I have thought about it, you know, and I think leaving it is best."

"Okay." Millie replied as she put her head down. An awkward silence followed until Rosie broke it.

"I bought you a couple of bits to see you through until you're up for shopping. Now it's not much, just a dress, a cardigan, and some underwear. You can pay me back when you get your first week's wages."

"Rose, you've done enough just putting a roof over my head..." Before Millie could continue Rosie cut in.

"You can't wear that skirt and top all the time; it don't fit you and they're the smallest things I've got. Answer me this, when was the last time you had something new to wear?"

Millie looked at the floor, unable to answer.

"Would you like me to answer that for you?"

Millie shook her head. "We both know it's been a while."

"A while? Millie, you've had the same clothes since you left the children's home." Rosie snapped back.

"I don't want anything he bought me anyway, this is supposed to be a fresh start." Millie stood and smiled at Rosie. "Thank you, I do appreciate all you've done for me, I just don't want you going short."

"You would do the same for me Mil if the tables were turned. Now let's see what you look like in this dress." Rosie grinned. "You can wear it tonight; we can go to the pub."

Millie's face went pale. "I don't know about going out, I'm happy to stay in."

"You need to go out Mil, start living a little." Rosie replied. "But if you don't want to, we can wait until you feel okay."

Millie nodded. "Thanks Rose, for being so understanding."

Chapter Seven

December 1975

Millie placed the last bauble on the tree and stood back to admire their work. "I love the Christmas tree." Millie gazed at the lights and brightly coloured baubles. She had always loved Christmas as a child. Not so much the gifts, living in a children's home you never got much but even so she was appreciative of what she did receive. It was more in the feeling, the way it made everyone happy, all being together. Millie sighed; it had been a long time since she had enjoyed a Christmas.

"Thanks for helping." Rosie replied as she placed two cups on the coffee table. "Mil come and sit down."

Millie joined Rosie on the sofa and stared at her. "Have I done something wrong?"

"No, of course you haven't, but you've been locked away in this flat since the end of September and it's now December. We didn't even go out for your birthday. You need to get out..."

Millie cut in. "You want me out?" She asked frantically.

"No, that's not what I mean." Rosie sighed.

"Then what do you mean?" Millie asked, blinking away the building tears.

"I mean out, tonight to be precise, we are all going to the pub. Look Mil you can't spend the rest of your life locked up in this flat, all you're doing is swapping one prison for another." Rosie explained.

"Maybe it's what I'm used to..." Millie trailed off as she was transported back in time.

Millie sat on the bed watching Levi get dressed ready for the pub. She had asked if she could come and ended up getting a black eye, it still throbbed. 'It's Christmas Millie, why would I want to spend it with you he had told her. She didn't reply which made him angrier. She noticed him watching her from the corner of her eye and put her head down, her heart rate fastened as she tried to control her breathing. She didn't want another slap. As Levi approached her, he pushed her back onto the bed and straddled her. He pulled at her clothes, and they ripped with his effort. Millie had learned not to struggle with him, she just lay there and let him have his way. She drifted off to another life, one where she was safe. When he had finished, he let out a moan and then stood and continued getting dressed. When Millie heard the front door slam, she stood and walked to the bedroom door to open it, but it was locked. He had locked her in. That Christmas she spent in her room, alone. That was her first Christmas as Mrs Cooper, from then on in, they got worse.

After dinner Millie walked across the road with Scot by her side. She was grateful that he held her hand, she didn't think she was going to make it out of the front door. When the tears started, he had thrown his arms around her and told he would be with her every step of the way.

"You know it's been great seeing you Mil, talking about old times again." Scot smiled. "And I know I've said it before but I'm glad you're back in Stepney. It's where you belong, it's where we all belong."

Millie stared up into his big brown eyes and smiled back at him. His hair had been cut short, he had never liked his afro, he used to complain all the time in the children's home. So much so that they cut it all off for him one November and then he complained his head was cold, so they had to buy him a woolly hat. He was taller than Rosie, his twin, easily 6ft, and often fell on the wrong side of the law. He had a kind heart though, towards Rosie and Millie and Millie loved him for that. He would be the brother she would choose if she could. "Tonight's been great, just what the doctor ordered, and yes, I'm glad I'm back too." Millie replied as she looked up at the pub. She wasn't sure she was ready for this. Before her nerves got the better of her, she focused on the building. It was huge, red brick with three floors. It had been a familiar sight growing up as it was down the road from the children's home. It had two balconies on the first floor, one at the front and one on the side. She looked at the huge sign and said it aloud. "The Old Artichoke."

Scot laughed. "It's good to see you can still read."

"I don't think I can do this." Millie replied as she pulled back.

"Sure ya can, you've been through worse Mil. Now take a deep breath..... let's go." Scot reassured her.

Making their way to the door, Millie walked in behind Rosie and Bobby with Scot behind her. She could feel his hand on the small of her back, as if to guide her in, or was it to force her in? She hadn't decided. As she walked in, her eyes took in the room, it was large, about twenty tables in this part. Smoke hung in the air and that familiar smell of beer hops filled her nose. The whitewashed walls had photographs on them. On the left-hand wall the photos were old looking of men from years ago, they were holding guns. Above the photos were the words 'The Sidney Street Siege, 1911'. Other various photos hung on the wall opposite. They were all black and white too, relating no doubt to the pub or area from years gone by. In front of her stood the bar, the width of the room. Millie swallowed her nerves down and followed the others to a vacant table. Once seated she scanned the pub. It was busy, with people chatting and laughing. A large table next to the bar caught her eye. Men all dressed in expensive suits, they sat and sipped scotch like they owned the place. Millie's eyes nearly popped out of her head when she spotted the man from the hospital. He sat there staring straight at her with a cocky grin on his face. She looked away and was pleased when Bobby and Scot came back carrying drinks.

"Here you go ladies, enjoy." Bobby placed the drinks down in front of them and took a seat.

Scot threw a couple of bags of crisps onto the table. "That should keep us going. Excuse me for a minute. I just need to have a word with someone." Scot turned and made his way over to the table of men while Millie watched him.

Millie tried to listen to what they were saying but the pub was too noisy. "Who is he talking to?"

Rosie looked over her shoulder and frowned. "You should recognise one of them, you met him in the hospital. Paul Kelly. That lot." Rosie motioned with her thumb. "Think they own this town."

"Why's Scot talking to them?"

"I think he is into something dodgy. All the extra cash he's been flinging about. Well this proves that I'm right. He's a mug getting involved with them." Rosie replied.

Millie noticed the bitterness in Rosie's voice. She turned her head and watched Scot with Paul Kelly. "He's shaking his hand, Rose."

"I don't know what he's up to, but it will all end in tears." Rosie sighed.

Chapter Eight

Millie watched from the window of the flat, as all the people left the pub. She had ended up enjoying tonight. The atmosphere was good, and once she had pushed the memory of Levi out of her head, she had relaxed a little. Scot had taken off just before they had made their way home and Rosie and Bobby had gone straight to bed. The noise they were making made Millie feel uncomfortable, it was like she was an imposter in their home. The sad thing was she didn't really belong there; she didn't belong anywhere. "24 years old and what have you got to show for your life?" She asked herself out loud. Without hesitation, Millie put her shoes and coat back on, she grabbed Rosie's door key and went outside for a walk. She needed to think. Looking up at the sky, she allowed the rain to mingle with her tears. The freezing droplets of water stung her face, but she found comfort in the feeling. Maybe the pain was what she deserved. Millie put her head down and wiped the water from her eyes and face. She didn't want to dwell on the past. She continued on her way and crossed the road. She walked not knowing where she was going, she just walked until she stopped outside a large house. As Millie gazed longingly at the house, a feeling of calm washed over her, her body was filled with a warmth she hadn't experienced for an exceptionally long time. She knew this house inside and out. It was the house she had grown up in with Rosie and Scot. The children's home. Millie stared at the windows and drank in every feature. This was her happy place. Not that she knew it when she was there, she couldn't wait to leave. And when she did, she met Levi. The world was exciting, he was exciting. She had so many hopes and dreams and then they were gone in an instant. Millie turned and made her way back along the road and stood outside the Artichoke. "Nothing ventured nothing gained." She told herself. She walked to the main door and tried the handle, but it was locked, so instead she banged loudly and waited.

As the door flew open Finn the landlord stood glaring down at her. His eyes hard and menacing. "What do you want?"

Millie took a step back before she spoke. "I want a job." She watched his eyes as he looked her up and down and then without warning he slammed the door in her face. Millie stood with her mouth open. She was used to being treated like she didn't exist by Elijah and his family, but she hadn't expected it from a total stranger. Again she knocked on the door, harder this time and waited for him to answer it.

"Look kid, shouldn't you be in bed by now, your parents will worry." Finn pointed to the road. "Now get lost."

Millie swallowed down her fear and took a deep breath. "Firstly sir I have no parents and secondly I have no one to worry about me so please, if you have any jobs going, I would be grateful if you would consider me?"

"Well firstly you ain't old enough to work in a pub, what are you, twelve? And secondly you wouldn't handle it, it's rough in here and I don't need a barmaid that I have to babysit. Now bugger off!"

Millie watched as Finn grabbed the door ready to slam it shut. Before he did, she replied. "I'm twenty-four so I am old enough and as for a babysitter, I've experienced and lived through more shit than you could only dream of. I'm also reliable, punctual and a hard worker.... Now are you going to give me a job or are you scared I'll prove you wrong?" Millie plunged her hands into her pockets as she felt them starting to tremble. She watched the man's face soften and held his stare.

"Fine. Be here tomorrow at eleven forty-five. You can have a trial shift. If you cut it, I'll give you a job, if not, I don't want to see your mush ever again. Okay?"

"Okay. Deal." Millie held her hand out ready to shake on it and watched the man's face crease with amusement. "You won't regret this."

"I'd better not. Now get off home."

Millie stood back as the door shut. She felt a buzz inside her body. A feeling she hadn't felt for quite some time. She had done it. She had got herself a job. The smile took over her whole face and in an instant, she forgot about all the hardships she had endured. Life was on the up. Millie looked up at the flat. She didn't fancy listening to Rosie and Bobby going at it, so she walked to the bus stop and sat down. The rain had turned to sleet, and the sky was beginning to turn white. It would be snowing soon. With only a few days until Christmas Millie's smile fell. Would this year be better than the last? It would be her first without Levi. No more keeping her head down and mouth shut in case she said the wrong thing. No more insults and put downs from Flo. No more being forced to.... Millie squeezed her eyes shut. No She wouldn't be forced to do that again. Things would be better.

It was after Midnight when Millie decided to head back to the flat. The faint glow of street lamps lined the road. The sleet had turned to snow and with the unusual quietness, the area had an eerie feel. But despite being eerie Millie preferred it. The peace and quiet, the loneliness, these had become her sanctuary.

Millie unlocked the door and went to step inside but before she walked over the threshold, she looked up the street and noticed head-lights heading towards her. She jumped into the doorway and stood back in the darkness. Her eyes widened as she witnessed the procession of trucks, each one pulled a caravan. Millie stood unable to move, a tight knot formed in her gut. Slowly one by one the trucks passed, while Millie held her breath. Once the last of them vanished into the distance it was only then she was able to move. She closed the front door and rested back against it trying to calm herself. Millie's body trembled. The gipsies were coming to town and with them there would be trouble.

Chapter Nine

"Why can't you just be happy for me?" Millie picked up Rosie's lipstick and applied it, after she smacked her lips together, she then pouted at herself in the bedroom mirror.

"Because you've only been out of hospital a few months and last night you had a meltdown at the thought of leaving the flat." Rosie sighed.

Millie felt a film of sweat form on her forehead and her pulse raced. She pushed the memory away. "Look I know what you're saying, but it's now or never. Isn't that what you told me last night?" Millie turned to Rosie and gave her a sad smile. "I need to start taking control of my life."

"I don't want you overdoing it, okay."

"Okay.... I'm only going to be serving drinks so stop fussing. Anyway, shouldn't you be getting off to work, you'll be late." Millie watched as Rosie glanced at the clock.

"This conversation isn't over. I'll see you later."

Millie listened to the front door slam before looking back in the mirror. "You are no good at applying makeup girl." Wiping the lipstick off she attempted to try again. At least she had a couple of hours to practise. Four times she attempted to do her makeup and each time she washed it off. On her last attempt she put on a bit of mascara and a light coating of lipstick. Now content she looked up at the clock. It was eleven fifteen. Her nerves had started to get the better of her, so she decided to go now rather than chicken out. She made her way across the road and knocked loudly on the door; Millie smiled as it was opened.

"You're early." Finn told her.

"Better to be early than late." Millie replied, trying to sound more confident than she felt. "My name's Millie, by the way."

"You'd better come in then Millie." Finn stepped back and ushered her in. "Go and put the kettle on, you may as well make yourself useful. It's just through there." Millie followed Finn's direction and walked behind the bar. The place looked like it could do with a good clean. Dust was covering the glass shelves and there were sticky patches where the optics had dripped. She ignored her urge to clean and walked through to the back room. Millie took a deep breath as she looked at the mess. Cups and plates were piled up in the sink, and those that didn't fit were piled up on the side. There was a table in the middle of the kitchen with more dirty cups on. Millie shook her head; it was the one thing she couldn't stand. Mess. She rolled up her sleeves and started to clear the dirty crockery from the sink before filling the bowel with clean hot water.

Millie emerged twenty minutes later with the cups and handed one to Finn.

"You're gonna have to speed up a bit if you want to work here. That should have only taken you five minutes." Finn took a sip then placed the cup on the bar. "At least you make a good cuppa."

"I couldn't help but notice the washing up needed doing, so I did it, I thought it would save you the job as I'm working here." Millie replied.

"And that's another thing, you do the jobs I tell you to do. Understand."

"Yes sir, sorry." Millie turned before Finn could see her eyes water and looked at all the optics. "So where shall I start?"

"That box of mixers needs to go in that fridge there, and make sure you keep them in straight lines. I'll open up." Finn walked to the door and unlocked it. Next, he walked to the fire and placed another log on it while Millie studied him.

She couldn't make out his age, more than likely early fifties she guessed. He had a strong southern Irish accent that rolled off his tongue and his hair was dark but greying at the sides. He reminded Millie of a boxer. His nose was squashed, like it had been broken. "What should I call you. Boss?"

"My name's Finn. If you've finished putting the mixers away, you can wipe the optics over. Now it won't be busy this lunchtime so you can manage on your own."

"What?" Millie looked at Finn with her mouth open.

"Millie, you have worked in a pub before?"

"Not exactly." Millie felt her face redden.

"Jesus fecking Christ.... Have you any experience at all? With anything?" Finn asked.

"Not pub wise. No." Millie noticed Finn's face turn a purple colour.

"How do you expect to work in a pub if you don't know how? What happens if there's trouble, can you even defend yourself?"

"I don't need to defend myself. I can take a good hiding, better than anyone. Look I'm sorry I've wasted your time." Millie grabbed her bag and coat and headed towards the door.

"So you're a quitter too."

"I'd rather walk out now than listen to another person telling me how useless I am." Millie could feel the tears building and did her best to sniff them back. She took a quick look at Finn and was surprised to see his mouth drop open; he looked like he had been punched in the gut.

"Whoa kid. Where did all that come from?"

Millie ignored him and rushed towards the door. As she reached it, she stopped and turned around. "It's come from the way I've been treated most of my life."

"Stop Millie. Come back."

Millie watched as Finn rubbed the back of his neck. He looked shocked, but his face had softened.

"Do you know why you're here?" Finn asked.

"Because I asked for a job."

"Yes, and I told you to get lost, but you didn't. You persevered. That's why you're here. You wouldn't take no for an answer. That's a good attitude to have child, it will see you through life. If you want experience, you best get back behind the bar."

Millie paused. "You gonna teach me then?"

Finn nodded. "Looks like it."

"Okay, I guess I'll give you a second chance then." Millie smiled at Finn's expression. He looked gobsmacked.

* * *

By the end of her shift Millie had been able to run the bar without the help of Finn. He had sat on the other side of the bar just in case she had needed him he had told her, but she didn't. Millie had found she had taken to bar work like a duck to water. She often saw Finn watching her from the corner of his eye, but she pretended not to notice. By the time they had closed for the afternoon, Finn had agreed to give Millie regular shifts.

Millie poured Finn a scotch and herself a glass of wine, despite not being a drinker and sat at the bar. She then grabbed the local paper that was left there by one of the punters and turned to the 'for rent' section.

"What are you looking for?" Finn asked as he craned his neck.

"Somewhere to live, I can't stay at my friend's forever. Blimey, the flats are so expensive. It'll have to be a bedsit." Millie looked glumly at the prices. She scanned the rows of bedsits and decided they weren't much cheaper. She knew she would need one nearby. It wasn't safe at night to be travelling home late, only the other night a woman had been attacked.

"I've got a better idea." Finn replied.

"What's that?" Millie answered without looking at him, her mood had dipped at the lack of affordable rooms to rent.

"You can have a room here. I've got three spare bedrooms. I'll take the rent out of your wages."

Millie dropped the paper and stared at Finn. "Do you mean that?"

"I only say what I mean Millie. So when do you wanna move in?"

"Now!" Millie laughed, as her excitement bubbled over. She watched Finn nod his agreement and jumped off the stool. Without another word Millie went to collect her things. Within the hour she had packed her clothes away in her new bedroom and settled back on the bed with her white bunny. Life was on the up. She had a double bed to herself which was placed in the centre of the wall with two bedside cabinets either side. She had a chest of drawers and a wardrobe, all to herself. Now all she needed was some clothes.

"Millie. Stews in the pot help yourself." She heard Finn's voice as it travelled up the stairs.

Millie lovingly placed the white bunny in the centre of the bed and made her way down. "Thanks Finn, it smells delicious."

"Room to your liking?" Finn asked.

"It's perfect. Thank you." Millie replied as she scooped up the stew and dumped it on the plate. "I love dumplings, used to have them in the children's home...." Millie trailed off and then looked at Finn, who was staring back at her. After an awkward silence, Finn turned and walked towards the bar. Millie sank onto the chair and cursed herself. She didn't want people knowing about her life, she didn't want the pity that would come with it.

Millie cleaned up after dinner and then went through to the bar to start work. The evening shift flew by and before she knew it, she climbed the stairs to her new bedroom. Rosie hadn't taken the news too well, but she seemed consoled that Millie was just across the road. It seemed things were really on the up and Millie's excitement had bubbled inside her all evening. As she reached the bedroom she headed towards the window. It had been snowing on and off all day and Millie wanted to watch it, she found it calming. Her thoughts turned to Levi, and then without knowing it she thought about Elijah. Had she got away with murder or was it only a matter of time before she was found out? Millie's eyes widened as she spotted blue flashing lights heading up the street. Unable to move she stood and watched as the Police car approached the pub.

Chapter Ten

Paul stopped outside the Artichoke and watched as the Police car disappeared into the distance. He took a deep breath and got out of his motor. He needed a drink and as the lights were still on, he decided to knock. The door flew open, and he was met with Finn's angry face. "I know it's after-hours Finn, but I could really do with a drink mate." Paul smiled.

"You better come in then. Tough day?" Finn replied.

"You could say that. I'll have a scotch." Paul sat at the bar and watched Finn pour the drink. "Cheers."

"Cheers.... I thought it was the old bill knocking the door, I was about ready to tell them to feck off." Finn growled.

Paul laughed; he knew Finn hated the filth. More than likely, as much as he did, maybe more. "You're okay, they ain't out there, I didn't expect you to still be up, it was only because the light was on, I stopped."

"I've got an unexpected house guest, so I'm running late." Finn grabbed the bottle of scotch and refilled both glasses while Paul observed him.

"Anyone I know?" Paul took a swig of the new drink and rested his arms on the bar.

"A young woman, turned up at closing yesterday and had the balls to ask for a job, so I gave her one."

"And a home too! You are going soft in your old age Finn." Paul frowned.

Finn shook his head. "No, she's different, she's a fighter. Goes after what she wants, but there's also a sadness about her..."

"Sadness? Well, that's gonna be good for business then." Paul downed his drink in one, then grabbed the bottle of scotch, he refilled his glass and Finns.

"Anyway, enough about me, what's going on with you?" Finn asked.

"It's been a rough day." Paul replied with a long sigh.

Finn nodded. "I've had my fair share of them over the years, I take it it's Jamie we are talking about?"

Paul looked up and faced Finn. "It's more than him. It's like I'm carrying the weight of the world on my shoulders, trying to get things done. All I do is work and then go home to an empty bed." Paul downed his drink.

"That surprises me Paul, you've always got women hanging around you."

"They are what's known as Gangster groupies Finn, whilst they serve a purpose, they are only looking for excitement and money." Paul studied his glass before continuing. "I did actually meet someone."

"So what are you moping for?"

"I say I met someone; it was more like she ran into me.... I threw a few wisecracks because I couldn't string a coherent sentence together.... she actually took my breath away, and my brain apparently..... I just stood there like an idiot grinning." Paul shook his head. "I hardly slept that night, and then when I finally think she's gone, she turned up here in the pub last night."

"So did you talk to her, get her name, ask her out to dinner? Finn pressed.

"Nope, I sat staring at her like a fucking idiot.... next time though I will. Anyway, take no notice of me." Paul shook his head.

"If she's the one then you need to at least try, otherwise you'll always wonder." Finn filled both their glasses once more.

"You're right and I will. Next time." Paul sighed. "Anyway regarding work, Jamie is Jamie, no fucking help whatsoever and I'm fed up carrying his dead weight."

"I'm gonna give you a bit of advice son. Now it's up to you if you take it, but if it were me, I'd get rid of Jamie. Stop the partnership and go separate ways. All he does is swan around town making enemies, and he doesn't give a feck about you or anyone else. You need to step up and let everyone know you're the real boss, get someone you can trust to work with and next time you see this mystery woman, for feck's sake talk to her."

Paul nodded. "I know what you're saying makes sense, and when the time's right I will and regards the woman, like I said next time I will. Anyway, I best get going, that scotch is sliding down way too easy." Paul stood and made his way to the door. "And Finn, this stays between us."

Finn nodded. "Of course."

Paul slid onto the seat of his Range Rover and watched as the pub was plunged into darkness. His only thought being, would there be a next time?

Chapter Eleven

Millie looked at the clock. It was only 8.30am. She was desperate for the shops to open. She needed new clothes. Thanks to Finn giving her a sub, which was after he got over the shock of her asking him. He agreed and gave her half her wages. After getting dressed she decided to take a slow walk down the high street. Millie put on her coat and grabbed her keys.

As she walked, she took in all the brightly coloured displays in the shop windows. The Christmas trees all sparkled with their lights twinkling. Christmas Eve was her favourite day of the year. It always had been, even as a child. Every year she had wished for the same present. A mum and a dad, just like other kids had, but of course Father Christmas never delivered, so Christmas day was always a disappointment.

Millie breathed in the icy air as the freshly fallen snow crunched beneath her feet. Putting the thoughts of her real parents out of her mind she focused on her destination. She made her way to C&A where she was going to treat herself to a nice dress for tonight. Millie admired the dress display in the window while she waited for the shop to open but then the hairs on her arms stood up. She placed her hand against the wall to steady herself as she felt her vision blur. After a few deep breaths Millie's eyes darted around the street. There were people standing around chatting, others were plodding along in the snow. Millie scanned the area, not knowing what she was looking for until movement caught her eye. A woman was staring at her but when she spotted Millie staring back, she then turned and disappeared down an alleyway. Without hesitation, Millie half ran, and half slid across the road in pursuit. As she reached the alleyway, she saw the woman strolling off into the distance. "HEY YOU!" She called out, but the woman disappeared from sight. Millie shook her head, was she feeling jumpy because of Elijah's death, or was there another reason for feeling spooked? Deciding she was being paranoid Millie carried on back across the road to C&A and made her purchase quickly. She felt unsettled. Was someone really watching her or was she going mad? It was a feeling she couldn't shake. At the back of her mind Flo was always there, it was only a matter of time before she would catch up with her. Was this the reason for her paranoia?

Millie returned from her shopping trip and sat with Finn as he stirred the gravy. She kicked off her shoes and wiggled her toes. "Blimey my feet are like icicles."

"You need boots in this weather, boots and thick socks." Finn answered as he continued to stir the pot.

Millie watched him, it smelt good, and she felt her tummy rumble in agreement. Chicken had always been her favourite roast. Which was just as well because that was what they normally had in the children's home on a Sunday. She had never had a roast mid-week before and not on Christmas Eve. Was this what real families did? Her thoughts returned to her parents. "Finn, what's it like to have a mum and a dad?" Millie noticed him tense.

"That's a funny question to ask." Finn turned to look at her.

Millie noticed the sad look in his eyes and quickly changed the subject. "I guess it's gonna be busy tonight."

Finn pulled out a chair and sat opposite her. "You could try and find them."

Millie shook her head. "They never wanted me. Why would I look for them?"

"There may have been circumstances that lead to them giving you up."

"And what if I find them and they don't want me. Then what?" Millie stood up and walked through to the bar, with Finn following.

"You know I have a daughter, she's probably about your age now."

"Where is she?" Millie asked, surprised.

"I don't know. My wife left me and took my daughter with her, all I was left with was a note. I haven't seen them for twenty years. I did search for them, in the beginning, but I couldn't find them."

"I'm sorry Finn." Millie placed her hand on his arm and gave a little squeeze.

"The point is I did try Millie, and as much as it hurt not to find them, I'm glad I tried because otherwise I would have always wondered. What if? Maybe you should have a think, because we don't need to have 'What ifs' in our lives, we need 'I tried'."

"Maybe after Christmas. Tonight is for celebrating. Now do you think that roast is ready, I'm starving." Millie smiled.

"Come and help me dish up."

* * *

After dinner Millie and Finn opened the pub. It was packed with party revellers within the hour, as they all celebrated Christmas Eve. Music was playing from the jukebox and a few of the women were dancing around the tables as their men watched on. It was a wonderful sight for Mille, she had never experienced anything like it. Despite being run off her feet, she was loving it.

Millie smiled at Rosie when she approached the bar. "Alright Rose?"

"Well, I would've been better if you were on this side of the bar, but yeah, I guess I am. It's lovely having you back Mil."

Millie laughed. "It's good to be back. Hang on, I need to serve the holy table."

"The holy table?" Rosie quizzed.

"Yeah, that lot." Millie nodded towards Paul Kelly and his firm.

"Why do you call it the holy table?" Rosie laughed.

"Because they all think they're gods.... Look at them. You would think they owned the place and as for Paul Kelly well." Millie rolled her eyes.

"What about Paul Kelly?" Rosie pressed.

"He keeps smiling at me, it's making me feel a bit.... I dunno, weird?" Millie placed the seven glasses of whisky on a tray and carried it round to them. "There you go gentlemen." She announced with a curtsey as she handed one to Jamie Carter.

"Millie. Nice to see your dress sense has improved." Paul laughed.

"Mr Kelly. Shame your mouth hasn't." Millie watched as Paul's eyes twinkled with amusement.

"Careful boss, this one answer's back." One of the men replied.

Millie turned and walked away, ignoring them all. She could feel Paul's eyes on her and sure enough when she turned around, he was still staring at her with that stupid smile on his face.

"Millie stay away from them. They're bad news." Rosie warned her.

Millie watched as Rosie fidgeted in her seat. Her brow was creased, and she slowly shook her head.

"I have to serve them Rose, it's my job." Millie looked over to Paul Kelly and he was still staring back at her, he also raised his glass in a toast, and winked. Millie turned away and continued to serve the thirsty punters. She could feel her cheeks colouring up.

"I mean keep away from him." Rosie pointed out. "Our Mr Kelly is not a man to mess with Mil."

"I have no intention of messing with him in any way, shape, or form, so relax. Now do you wanna refill?" Millie smiled and looked over Rosie's shoulder as the door opened. Her heart sank when she spotted the travellers as they walked in. She could see they wanted to make a grand entrance by the way they walked. They were loud and they made sure to glare at the punters.

Millie watched as the bar went quiet. All eyes turned to the travellers. Millie spotted Levi's cousin Billy, at the back and wished the ground would have opened up and swallowed her. She knew the man at the front, his name was Duke Lee. Bare knuckle fighting champion of the Travellers.

"Do you know them Mill?" Rosie whispered.

"A couple of them. Keep quiet Rose and come behind the bar. You'll be safer." Millie felt a cold sweat cover her body.

"Why, what are they gonna do?" Rosie slid off of the stool and made her way to Millie.

"From the looks on their faces, they've come for a fight." Millie's head flicked to Paul. He got up and walked towards Duke.

"Can I help you?" Paul asked as he stood in front of Duke.

"Just come for a drink mush. This is a public house I take it?" Duke answered in his usual cocky manor.

Millie watched as Duke held eye contact with Paul, despite being a couple of inches shorter. She knew he could fight; she had heard Levi and his cousins boast about the illegal fights he had won.

"Not all public are welcome, So why don't you turn around and go back to where you came from." Paul replied.

"He's clenching his fists. That's not good." Millie whispered to Rosie. "Duck when I say." Millie grabbed Rosie's hand and waited for her to nod before refocusing on Duke.

"Ahh you see I would but I'm also on a bit of business. My cousin Rueben has gone missing, and this was the last place he was seen, so I really need to have a look around and see what's happened to him." Duke's head turned to Millie. "Eight pints of bitter please love."

Millie looked at Finn for approval, but he was too busy keeping an eye on the Travellers. "Sorry sir, the bars closed." Millie bit her lip as Duke glared at her. Her palms were starting to sweat along with the rest of her body.

"Don't I know you?" Billy called from the back.

Millie shook her head and looked at the floor. Her breathing was becoming erratic.

"Yes, I do.... You're Levi's wife. Glad you've moved on so quickly." Billy walked up to Duke. "Didn't even turn up for Levi's funeral."

Millie felt all eyes shift to her, while she stood glued to the spot.

"You can expect a visit from Flo, she can't wait to get her hands on you." Billy moved closer to the bar. "Now if I were you, I'd start pulling those pints."

Millie looked up at him as he banged his fists on the bar and jumped. She swallowed the fear that had built inside her and glanced at Finn, who just stood and stared at her. She looked back at Billy and took a deep breath before she replied. "You're not me though, are you?" Millie leant in closer. "The bars closed."

Millie held her breath as Billy pulled his fist back, ready to punch her in the face, but before he managed to strike, Paul had grabbed his head and rammed it into the bar three times in quick succession. The blood splatter hit Millie in the face before she managed to step back. Before she could blink she watched as the whole pub erupted into a bar fight.

Chapter Twelve

Finn picked up a chair and placed it on a table. Paul watched his weary face as he rubbed the back of his neck. He had aged in the last hour. Paul turned his attention to Millie as she swept the last of the glass up then emptied it into the bin. Paul continued to pace the floor, mumbling under his breath. He had a nasty gash on his forehead and the blood trickled down his cheek. The pub was now empty apart from those three.

Paul stopped pacing and pulled out a chair. "Sit." He motioned to Millie.

"What?" Millie paused. "Why?"

"Because we need to have a chat." Paul motioned to the chair. "Now." He watched her closely; she looked like a rabbit caught in the headlights of a speeding car. Her movements were slow and timid. When she was finally seated Paul began. "Are you a fucking gypsy?"

"No. No I'm not." Millie replied, startled.

"Why do you look guilty Millie?" Paul looked at her hands, they were shaking. He watched Millie put her head down, she didn't reply, so he tried again. "He seemed to know you pretty well. So how are you involved with them?"

"I married his cousin, Levi."

"So you're a gypsy lover. Fucking great. Don't you vet your bar staff before you give them a job, Finn?" Paul roared in disgust.

"Calm down Paul. She wasn't responsible for the fight. You know that." Finn reasoned.

Paul watched Millie as she stood up and walked towards the bar. "Where the fuck do you think you're going." He grabbed her arm and pulled her back.

"GET OFF!" Millie screamed out in panic as she pictured Levi.

Paul was momentarily shocked when he felt Millie lash out at him. He tried to catch her, but she bolted towards the door. Paul stopped and watched as Millie crumpled into Finn's arms. The sound of her sobs echoed around the bar.

"It's okay Millie. He's not going to hurt you." Finn smiled sadly. "We need to figure out what's going on, why are they here causing trouble Millie?"

"Finn, I don't know. Duke said his cousin Rueben is missing. If that's true they won't stop until they find him or his body. And then the real trouble will start." Millie replied as she sniffed back the tears.

"I think we all need a drink to calm us down. Finn, do you mind doing the honours." Paul sighed as he held out his hanky. "Here you've got snot hanging from your nose." He noticed her face colour up immediately.

"You're such a gentleman." Millie snatched the hanky and blew her nose. "Thanks." She held it out for Paul to take back.

Paul looked at the sodden hanky and shook his head. "It's okay, you keep it." Paul grabbed his drink and downed it in one. "You'd better bring the bottle Finn." Paul grabbed the bottle as Finn sat down and refilled his glass. "Right Millie, your reaction was a bit over the top for someone that knows nothing. Now start talking."

"You think I know why they are here?" Millie asked.

"I don't know. But like I said that reaction was way over the top.

Why are you scared?" Paul kept eye contact with her until she looked away.

"You grabbed me."

"Millie, you acted like a wild animal. That's not normal." Paul glanced at Finn. "Can you throw any light on your barmaid's' behaviour?"

"I think it's up to Millie to tell us.... Millie, you're safe here." Finn handed Millie her glass. "Take a sip, it will steady your nerves."

Millie took a long swig, and immediately spat it out. "That's disgusting."

Paul jumped up and attempted to brush off the whisky that sprayed him. "Fucking hell, can this night get any worse!" Paul motioned to Finn. "Get her a brandy, whisky's obviously not her drink."

"I don't drink." Millie replied pointedly.

"Here, sip this, it will calm your nerves." Finn placed the brandy onto the table as she took the glass.

Millie took a small sip and shuddered while Paul watched.

"It's a bit better than whisky." She said flatly.

"Right, can we get on." Paul took the glass out of Millie's hand and placed it down. "Now Millie what's going on?"

"I don't know what you want me to say. I don't know what's going on." Millie grabbed her glass and took another sip.

"I think she's a spy, Finn." Paul sat back and crossed his arms. He saw the annoyance spread across Millie's face.

"A spy?" Millie questioned. "A spy for what exactly?"

"A spy for the gipsies.... You were probably in on the drugs." Paul clocked the frown on Millie's face. "What ain't you telling us?"

"Look I'm not involved with the gipsies; I married one and I've paid the price ever since. I have nothing to do with them or their drugs." Millie grabbed the glass and swallowed the liquid down in one.

"So you know about the drugs then?" Paul sat forward. There was a change in her voice, he was certain she knew something.

"No. Not really.... I was in a car crash, that's how Levi died. The Police came to see me in hospital. They said they found drugs in the truck." Millie looked at Finn. "Can I have some more brandy please?"

"Millie, what drugs did they find?" Paul took her glass and poured a large measure.

"Cocaine."

"And you didn't know he was dealing?" Paul slid the glass towards her.

"Nope.... It was the first time I had heard the word drugs mentioned." Millie gripped the glass.

"So you're trying to tell me your husband flogged drugs and you didn't know anything about it!" Paul laughed. "Do I look stupid?" Paul stopped talking when Millie stood up.

"No I didn't, because he was out day and night getting pissed and no doubt shagging around and selling drugs while I was stuck with his mother being forced to...." Millie stopped dead.

"Millie." Paul placed his hands gently on her shoulders. "Forced to do what?"

Chapter Thirteen

The week that followed seemed to drag, Millie had kept her head down and avoided the sympathetic glances from Finn and the suspicious stares from Paul. Paul had tried to get her to open up, but she had refused, she would never tell, not even Rosie knew and that's how she wanted it to stay. Millie looked at the bedside clock, it was 7.30 am. She climbed out of bed, still weary from the lack of sleep. It was New Year's Eve and the pub was having a big party. Finn had arranged for some woman to play the piano and he was laying on a buffet. Millie didn't feel like celebrating. What did she have to celebrate, nothing now Flo knew where she was. It would only be a matter of time before she came to cause trouble.

"Is that you Millie?" Finn's voice carried up the stairs.

"Yeah, I'll be down in a minute." Millie made her way to the bathroom and had a quick wash. Today was going to be busy, which was just as well, she hoped it would take her mind off things.

When she entered the bar Millie wasn't surprised to see Paul Kelly and his men already there. "You lot are up early."

"Good morning, Millie, lovely to see you too." Jamie Carter replied.

Ignoring him she turned to Finn. "I'll go and pick up the rest of the food when the shops open."

"You're not going on your own Millie, it's not...." Finn stopped when Paul cut in.

"I'll take her."

Millie turned to Paul and glared. "I don't need a babysitter."

"Maybe not but you'll need help with all the bags, even you can't carry them all." Paul glared back.

"Fine." Millie turned and walked to the back room where she started to make herself a cup of tea.

"I'll have one of those." Paul Kelly's voice drifted over her shoulder.

"Can you stop following me? It's creepy." Millie opened the cupboard and grabbed two cups.

"Creepy?" Paul laughed. "Don't flatter yourself, love. You're connected to the gipsies, so while they are in town, I will be following you, just to make sure you ain't up to no good."

Millie continued to make the tea, that last comment had cut deep, although she would never admit it. 'Up to no good!' If only Paul knew the torture she had endured, maybe she should tell him. But would that get him off her back, and then again why should she have to tell her life story when all she wanted to do was forget it. Millie put the thought out of her mind and sat and drank her tea in silence. She could feel Paul's eyes on her. He made her nervous. She placed her cup down and stood up. "I'll get my shoes, if that's allowed." All she got back was a grunt.

After putting her shoes on she followed Paul outside. she climbed into his Range Rover as he held the door open for her, she had never been in such a luxurious motor. If it weren't for the fact, she was lumbered with him, she would have enjoyed it.

The drive to the high street was done in silence. Millie looked out of the passenger window, so she didn't have to look at him. Everywhere looked grotty. It was always the same after Christmas. The half-melted snow had turned to slush and now looked grey. At least the rubbish had been cleared. The shops would soon have their winter sale displays up, and the high street would be busy once again. Millie breathed a sigh of relief when Paul parked at the side of the road. "I need to go to the butchers first." Millie glanced at Paul as he got out. He didn't even have the courtesy of answering her. She watched as he stomped around to the passenger door and opened it.

"Come on then your majesty." Paul took Millie's arm and helped her out.

"What are you doing?" Millie felt his hand clench around hers, her heart missed a beat.

"Just keeping you safe."

"You think I'm gonna do a runner?" Millie asked more in surprise, although she felt a strange feeling of disappointment.

"I don't know Millie.... Are you?"

Millie pulled away from Paul in annoyance. "No Paul. Would anyone dare to run from the great Paul Kelly."

"Not if they had any sense." Paul replied. "And just so you know, I can run fast, when I have too."

Millie turned and walked towards the butchers; her heart sank. She had replaced one prison for another, despite her new captor being handsome. As she joined the queue Millie felt the familiar tingle as the hairs on her arms stood up, she looked around. That same feeling hit her. Was she being paranoid?

"What's wrong?" Paul asked.

"Nothing." Shaking her head she refocused on the counter. It must all be in her head. She turned and watched Paul as he walked to the door and scanned the street outside. "I didn't see anything."

"Then what was it that spooked you?" He asked suspiciously.

"I got a weird feeling, like I'm being watched." Millie thought back to the hospital. "It started in the hospital, a woman...." Millie trailed off. She was being ridiculous.

"Did you recognise her?"

Millie shook her head. "No."

"Was she a gypsy?"

"I don't know, I've never been able to get a good look at her." Millie watched Paul as his frustration came out in his voice.

"Is there anything you can tell me about her that might help find her?"

"She had blonde hair, I think." Millie jumped as Paul spun around to face her.

"Half the fucking world has blonde hair."

"I'm sorry." Millie turned her eyes to the ground. She didn't need another angry face condemning her.

"You don't need to be sorry.... How many times has this happened?"

Millie looked up at Paul, he was staring straight into her eyes. His face had softened, and he looked different. "A few now. It started in the hospital.... I don't know who it is, or even if it's the same person. It could be Levi's family.... Look, can we get the shopping and go home; I've got a lot to do before the party and I'd rather focus on that than some stalker."

Chapter Fourteen

Paul sat with his men, while one of them stood guard, and watched the door of the pub. He picked up his drink and studied the glass while swirling the whisky around. His mind kept drifting to Millie. He looked up as she walked through to the bar. His eyes were drawn to the low-cut top she was wearing. Her dress sense had certainly improved.

"Shall I set the rest of the food out Finn?" Millie called over.

"Yes love, get it all out now and then come and have a drink." Finn replied.

Paul stood up and walked through to the back room. "How are you feeling now Millie?"

"Okay I guess, although I can't help feeling there's gonna be trouble tonight."

"If they come through the door, I want you to come back here. Don't come out under any circumstances. Understand?" Paul took a step closer. He was so close he could smell her; he breathed in her scent while he watched her closely. He noticed her eyes twinkle with annoyance.

"I work here, my job is at the bar, not hiding in the back."

"I can't fight while I'm worried about you." Paul's voice rose and he struggled to contain his temper.

"It's not your job to worry about me. I'm a gypsy lover. Remember."

"Oh I remember all right, so tell me Millie, who's side are you on?" Paul took a step forward and watched as she took a step back. He had her trapped against the wall.

"You're scaring me." Millie whispered. "Just like they do."

Paul's eyes were drawn to Millie's chest, her breathing deepened, and he could see her chest rise and fall with each breath. Annoyed with himself he stepped back and ran his fingers through his hair. "And you frustrate me, Millie." Paul turned and made his way back to the bar. As he joined the rest of the men, Finn placed a shotgun on the table.

"I've brought Bertha out of retirement."

Paul laughed as Finn patted the shotgun. "Let's hope we won't be needing that, but just in case place it behind the bar, so you can get to it." Paul looked up at Millie as she carried a large tray of sausage rolls through. He saw her eyes go wide as she looked at the shotgun. "Put it away Finn, out of sight."

Paul sighed as Jamie pulled his gun out and waved it in the air. "Don't worry, we're all packing tonight."

"You'd better open up Finn or the punters will be knocking down the door." Paul stood and made his way over to Millie. "I'm gonna ask one last time, go into the back if trouble starts. Please." Satisfied when Millie gave him a nod he smiled. "It's going to be okay Millie, it's just a precaution."

Paul made his way to his table and joined his men. He watched Millie as she prepared the bar ready for the first lot of punters that entered. He stared thoughtfully at her and drank in all her features. The way she flicked her hair back. The annoyed expression she would give him when she caught him watching her. Paul smiled, she always made him smile and yet she didn't know it. Paul watched Millie's face light up when Rosie walked in. He felt a pang of jealousy, he wanted her to look at him like that. He wanted to be the one that made her smile. Paul stood up and walked to the bar. He needed to hear her voice, but instead he heard Rosie's.

"But do yourself a favour and don't experience it with him Mil, it will only bring you heartache." Rosie said.

Paul knew she was talking about him, he caught Millie's eye and held up his glass, he needed a refill. As Millie walked over with the whiskey bottle Paul smiled. "There are worse people you could experience it with." He noticed Millie's eyes go wide. "Yeah, I heard that comment."

"She worries about me, and for the record there's nothing going on between us." Millie replied.

Paul picked up his drink and held it up. "Yet." He added and then made his way back to the table. His heart was racing. He took his seat and took a large sip of his drink to calm his nerves. When he looked back over to Millie she was in deep conversation with Rosie. Paul looked at the door when it opened. In walked an old gypsy woman. He rose from his seat and stood at the bar, ready. Behind her walked Billy, the mouthy bastard that had a go at Millie. Paul's eyes flicked to Millie when he heard the glass smash that she was holding. Her complexion had paled, and she stood deadly still. Paul's temper flared as he refocused on the old woman.

"Well. Well. Well. What have we here then?" The woman sneered at Millie.

Paul knew straight away who it was. Flo Cooper. Millie's mother-in-law.

Chapter Fifteen

Millie took a deep breath; she knew Flo would see the shock on her face, but she also knew that she had to face her. Flo looked just the same as the last time she had seen her. Her black hair plaited and hung down her back and her hard weathered face wore the same sneer it always had when she had spoken to Millie. "What do you want, Flo?" Millie swallowed down her nerves as the colour drained from her face. Before Flo could answer Paul Kelly stood at her side.

"She said, what do you want?" Paul growled.

"I've come to take my darling daughter-in-law home where she belongs." Flo smiled.

"Millie, do you belong with this thing?" Paul asked.

Millie shook her head slowly. "No. I don't." Millie looked up as the door opened, and in walked Duke followed by ten men. She glanced at Paul and noticed he tensed. His hands immediately balled into fists.

"Get in the back Millie." Paul called over his shoulder.

"Rose." Millie waved at her to follow. As she shut the door, she heard the first crash as the fighting broke out.

"Millie?"

Millie felt Rosie's hands grab her as she slid to the floor, she pulled her knees up and hugged them while rocking backwards and forwards. Then the tears came. Two arms hugged her as she sat there and sobbed. The noise of shouting and crashing was filling her head. She couldn't think. "I can't do this Rose. I can't live like this."

"Then don't. Look we can move away, Bethnal Green's only up the road but it can be a new start." Rosie wiped at Millie's eyes.

"Run away you mean.... I've been running and hiding all my life, I'm tired Rose. Tired of being treated like scum." Standing up, Millie straightened her skirt. "It stops now."

"What are you gonna do? Millie.... Where are you going?" Rosie asked.

Millie opened the door to the bar; she was met with arms and fists flying everywhere. Flo was in the corner whacking anyone that came near her with an ashtray. Millie felt the anger build until she thought she was going to burst. She grabbed the shotgun from underneath the bar, cocked it and pointed it towards the ceiling. She squeezed the trigger twice, in quick succession. The two shells hit the ceiling causing plaster to fall. It looked like it was snowing and the four people standing underneath quickly ducked away. The sound continued to ring inside her head. Everyone stopped and looked at her. "Enough.... I've had enough." She felt Paul tug at the gun.

"Let's put that down before you actually kill someone."

Momentarily stunned, the vision of Elijah's twisted body filled Millie's mind. Shaking her head, as if to blot out the memory, she pulled the gun away from his grasp. "If I had intended to kill someone, trust me, they would already be dead." Millie turned her attention to Duke. "Why are you here?" She watched as Duke rubbed blood from his lip.

"I told you. My cousin Rueben is missing, and this was the last place he was seen."

"But he hasn't been here, not in here anyway. So why do you think he had?" Millie watched Duke frown.

"I was told this was the last place he was seen."

"Well whoever told you that wasn't telling you the truth. Now if you want to sit and talk about it sensibly then do so, but if you plan on wrecking this pub then I must insist you leave. The choice is yours."

"I don't take orders from little girls." Duke replied.

Millie smiled. "I'm the one holding the gun."

Millie almost burst out laughing as Duke's face turned purple. "Now what's it to be?"

Duke nodded. "Okay. We'll talk, but if I don't get the answers I want, then this." Millie watched as Duke pointed around him. "Will be the least of your problems."

Millie noticed Flo out of the corner of her eye. She started to walk towards the bar. "What do you want now, old woman?"

"Duke, she was married to my Levi. She's the only family I've got left. She belongs with me."

"I belong with no-one, especially not you. I had enough of the way you and your son treated me. Do you really think I would go back to that?" Millie replied bitterly.

"It doesn't matter what you want, girl. You belong to me, especially now I've lost my Elijah too." Flo replied with a sneer.

Millie glanced at Rosie, who had the same look of dread on her face. She then glanced at Paul who was watching her closely. She took a deep breath then refocused on Flo. "Levi's dead and I belong to no one, especially not with some evil old cow. Now get your dirty scheming arse out of this pub." Millie raised the gun and aimed it at Flo's head.

"This isn't over girl." Flo scowled.

Millie raised the gun higher. "Now get out."

Millie breathed a sigh of relief as Flo turned and walked out her thoughts turned to what Flo would do next. She knew this wasn't over. Millie was brought out of her thoughts and turned to Duke as he burst out laughing. "What's so funny?"

"The guns empty, you used both barrels."

"Give me the gun Millie, please." Paul held out his hand.

"Maybe you should have a chat with Duke in the back while everyone else helps straighten this place out." Millie surveyed the room. It wasn't as bad as last time but there were still upturned tables and chairs scattered around the bar. At least cleaning this mess up would keep her mind off of Flo's retaliation.

Chapter Sixteen

Paul sat at the table opposite Duke. Just staring. "Okay. Talk." He rubbed his scar, it was itching and starting to give him a headache.

"Where's Rueben?" Duke stared back.

"Who the fuck is Rueben and more to the point, how would I know where he is?" Paul leaned forward and studied Duke. "You know this is my manor, if this Rueben were about, I would have heard about it." Paul watched as Duke pulled out a packet of cigarettes and then lit one. He hated smoking, he hated the smell it left in the air, the way smokers smelt like ashtrays and the way they threw their dog ends onto the street.

"Don't mind if I smoke, do ya?" Duke asked as he took a long drag on the cigarette.

Paul waved the smoke away and ignored the question, instead he carried on. "Can you get to the point; I've got things to do."

"Fine." Duke replied before stubbing the cigarette out on a saucer. "Someone knows about it. The fingers been pointed at your mob." Duke paused. "Who else would have the balls to top a traveller."

"I would start with whoever told you he was here....and what was he doing in Stepney?" Paul sat back and folded his arms.

"Drugs." Duke replied flatly.

"Drugs? I control the drugs on this manor, and I haven't heard of anyone else selling around here. If I had of, I would've topped him, and you would know it's me." Paul ignored Duke's glare and carried on. "The woman who came in for the girl, Millie. You tell her to stay away, because I will kill her if she comes anywhere near Millie again."

"More threats Paul.... I don't give a shit about some girl or Flo, but I will tear this town apart to find out what's happened to Rueben, that's your final warning."

Paul watched as Duke stood up and left. He blew out slowly as he looked at the bent up dog end that was still smoking. Paul grabbed it and stubbed it out properly and then went and joined his men at the bar. "They gone?"

Jamie Carter nodded. "Yeah, but I've got a feeling they'll be back."

Paul turned and looked at Millie. "Are you okay?" He could see she looked shaken; the colour still hadn't returned to her cheeks.

"Yes." Millie replied as she straightened the plates of food. "Lucky this lot didn't go over."

"We'll talk later." Looking around the pub Paul pointed to the piano. "It's New Year's Eve. So let's celebrate." Paul watched as the pianist took her seat and started playing despite looking more than a little dishevelled.

"Look at me fecking ceiling!" Finn shouted. "I'm grateful for you stopping the fight, Mill but did you have to put two fecking great big holes up there." Finn pointed up as another flurry of plaster drifted down and made Finn sneeze.

"It was either that or kill someone Finn." Paul replied before Millie could. "And I'll pay to get it fixed, now come on, get a round of drinks for everyone, on me."

Paul sat and watched Millie for the rest of the evening, she was putting on a good front, but he could see she was worried, and he couldn't have that. In fact, he wouldn't have that. He had posted a couple of his men out the front as a precaution, but he didn't expect any more trouble tonight. He glanced at his watch; it was nearly midnight.

After everyone had sung Auld Lang Syne, the pub started to empty. Paul watched Millie as she placed the dirty glasses on the bar. He looked over to Finn. He looked done in.

"Why don't you go up once you've locked up. I'll finish tidying this lot then I'll be hitting the sack." Millie told Finn.

"No child, you should go get to bed, I think you've done enough for one day." Finn replied earnestly.

"I'll lock up." Paul informed them both. "I'll be staying here tonight with a couple of my men, just in case."

"Just in case what? You don't think they'll come back so soon.... Bethnal Green's looking more tempting by the minute." Millie added.

"No. I don't know. Look, it's just a precaution. And what's Bethnal Green got to do with it?" Paul rubbed his scar as his temper started to flare.

"Nothing, it's got nothing to do with anything. Okay Finn, I'll call it a night." Millie replied.

Paul watched as Millie placed a small kiss on Finn's cheek and then disappeared into the back. He felt a small tinge of jealousy and had to shake his head to stop it before he followed her through to the back. "Where do you think you're going?"

"To bed, it's been a long day.... We can talk in the morning." Millie replied.

"We will talk now. I'm not daft Millie, that day in the hospital when you ran into me, you had been out, and when that pikey bitch mentioned her old man was dead you looked at Rosie straight away. You both looked guilty." Paul watched Millie's shoulders slump. "Look, I don't care about some dead pikey, but we still need to talk."

"What have we got to talk about?" Millie yawned.

"Come and sit down." Paul pointed to the table and waited for

Millie to sit. "You went pale when that woman spoke to you. What's that about?"

"She's Levi's mum. We've never got on." Millie put her head down.

"If you've never got on then why does she want you back with her?" Paul placed his finger under Millie's chin and lifted her head slightly. "Millie?" He asked softly.

"Now Levi's gone.... I'm her meal ticket."

Paul wiped away the lone tear that trickled down Millie's cheek. "What did she make you do?"

"She." Millie took a deep breath. "I can't, I'm sorry. It's the past and that's where I want it left.... buried."

"You need to face whatever's happened Millie, because some things won't stay buried until you do." Paul placed his hand on Millie's, it was soft and warm. He leant forward without thinking and brushed his lips against hers, the moment sent shockwaves through him. Pulling back, he stood abruptly. "You'd better get some sleep." He walked back out to the bar, annoyed with himself. Whatever this feeling was, he was going to fight it.

Chapter Seventeen

January 1976

Millie was enjoying the January sales; they were in full swing. The shoppers were out in their droves, despite the freezing temperatures. All the Christmas decorations were down and everywhere looked drab. Millie hated this time of year, the little bit of sparkle that Christmas brought, vanished. Millie watched Rosie as she held a dress up. "It suits you Rose. You should buy it."

"And what are you going to treat yourself too?" Rosie grabbed another dress off of the rail and thrust it towards Millie. "Try this one. It will compliment your eye colour."

Millie held the dress up to her body and looked in the mirror. "It's a bit short."

"With legs like those girl you should have them on display, come on." Rosie headed towards the changing room, dragging Millie with her. "We'll go Wimpy after. My treat."

"Fine." Millie frowned. She didn't need a dress like this, she never went out and it was too good to wear for work. "It's a bit tight." She told Rosie as she had squeezed into it.

"It's perfect. You look amazing, like one of those models." Rosie replied in admiration.

"I don't think you get many 5'2" models about Rose." Millie laughed.

"Why do you do that?" Rosie stood in front of Millie and placed her hands on her hips.

"Do what?" Millie frowned.

"Always put yourself down.... Paul Kelly obviously fancies you, or he wouldn't have kissed you."

"That was three days ago. I haven't seen him since." Millie thought back to New Year's Eve. "I know he kissed me but when he pulled back, I could see he regretted it."

"Did you...regret it?" Rosie asked.

Millie shook her head slowly. "No. It's gonna sound stupid..." Millie trailed off.

"No, it won't, just say what you're thinking." Rosie prompted.

"It wasn't like a kiss I've ever had; it was soft and warm, and I felt something, oh I don't know." Millie stepped out of the dress and replaced it back onto the hanger.

"Nothing happened since?" Rosie raised an eyebrow.

Millie pulled her jeans back on. "No, I haven't seen him. His men have been in, guarding the place. When he comes in it's gonna be awkward.... Let's pay." Millie stopped when she caught a woman staring at her from across the shop. "That woman's been following me."

"What woman?" Rosie followed Millie's gaze.

"There, near the door." Millie pointed as the woman turned and left.

"Are you sure it's the same woman?"

"I think so.... Sometimes I get a sense of being watched which is worse, and other times I see her." Millie shivered.

"Maybe you should tell Paul Kelly." Rose handed her money over and looked at Millie. "What?"

"I'm responsible for my own life. Not Paul Kelly. Can you stop talking about him? Please." Millie grabbed the bag from the cashier. "Thank you." Then walked to the door. She looked up and down the high street, but the woman had disappeared.

"I think the lady protests too much." Rosie laughed. "Look I don't want you getting involved with Paul Kelly, his reputation is shocking, but...."

"There is no but. Now are you buying lunch or not?" Millie slipped her arm through Rosie's as they made their way to the Wimpy.

Millie ate quickly so she could return to work and help Finn set up the bar. She walked back with Rosie and the two women gossiped about old times. It was refreshing for Millie to have her mind taken off Paul Kelly, Flo and the gypsy feud. Her head had started to hurt again with all the thoughts that ran through it. All the worry she had and the consequences she knew would come. By the time Millie returned home she made her way up the stairs and dropped her bags on the bed. She had never spent so much money on herself. As she unpacked the bags, she pulled out a pair of briefs, not her normal type. These were lacy. As she held them up there came a knock at her door. "Yes?" The door opened slowly, and Millie's face dropped. "What do you want?" Millie studied Paul's face, he looked nervous.

"I've come to see if you're alright?" Paul closed the door behind him.

"I'm fine.... Are you alright?" Millie watched Paul's eyes travel to the garment she was holding. She immediately screwed them up into a ball and tucked them into the drawer of her bedside cabinet.

"Yes.... I thought you might be ready to talk." Paul tucked his hands in his pockets.

Millie smiled; the great Paul Kelly was nervous. "What do you want to talk about?"

"The gipsies aren't gonna go away you know, not until they find who's responsible for this Rueben's death. You're the only link Millie, so what do you know?" Paul asked.

"Why do you think I know anything.... I was a prisoner, Paul. I hardly went out and if I did, I had to be quick.... I told you all I know."

"Levi had cocaine in his pickup truck." Millie sighed as Paul continued. "Did he see Rueben?"

"Yes, but I don't know what they got up to." Millie shrugged.

"Duke said Rueben was selling drugs. Was Levi?"

"I wouldn't be privy to info like that, I was an outsider. I've spent the last six years of my life being told what to do, and when to do it. You once asked me whose side I'm on, well to be perfectly truthful, it's not theirs but then it's not yours either, it's mine. I'm on my side, because at the end of the day I'm the only one that's gonna look after me." Millie watched as Paul's face hardened.

"I'm on your side Millie, you may not believe that but it's true. Who stopped that pikey from smashing you in the face...Me. Who was at your side when that pikey bitch demanded you go with her....Me. So don't act like you're all alone because we both know you ain't."

"So where have you been for the last three days?" Millie walked towards Paul and stood in front of him. "You kissed me and then you ran out of here like I was a leper."

"You kissed me back." Paul replied.

"Yes, I did, but I think we can both agree it was a mistake. Now if you don't mind, I need to get on." Millie nodded to the door. "And close it after yourself."

"I still need to know about Levi." Paul crossed his arms.. "So, I won't be going anywhere until I know everything."

"If anyone will know it will be his mother, Flo." Millie replied.

"Then we need to have a word with her, get your coat." Paul grabbed the handle of the door.

"I'm not going." Millie stepped back as she swallowed down the bile that came up her throat. "You can't make me." The colour drained from her face as she stumbled back onto the bed. Her body started to tremble, and she lost all control.

"What are you scared of.... What did she do to you?"

Millie stood in Flo's front room; the coal man stood in the doorway smiling at Flo. "One bag of coal for a look or two for a look and a feel." Flo nodded and turned to Millie. 'Take ya top off girl and hurry up." Flo demanded. Millie stood her ground and shook her head. 'Don't make me fucking angry, or I'll tell Levi you been out flirting. Now what's it to be?" Flo grinned. Millie knew Levi would give her a good hiding if he thought she had been out, so there was no choice. She pulled her top over her head and stood there while the coal man enjoyed himself.

"Get out Paul." Millie whispered as the memories flooded her mind once again.

"No. Not until you tell me what happened." Paul moved closer.

"I'm sorry. I can't." Millie pulled herself up and sat on the edge of the bed.

"You know, when I first met you, I thought, she's a fighter. You answered back and stood up for yourself, but here you are, letting one woman control you."

"She's not controlling me." Millie snapped.

"No.... Well what is she doing then? You're sat here too scared to face her, looks like control to me."

Millie felt the bed move as Paul sat next to her. "You won't leave me there?" She asked him.

"Of course, I wouldn't. I'll take a couple of the boys to keep watch while we go in and talk to her. I've got a feeling she'll say more with you there." Paul smiled. "Shall we go then?"

Millie nodded her head. It was time to face her fears. "Okay."

Chapter Eighteen

The drive to Flo's was done mostly in silence, Paul really wanted to ask Millie out to dinner, but judging by the look on her face, now wasn't the right time to ask. Instead, he sat staring at the house. He was disgusted, it was a tip. There was rubbish in the front garden and the garden gate was hanging off. He glanced across to Millie, to see if she was okay but judging by the grip she had on the door handle, she was anything but. "Ready?" She didn't reply, all he got was a nod. "I'll do all the talking." Paul Jumped out of his Range Rover and walked around to Millie's side. He helped her out and then waved to his men in the car behind to follow. The four of them stood at the door while two men kept watch from the road. After knocking loudly Paul stood back and waited. As soon as the door opened, he stuck his foot in and pushed, which caused Flo to fly backwards onto her arse.

"What the fuck...." Flo mumbled.

Paul laughed; her expression was priceless. "Get up." Paul dragged her up onto her feet and pulled her into the front room. He pulled out a chair from the table, then pushed her into the seat. He nodded for his men to tie her up. "We need a little chat about your no-good son."

"You'll regret this girl." Flo spat at Millie. "Just you wait."

Paul pulled Millie behind him. "You will address me ya pikey bitch. Now, what was your son doing with drugs in his truck?" Paul waited for an answer, but none came. "Roll out the tool kit boys." Paul waited, he wanted to take his time. She had to be scared enough to tell the truth. Paul studied the instruments then ran his hand over them, then stopped when he reached a pair of pliers. "Hold her hand still."

"Get off, I don't know anything. Millie tell them, the men's business is their own." Flo pleaded.

Paul looked at Millie, she was standing back with her arms wrapped around herself, probably a form of comfort Paul thought. How he would love to wrap his own arms around her and keep her safe, he knew she was scared, he could see it in her eyes. As his temper flared, he turned back to Flo, he would make her pay for what she had done to Millie. "This little pinkie doesn't need a nail." Paul placed the pliers against her nail and squeezed them shut. "Now I've been told this hurts." As he slowly pulled, Flo screamed out in panic.

"What do you want to know? Please. I'll tell you anything." Flo begged.

Paul opened his mouth to speak but then caught sight of Millie as she stepped forward, Paul nodded when she looked at him.

"Was Levi selling drugs?" Millie asked.

"Yes, he and Rueben were selling them, but they were on a wage, they didn't get the profit." Flo answered.

"Who were they selling them for?" Paul asked in a much firmer voice than Millie had used. He realised it had to be a major player to provide that much.

"I don't know. Levi never said." Flo looked at Millie. "You know what he was like. Everything was a secret."

Millie took another step forward as Paul watched. "But you knew he was selling drugs.... He never told me anything, Flo. I was treated like shit, not only by him but also by you."

Paul pulled Millie back, more than a little surprised that she had found her backbone. "Was he told where to sell them?" Paul asked.

Flo nodded. "Stepney. The Black Bear and The Woodman. That's all I know."

"When did he pick up the drugs and from where?" Paul studied the pliers. "Seems a shame to have come all this way and not use them."

"Wait. He often went over to Bethnal Green, but I'm not sure. Look I've never seen the drugs, Levi would bung me some money when he had a good night. I don't know anything else; I swear."

Paul laughed then looked at Millie. "Do you believe her?"

Millie shook her head. "No."

Paul passed the pliers to one of his men. "Pull her thumb nails out." He grabbed Millie and led her out of the house before the screams became too much.

"Did you have to do that?" Millie asked.

"All what she did to you, and you ask me that." Paul replied as he opened the car door. "Get in."

"It wasn't your job to dish out punishment on my behalf." Millie argued.

The rest of the journey was made in silence. While Paul glanced every so often in Millie's direction. She did not look happy.

After dropping Millie back at the pub, he made his way to see Ronnie. He pulled through the tall metal gates and parked next to Ronnie's Jag. Paul sat for a moment as he tried to get his temper under control. Eventually giving up he entered the porta cabin and found Ronnie Taylor sitting behind his desk. He had a stack of paperwork in front of him. "Ron." Paul nodded his head.

"Come in and take a seat son. Bloody paperwork does my bonce in, anyway how are you.... You alright?" Ronnie asked.

"Yeah, could do with a drink though." Paul was still fuming with Millie. He didn't get a thank you, he didn't even get a goodbye, and the way she slammed the car door was un-fucking believable.

"Okay son, do you wanna talk about it." Ronnie poured the Whisky and handed one to Paul.

"No.... I would rather concentrate on business." Paul downed his drink and handed Ronnie the glass for a refill. "Fucking women. I will never understand them, ungrateful little cow, everything I've done, and she gets the hump."

Ronnie smiled. "That's women for ya... So, who is she?"

Paul knocked back the next drink. "She's a nobody, a fucking pain in the arse nobody."

"Yep. I can see she's a nobody by the way you can't stop talking about her." Ronnie refilled Paul's glass and sat back.

Paul looked down at his drink and sighed. "I've always been in control of my life, my feelings. I know where I'm heading, I know what I want, and then out of the blue, bang. She's come along and now I don't know what the fuck I'm doing." Paul gulped his drink down and banged the glass on the desk.

"You need to tell her how you feel, son." Ronnie finally replied.

Paul looked at Ronnie in disbelief. "Have you listened to anything I've said?"

"Son. I've heard every word you haven't said, forty minutes you've gone on about this woman. I'm telling you, that's love. And I'll go one further, go and tell her before someone else snaps her up. Then we can get some bloody work done, now go, I'll see you next Friday to sign the contracts." Ronnie placed the unread paperwork into his desk drawer. "One more thing. What's her name?"

"Millie." Paul replied stiffly before he marched out, annoyed with himself. He was a businessman; no woman should interfere with business. Jumping into his car, he reversed out onto the road without looking, causing a car to swerve and beep. "FUCK OFF!" Paul screamed, while sticking his middle finger up, then zoomed off to the pub.

* * *

As Paul pulled up outside the pub, thirty minutes later, he checked himself in the mirror. He noticed his scar which had turned red. It always went red when he was angry, so he closed his eyes and took a few deep breaths to calm himself. When he was ready, he made his way to the door. On entering, the first thing he saw was Millie, chatting to Jamie Carter. Clenching and unclenching his fists he made his way to the bar.

"Here's the man himself." Jamie laughed.

"Exactly where have you been while the rest of us have been working?" Paul asked as he glanced at Millie; she still didn't look happy. "Whisky if it's not too much trouble." Paul refocused on Jamie. "We need to go and see Duke and put a stop to this shit once and for all."

"Are you stupid.... That will cause a never-ending war." Jamie placed his glass on the bar. "I'll have a refill too love."

"If we do nothing, we're gonna get every Tom, Dick, and Harry trying their luck. We need to put a stop to it now, and she isn't your love." Paul grabbed the glass as Millie went to put it down and knocked it back in one. "Same again."

"Please." She replied.

Paul studied her face for a second. She looked cross. Her eyes looked defiant, and she held eye contact. Paul didn't know if he wanted to laugh or kiss her. He decided neither would be appropriate. "Please, and one for yourself sweetheart." Paul held in his laughter as Millie huffed.

"Is something going on between you two?" Jamie whispered.

"No.... Yes.... I don't know. I don't know what's going on." Paul sighed. Maybe Ronnie had a point after all. "Anyway, back to business. I want every man we can get to pay the pikeys a visit tomorrow night. Get the word out. We'll meet at the warehouse at 7pm."

Chapter Nineteen

Millie lay in bed and thought about the conversation she had listened in on. Paul taking on the travellers was nuts. Her heart thumped in her chest, with just the thought. She looked at the clock, it was only 6.30am. She pulled the covers back and swung her legs out of the bed. She needed a plan. She reached out and grabbed her white bunny and studied it. It needed a wash and re-stuffing. This was the only possession she'd had all her life. A gift from the mother that never wanted her. So why was it so precious? Millie shrugged and placed the bunny on the bed. She didn't have time for sentiment, she had things to do.

After washing and dressing she grabbed some breakfast and then waited outside the pub. The taxi pulled up and Millie jumped in.

"Are you sure you want to go there, miss?" The taxi driver asked as he looked in the rear-view mirror.

"Yes. I'm sure." Millie smiled. She wasn't though. What sane person in their right mind would want to go there?

After fifteen minutes the taxi ground to a halt. "This is as far as I go love. Are you certain you want to be dropped off here?" He asked again.

"Yes. Here's your money. Thank you." Millie jumped out of the taxi and looked up ahead. It was the start of a dirt track, mud was churned up in places and there were old bricks and rubble thrown down, Millie assumed it was so that the motors didn't get stuck. The track was tree lined and although most of the trees had lost their leaves, Millie could imagine just how beautiful they would look in the summer. She was an outdoor girl, she much preferred to spend her time outside with nature rather than cooped up in a house. She had imagined having a little garden when she got married, that didn't quite work out though. Instead, she got a prison. Sighing to herself, she began the walk. She could hear the dogs barking and hoped they would be chained up. They didn't sound friendly. She spotted children playing with an old car tyre, they stopped when they saw her. She noticed curtains twitching and expected to be ambushed any minute. She looked around and surveyed the Traveller camp.

"Can I help you girl?" An old woman asked.

"I'm here to see Duke Lee. Could you point me in the right direction please?" Millie felt more than one pair of eyes on her. She cursed herself for coming here alone.

"Mushy boy, go and get Duke." She hollered to one of the boys. He took off and ran to a trailer at the other end of the camp.

"Thank you." Millie replied to the old woman. She stood deadly still on the spot and waited for Duke to show. A couple of minutes later he came walking down the muddy lane.

"What do you want?" Duke asked gruffly.

Millie noticed his unfriendly tone. "I want to talk to you about this drugs business." Millie pointed to his trailer. "In private."

"You'd better follow me then." Duke turned and walked off with Millie following. He pulled open his door and waved for her to go in. "Start talking."

Millie perched on the edge of a bunk and looked around. The caravan was clean and tidy, which didn't really surprise her. She knew most travellers were clean and tidy. Even Flo kept her house sparkling. "This war you've got going on with Paul, it needs to stop."

Millie stopped talking when Duke burst out laughing. "I don't see what's so funny Duke. This is going to hurt people I care about."

"Who do you think you are coming here to my home, telling me what to do gorger girl." Duke cracked his knuckles. "Rueben has gone missing and the last place he was seen was in Stepney. Your pub to be precise. Now tell me girl, what would you do if someone hurt one of your own, or worse?"

"That's just it though Duke. He has never been in the Artichoke. We went to see Flo, the pubs he was dealing in were the Black Bull and the Woodman. Levi and Rueben that is. And they were working for someone else, but I don't know who." Millie watched Duke's face change. He looked like he was thinking it over. "So, we need to find out who they were working for."

"Look, Millie?"

Millie nodded.

"Millie. You shouldn't be involved in men's business, you're gonna end up getting hurt because this will only stop when I get answers."

"But I am involved. Every time you come and smash the pub up, I'm the one that has to clean it, and what happens when innocent people get caught in the crossfire, for something that wasn't their fault. I've finally got a home where feel safe and now, you're taking it away from me." Millie fought the tears as they pricked her eyes. "I know how these things play out I..." Millie stopped when the door opened, and a woman walked in.

"This is Connie, my wife." Duke nodded.

Millie smiled politely. "Hello." She studied the woman briefly. She was petite with long blonde hair. She seemed nervous; it made Millie wonder if Duke treated his wife the same way Levi had treated his?

"Hello." Connie replied then walked to the other end of the trailer.

There was another knock at the door and when it opened Billy, Levi's cousin stepped in. "What's that fucking bitch doing here?"

"Remember you're in my home Billy boy, I won't have you speaking like that in front of Connie. Now what's this about?" Duke asked.

"Her boyfriend hurt Flo, pulled her nails out, and she watched. I'm gonna smash you to pieces you fucking gorger scum." Billy replied.

"Is this true?" Duke asked as he approached Millie. "Answer the question." He demanded.

"We went to find out if Levi was selling drugs." Millie flinched as Billy moved towards her, her heartbeat was thumping in her chest and her whole body started to shake.

"Get away from her." Connie shouted. "You don't come in here threatening young girls. Duke, kick him out."

Millie watched as Duke took hold of Billy as he fought to get to her. "You heard Connie, get out."

"So, she gets away with it, You going soft?" Billy spat.

Duke held him at the open door and then punched him in the face, Billy fell back and landed flat on his back. "You don't ever come here again; be thankful I'm letting you walk away." Duke then pulled the door shut. "You had better start talking, girl."

"I told you; we went to find out if Levi was selling drugs, and do you know what? I don't care if Paul hurt her, she did far worse to me when I was married to Levi. My life was hell." Millie moved towards the door.

"Hang on." Connie called. "Duke, if that's true you can't punish her, that Flo's a right piece of work, I've never liked her. It's about time someone taught her a lesson, and look at her, she's just a child."

"I can't let what happened to Flo go unpunished, you know that." Duke replied as he rolled his eyes.

"And why not, you don't like that lot anyway." Connie replied as she folded her arms.

"Fine." Duke huffed. "Look Millie, I'm sorry you're caught up in this mess, but take my advice and keep out of it, thanks to my wife you've been let off the hook for Flo, but it won't happen again.... Now if you don't mind, I've got work to do." Duke pushed open the door and motioned for Millie to leave.

Millie looked up as Connie cut in. "Duke Lee, you can't leave that girl to make her own way home."

Duke sighed. "She made her own way here so I'm sure she's more than capable."

"It's fine, I can get a bus from the end of the road." Millie replied quickly before another row broke out.

"No, you won't. Billy might be waiting; Duke can drop you off." Connie grabbed the kettle and walked to the door.

Millie watched as she filled it with water from a large milk urn that stood just outside the trailer. "I don't want to cause no trouble, I think we already have enough, don't you?" Millie noticed the look Connie gave Duke, she almost wanted to laugh.

"It's fine. I'll drop you back." Duke turned and kissed Connie on the cheek. "Happy now?"

Connie nodded with a small smile while Millie stood there and witnessed the small show of affection between them. "Thank you. It was nice meeting you Connie." As Millie walked towards the door, two boys pushed their way through.

"Mind your manners boy's, we have a guest." Duke clipped them both around the head. "These two are my boy's. Jes and Aron."

"Hello pretty lady." Jes grinned.

Connie walked over and pulled him away. "Enough of that Jes, you should go Millie."

Millie stood there slightly confused. Connie had seemed friendly at first but now she seemed.... angry? Millie nodded and left without another word.

The journey back was quick, Millie had the luxury of listening to Dean Martin belting out of the door speakers. 'Trailer for sale or rent' Millie knew the words. Levi listened to the same music, although he preferred Connie Francis.

Duke pulled up outside the pub, Millie closed her eyes when she saw Paul walking towards the motor. He opened the door and pulled her out. "Paul."

"Millie, so you are on their side then." Paul glared.

Millie watched as Duke climbed out and walked around to meet him. "She came to see me about Rueben and Levi. And if she's on anyone's side it's yours."

"I don't want all this trouble Paul. Please." Millie begged. The tension was so thick Millie could taste it. She saw Paul's fists were clenched and glanced at Duke, he was staring directly at Paul, his eyes narrowed.

"Get inside, we'll talk later." Paul replied.

"That's right Millie, do as you're told." Duke laughed.

Paul threw the first punch as Millie watched in horror. The two men started trading blow for blow while Millie stood by helplessly. "STOP!" She cried, but it was in vain, she doubted they could hear her. People started to crowd around the two men as the fight became more violent. As if in slow motion Millie watched Duke throw a punch straight into Paul's face. The blood trickled from his lip immediately, and he staggered back a few steps. Before Millie could blink, Paul charged at Duke and both men ended up on the ground. Duke had a cut to his right eye which had blood dripping from it. Millie looked across the road as the sirens caught her ear. Two Police vans had turned up. Millie mingled in with the crowd as the two men were arrested, handcuffed and each placed into a van. Millie cursed; she had made things a whole lot worse.

Chapter Twenty

Millie closed up and headed to the bar. She needed a drink. Paul hadn't been in since he was released from the Police station. Her only contact had been a phone call, where he had demanded she keep out of his business. That had ended up in a full blown shouting match, and she had put the phone down on him. He did phone back, but she had refused to answer. More than likely because deep down she thought he was right. Both men had been kept in a cell overnight and then charged with disturbing the peace and she felt guilty. She should have been charged, not them. Finn had told her not to worry but how could she not, after all it had been her interfering that had caused this mess. Maybe she should change her name to chaos. Her thoughts went to Connie, she seemed nice at first, the way she demanded Duke drop her back. But then she turned when her boys came in. Sighing she rolled her eyes, too many people pretend to be nice. Putting the whole shit show out of her mind Millie grabbed a glass from the shelf. It had been a long day, and her feet were aching. "Do you want a drink, Finn?" She called through to the back. Minutes later he joined her.

She took a sip of her wine and closed her eyes. "Did you hear about that new plane they've got Finn, Concord, did its first commercial flight, to Bahrain? I wonder if you get motion sickness on it?"

"Heard it on the news. Whatever will they think of next." Finn remarked.

Millie noticed the bags under his eyes, he looked tired. She didn't blame him. This feud had started to affect his business. Millie had heard a few of the regulars had started to drink up the road. She didn't blame them either, who would want to drink in a war zone.

"At least Duke and his mob haven't been in, I don't think I could deal with clearing up after that lot." Millie placed her glass down and thought of Connie again, the way she was protective over her sons. What must it be like to have a family? "Finn?"

"Yes Millie. I know that tone." Finn replied.

"Do you remember you said I could look for my real parents, where would I start?" Millie watched Finn take a large gulp of his drink.

"Records, birth deaths and marriages maybe? Or you could try the hospital.... So what's brought this on?"

Millie thought for a moment. What had brought this on? "I don't know, I.... I'm curious, I guess. It's like half my life is a secret. I feel half empty if that makes sense." Millie took a sip of her wine. Was it what she wanted or was it what she needed.

"What if they don't want to know you?" Finn asked.

Millie nodded. "I'm prepared for them to not want me. I'm used to that feeling now."

Before Finn replied there was a knock at the door. "Who the fecking hell is that at this time of night." Finn walked towards the door and cursed under his breath, while Millie watched and giggled. She would never tire of listening to Finn moan, the way he said fuck made it sound almost nice. The Irish accent was her favourite.

"Too late for a night cap Finn?" Paul asked.

"For you, no." Finn replied. Millie watched as he opened the door and ushered Paul in.

"Millie." Paul nodded. "You're in my seat."

Millie watched as Paul's eyes twinkled, he was in a good mood. "Looks like you'll have to find yourself another." Millie returned his smile. Her heart started to race as he walked towards her.

"So why are you two up so late?" Paul asked, looking between the two of them. "Anything happened?"

"No, just a busy night. We're having a nightcap." Finn grabbed a glass and poured Paul a drink. "Here."

Paul took the drink and downed it in one. "Have you had a good day, Millie?"

Finn stood and yawned. "Think I'll hit the hay. Make sure you lock up after Paul goes Millie."

Millie nodded and returned her attention to Paul. She could smell his cologne. She watched his hand wrap around his glass and looked up into his eyes. He was staring straight back at her. She felt her tummy flutter. She dropped her eyes to her own drink before she replied. "I'm sure you haven't come here to ask about my day, so what do you want?" Sitting back in her seat she waited for the bollocking that she was certain would follow. Millie glanced up and watched as Paul's face flushed pink.

"I came to ask you to dinner Miss Snotty." Paul blew out slowly.

"I'm not snotty." Millie snapped. "So go on, ask me then."

"I thought I just did." Paul replied sharply.

"Okay." Millie took a sip of her drink and kept her eyes down.

"Okay what?" Paul asked, sounding confused.

"Okay, I'll have dinner with you." Millie felt Paul's arm slip around her waist. Her breathing fastened as he pulled her towards him.

"Well, that wasn't so hard, was it?" Paul's mouth was only inches from hers.

"No." Millie whispered just before Paul's lips touched hers. The kiss was soft and gentle. Millie felt her heart rate increase as Paul teased her with his tongue. As he pulled back, Millie opened her eyes and looked at him. "This is a bad idea."

"I know." Paul replied before kissing her again.

Millie pulled away first this time. "A really bad idea."

"I know." Paul leant forward one more time.

Millie felt a stirring deep inside, a tingling sensation that filled her body. As Paul started to kiss her ear she struggled to breath. She tilted her head back as he continued to kiss down her neck. Millie jumped as a loud crash filled the room. Her eyes were drawn to the middle of the room where a bottle had landed, as it touched the floor it smashed, and flames seemed to erupt.

"Get in the back." Paul shouted as he grabbed her hand.

Millie pulled away. "No. The flames are spreading." She ran into the back room and grabbed the tablecloth then returned to Paul to help put the fire out.

"What the feck was that?" Finn asked as he ran into the room. "Jesus Fecking Christ." He grabbed the tablecloth and started to stamp the flames out. "Those Fecking pikeys. I'm gonna kill 'em me self."

"We don't know it was them." Millie coughed as the smoke hung in the air. "Why would they try to set fire to the pub?" Millie made her way to the door and watched Paul as he stood outside scanning the horizon.

"Who else would do something so stupid.... It's got to have been them." Paul turned and made his way back into the pub. "I'll have to leave men here day and night. Just in case they try something again."

"Maybe Millie can stay at Rosie's until this is over." Finn suggested.

"Good idea." Paul nodded. "She can pack a bag."

Millie watched the two men discuss her like she wasn't there. Just like everyone else in her life they were deciding her future, without asking her. "You do know I'm standing right here, and I can hear every word you're saying?"

"Look Mil, it's for your own safety." Paul replied.

"No Paul. I'm not going anywhere. This is my home, and I will be staying here, so you had both better get used to it." Millie planted both hands on her hips in defiance, as she watched Paul blow out slowly.

"Mil, it's too dangerous for you to stay here, it's not the time to play the martyr. Now go and pack a bag." Paul argued.

"No." Millie's mouth dropped open as Paul marched towards her. He picked her up and threw her over his shoulder. "Put me down!" Millie demanded as she pummelled on his back. "You can't make me."

"I can and I will.... Look, it's only for night-time, you can still work, just sleep somewhere safe." Paul placed Millie down in her bedroom. "It's only until we sort this mess. Now please, humour me."

"I have nowhere else to stay. This is my home." Millie looked around the bedroom, it was hers, why should she be kicked out by some stupid feud.

"Fine. You can stay at mine." Paul laughed. "We can finish what we started earlier."

"I am not staying at yours." Millie glared back in defiance.

Chapter Twenty-One

Millie opened her eyes slowly and looked around the strange room, it took her a few minutes to realise where she was. Paul Kelly's. As she sat up, she caught the smell of bacon frying causing her tummy to rumble. She pushed the covers off and followed the smell.

"About time. I was gonna wake you, hope you're hungry." Paul called over his shoulder as he stood at the stove.

Millie's eyes took in his bare torso, he was wearing jeans and nothing else. She knew he was toned; she could see the bulging muscles through his t-shirts. Not so much when he wore a suit. "Yeah, I guess I am."

"Good, take a seat at the table, it's nearly ready. How many sugars do you want?" He asked her.

"One please." Millie made her way to the table and sat down. She looked around the open plan room, impressed at the tidiness. Paul had a large sofa that faced the television, and a bar was in the corner with bottles placed on a tray on top. She dug her toes into the plush carpet. He definitely liked the finer things in life. She glanced out of the window; the sky was bright. "Can't believe it's March already."

Millie thought back to Levi. Seven months had passed since his death.

"Has the year been good for you so far?" Paul replied as he placed a plate in front of Millie.

"Thanks.... It's been better than the last six years." Millie took a bite of the bacon and savoured the flavour. "You can cook." Millie smiled.

"You sound surprised, although I wouldn't class frying a bit of bacon as cooking." Paul grinned. "But a compliment is always welcome."

Millie watched Paul as he shoved a huge forkful of sausage, egg, and beans into his mouth. "You know you'd get more in if you used a shovel."

"What can I say, I'm a growing boy." Paul replied.

"At thirty-one you're still growing?" Millie laughed. "Well I suppose your t-shirts might stretch an inch or two more."

"Nice of you to notice.... I didn't realise you'd been perving on me." Paul winked.

"What. No.... I don't perv." Millie placed her knife and fork down. She could feel the heat spreading over her body. She closed her eyes wishing the redness away.

"I love it when you blush." Paul replied.

"I'm not blushing, it's hot in here, that's all." Millie grabbed her tea and took a small sip.

"Must be really hot considering the colour you've gone." Paul laughed. "Get dressed, I'll drop you back."

Millie showered and dressed and then made her way down to Paul's car. As he climbed in beside her, she could feel his eyes on her. "Are you okay?" Paul asked.

"Yeah. Why do you ask?" Millie turned to face him.

"You look embarrassed." Paul changed gear as he headed to the pub. "We kissed, that's all."

"I know." Millie replied as she placed her hands in her lap. "We have kissed before Mil." Paul paused. "You do know I would never force you to do anything you didn't want to do?"

"I know." Millie smiled, she felt safe around Paul. Even when he was angry.

"Look I need to get over and see Ronnie, the man I told you about, we can discuss this later if you want." Paul stopped the motor outside the Artichoke and leant over to Millie. He pulled her closer for a kiss. Millie closed her eyes and savoured the moment. She then watched Paul as he got out and walked around to her side, he opened the door and helped her out. He was a gentleman, Millie liked this about him. She felt protected when she was with him. Even from the very beginning.

Millie walked into the pub with a smile on her face until she spotted the damage the fire had done. It wasn't much but even so, what if they had all been asleep. Would they have heard it or would they now be laying on a mortuary slab. Millie shivered at the thought, she put it to the back of her mind and busied herself until the pub opened at lunchtime. She had washed all the shelves down, and then started on the woodwork. The smoke smell was almost gone, probably because the cigarette smoke and beer hops masked it, she thought. Millie stood at the bar when Finn opened up, every time the door opened Millie held her breath hoping it was Paul and every time it wasn't found herself feeling disappointed. Ignoring the door, the next time it opened, she was surprised when she heard Rosie call her name.

"Hey Mil, what happened here?" Rosie asked.

"Fire, last night. Someone put a bottle through the window, lucky we were up, god knows what would have happened if we were asleep." Millie shuddered. "Anyway, how are you?"

"Well, I'm doing better than you; you should have knocked at mine and stayed there." Rosie replied.

"It's okay, I didn't stay here last night." Millie felt her face flush and wished she hadn't told Rosie that bit of information. She looked at Rosie and noticed the suspicion in her eyes.

"Where did you sleep?" Rosie asked. "And don't lie."

Millie sighed. "I stayed at Paul's and before you get the wrong idea, he slept on the sofa."

"What." Rosie frowned. "Why?"

"Because he's a gentleman." Millie watched as Rosie burst out laughing.

"I bet all the girls say that." Rosie replied once she had stopped laughing.

"What do you mean, all the girls? How many has he got?" Millie felt her heart sink. Of course, it was too good to be true.

"I'm sorry Mil, I didn't mean to upset you and yeah maybe he is a gentleman to you, but don't forget what he really is, what he really does." Rosie sighed. "You know I don't like the idea of you and him.... I just don't want you to get hurt."

Millie placed her hand on Rosie's and smiled. "I know."

* * *

Millie sat in the back room sipping her tea and eating a cheese sandwich. Finn had disappeared to the bookies for an hour, so she sat enjoying the peace. It had been a quiet shift; news of the fire attack had obviously spread. Paul and Finn were adamant it was the Travellers, but Millie wondered if it had anything to do with Flo. Flo wasn't the type of person to let things go, Millie knew only too well what Flo Cooper was like. She placed her elbows on the table and rested her chin on her hands, she was collecting enemies like people collected stamps.

"Hello."

Paul's voice broke through Millie's thoughts, she turned and smiled at him. "Hello."

"I could do with one of those." Paul motioned to Millie's cup of tea.

"Take a seat, and I'll make it." Millie busied herself as she made the tea, but Rosie's words popped into her mind. "Paul?"

Millie turned and looked directly at him. "How many women have you got?"

"What?"

"How many w...." Millie stopped when Paul cut in.

"I heard the question Mil.... Where the fuck did that come from?" Paul shook his head and blew out slowly.

Millie guessed it was to control his temper. "I just wondered, that's all."

"The fact that I've spent every possible minute with you should be a clue." Paul's voice rose. "Jealousy isn't a good look Mil, don't worry about the tea." Paul stood up and walked to the door. "I'll come back later, if you decide you can trust me."

Millie watched him leave, while her stomach sank to the floor. Annoyed with herself she threw the cup into the sink and watched as it smashed into tiny pieces, just like her life.

Chapter Twenty-Two

The pub was quiet, and Millie was bored. She watched Finn as he chatted to some of the locals. It was 7.30 and there were only a handful of punters in. This war had put people off of coming here. It left Millie with a feeling of unease.

"Finn, I'm just going upstairs; I won't be long." She called over before heading through to the back. She climbed the stairs quickly and then flopped down onto her bed, she grabbed her white bunny and held it to her chest. This was the one thing that comforted her. Why? She wasn't sure. It was the one thing she had had all her life. The one thing she was found with when she was left at the children's home. Millie held it up above her and watched as its ears flopped towards her, one ear had a brown mark where Levi had held a flame to it. The bunny was only small, about eight inches in height but despite its size it had the power to soothe her, and over the last six years it had done that many times....

'MILLIE, GET YOUR ARSE UP HERE.' Levi bellowed. Millie ran up the stairs and flew into the bedroom, her heart racing at the thought of another punishment. 'What's wrong...?' Millie stopped as

Levi lit a match and held it next to her bunny. She could see the ear beginning to singe. 'Why is this fucking thing on the bed, you're nineteen not nine.' Levi scowled. Millie stepped back as Levi thrust the match onto her arm, she felt her skin blister immediately but didn't scream. It would only make him angrier.

Millie placed the bunny back onto her bed and wiped at her eyes with her sleeve. She then rubbed at her arm where the scar was. It was small but she could still remember the pain. She gave herself a minute to compose herself and then made her way back downstairs.

Millie stood at the bar and grabbed the newspaper, she needed to do something to keep her mind off of Paul. It had been two days since she had seen him. She had stayed at Rosie's the night before, as Finn wouldn't let her sleep at the pub. As she turned the page an article jumped out at her. There on the third page was a picture of Levi's cousin Billy. The caption read, 'Body found' Millie felt the sickness build in her stomach and as her mouth watered, she ran to the ladies' toilets. She bent over and emptied the contents of her stomach into the toilet bowl, while she attempted to hold herself upright. A film of sweat had gathered on her forehead and her legs were in danger of giving way. After she wiped her mouth with the back of her hand, she then flushed the chain. Her mind was racing. Had Paul done this?

"Mil.... Mil?" Finn's voice bellowed through the closed door.

"I'm okay." Millie replied through heavy breaths. "Just something I ate." Millie washed her hands and splashed cold water onto her face. As she looked at herself in the mirror, she shook her head. She made her way back to the bar, under the suspicious gaze of Finn. She did her best to look normal, but she doubted she was pulling it off.

"Come and sit down, you look awful." Finn ordered.

"I'm okay, honestly Finn."

"Well, the fact you've gone as pale as a ghost suggests otherwise. Now sit." Finn pulled out a chair.

"Fine." Millie conceded. As she looked up, she spotted Paul walking towards her holding a large bouquet of flowers. "Oh great."

"What's happened, Mil are you okay?" Paul asked as he knelt down next to her.

Millie jumped up and grabbed the newspaper from the bar, she then slapped it onto the table in front of Paul. Paul stood up and stared at the picture, Millie could see his eyes moving as he read down the article.

"So, you're not only accusing me of being a womaniser but also a murderer?" Paul sighed.

"Are you saying you didn't kill him?" Millie studied Paul's face closely, he looked hurt, but soon composed himself.

"No Millie, I didn't and while we are on the subject, I haven't got any other women either." Paul pushed his hand through his hair while Millie watched.

"Okay. So, who did?" Millie asked, ignoring his shot about the women.

"I don't know and to be perfectly honest, I don't care.... What I do care about is you and what you think of me with regards to all these women."

"Maybe you two could take this in the back." Finn shouted over. "Unless you want all and sundry knowing your business."

Millie followed Paul into the back room. She sat at the table with Paul sitting next to her. Her heart was beating too fast, she wasn't sure if it was from anger, fright or just the feeling she got from being close to him. She looked down when he covered her hand with his. It felt warm and comforting, but she pulled away regardless. "You do realise what this means?"

"No, what does it mean?" Paul asked as he moved his chair closer.

Millie felt his leg touch hers and it sent a tiny shiver through her body. She needed to be strong, one of them had to. "If I thought you had done it, Duke will too."

"I'm not worried about Duke." Paul shrugged.

"Well, you should be, he could hurt you." Millie put her head down as her eyes misted up.

"You're worried about me." Paul smiled. "You know I asked you out to dinner once and you said yes, but we never went. Let me take you out tonight, we can talk about anything you want, ask me anything you want, and I promise I'll answer truthfully."

Millie didn't know if she wanted to punch him or laugh at him. He had been missing for two days and now wanted to pick up as though everything were normal. "This isn't the time for dinner Paul."

"Everyone has to eat." Paul mumbled.

Millie watched as Paul rolled his eyes. "You are truly amazing. You disappear for two days and then expect me to go to dinner with you." Millie shook head slowly. "No Paul."

"I've been working Mil and not enjoying myself with other women. That is what you think isn't it?" Paul replied.

Millie studied his face, he looked hurt, but could she trust him? Could she trust any man again? "I don't know what I think, and to be perfectly honest, this isn't the time to discuss dinner or your social life. Billy's dead and we will get the blame."

"Let me worry about that, if or when it happens." Paul replied.

"You really don't get it do you?" Millie asked him.

"Get what Mil?" Paul replied. "Why are you so worried about a dead pikey?"

Millie looked straight into Paul's eyes. "Because we've all been handed a death sentence."

Chapter Twenty-Three

It had been a couple of days since Millie had seen the newspaper article and so far, all seemed quiet. Paul had been on the lookout for Duke, much to Millie's dismay, but he had seemed to have vanished. The caravans had gone from where they were. Millie knew only too well they would return and with them vengeance. After spending the last couple of nights at Paul's she had felt closer to him. It had turned out he had spent the missing night up the hospital with his gran. She had had a fall and Paul had gone to the hospital with her. Millie liked the fact he was a family man. That was something she had no experience with. A family. Millie picked up a cloth and wiped down the bar for the fourth time. Trade had picked up a bit since the fire, but the pub was nowhere as busy as it had been. She wondered if it ever would be. Millie looked up as the door opened and spotted Paul. He was staring back at her with a smile as he walked towards her. She felt the butterflies intensify the nearer he got. "Hello." Millie felt her face flush, she could see Paul found it amusing. "Whiskey?"

"Please and one for yourself." Paul pulled out a wad of notes.

"I know prices have gone up, but I don't think you'll need that much." Millie turned and reached for the bottle. "Single or double?"

"Double, in fact leave the bottle." Paul slapped some notes on the bar and placed his hand on Millie's. "Have you been okay, no signs of trouble?"

"Everything is fine here." Millie pulled her hand away. "Paul, people will think we 'you know' we don't need gossip on top of everything else."

"What's, 'you know'? Christ Mil you've gone red." Paul laughed.

Millie leaned over the bar. "You know exactly what I mean, Paul Kelly."

"Oh, you mean they will think we slept together?" Paul grinned.

Millie looked around the room. "Stop it. Someone might hear." She whispered.

"I don't give a shit if they do, in fact."

Millie watched as Paul marched behind the bar. Before she could protest, he had grabbed her and pulled her in for a kiss. Millie heard the whistles and shouts go up from around the pub. She watched Paul's face as he pulled back.

"There, no need to hide it now, is there?" Paul made his way back to his bar stool. "We're official, and that lot can gossip all they like."

Millie's head turned to Rosie as she walked towards the bar. "Oh great. Now look what you've done." Millie smiled as Rosie stopped next to Paul.

"What's this, do I detect romance in the air?" Rosie asked, returning Millie's smile.

"I'll leave you two to it." Paul replied, as he made his way to his table.

Millie knew her face had coloured up; she could feel the heat radiating off her skin. "Rose I...."

"Look, if you're happy then I am too, just be careful and whatever you do, don't get involved in his business.... I knew you liked him, every time he came in here you went red, oh I'll have a wine please, maybe you can find out what Scot's doing with that lot." Rosie motioned with her thumb.

Millie placed the glass on the bar and looked at Rosie. "Do you ever take a breath when you're talking?" Millie looked over and watched the group of men. "Don't you think Scot's old enough to know what he's doing; he may not like you interfering in his life."

"He's my twin Mil, I'm the sensible one, he's the reckless one. He needs guidance, even if he doesn't know it." Rosie replied before sipping her wine.

"And what about me, am I reckless?" Millie glanced at Paul and was met with a smile and a wink.

"Our hearts control our heads Mil, like I said I knew you liked him. I've got to say though, Paul Kelly's always appeared as the cold, business only type. Seems he's got a thing for you too. Just be careful."

Millie nodded. "Okay, can we talk about something else now. Hang on, let me serve Harry." Millie walked along the bar and smiled at the old man waiting for his pint. "Nice to see you Harry, there you go."

"Thanks Millie, did you hear about Harold Wilson? He's resigned." Harry grabbed his pint and took a large mouthful.

"Yes, Finn told me." Millie handed him his change.

"Countries up the swanny, bleedin' politicians, right love, chat later." Harry turned and walked to a table while Millie watched him. She smiled to herself; Harry always had something to moan about. Politics, the price of food, even the music of today. To him everything was better in the fifties.

Millie made her way back to Rose. "Right, where were we? Ah yes, I've something else I wanna tell you. Rose, I want to find my parents."

"What's brought this on, I thought you weren't bothered?" Rosie frowned.

"I'm not, I mean I wasn't, but if there's a chance I could find them, well.... Wouldn't you want to know where you came from?"

Millie grabbed Rosie's glass and took a sip. "It's always there in the back of my mind." Millie's hands trembled slightly as she placed the glass down.

"Hey, it's okay. When and where do we start?" Rosie grinned.

"We need to start with the parish records of births, deaths and marriages." Millie topped up Rosie's glass. "I've only got a small birth certificate, it hasn't got any details on it, maybe if I can get a full one it might have something on it."

"Okay I finish work at 3pm on Monday, we'll go then. Now let's enjoy tonight."

Millie didn't reply, she just smiled as her mind wandered off to her parents. The one question that had plagued her all of her life was why didn't they want her?

Chapter Twenty-Four

Paul kept one eye on the door and the other on Millie. He didn't like the fact she was worried about the gipsies; it was his job to worry, not hers. What sort of a man was he if he couldn't make her feel safe, and he did, he wanted to make her feel safe. Everything he had wanted in life was standing right there, behind the bar. He often wondered if he was good enough for her. She had had such a hard life and yet she still cared about others. It made him feel warm inside, the way she was. They had spent hours talking, telling each other things that they hadn't shared with anyone else. He felt closer to her than he felt to his own family. Especially his dad. His dad was a drinker, always had been for as long as Paul could remember. He worked hard and drank hard, while his mum had to bring up him and his brother on pennies. Paul felt a loathing towards his old man. Ronnie had taught him to look after your family first, 'after all son, that's why we do this line of work, to give our loved ones a better life' Ronnie had said. Ronnie was a top bloke and would have made a great dad. Paul felt blessed to have him in his life.

"Duke's in the Woodman." Jamie announced as he stood at the end of the table.

Drawn from his thoughts Paul looked up at Jamie. "You are sure he's in there?"

"I saw him going in as I drove past." Jamie replied.

"Well, we better go and pay him a visit then." Paul stood and looked at Millie. "Hang on a minute." He motioned Millie to the end of the bar. "I've gotta pop out but I'll be back before closing." He pecked her on the lips and left without waiting for a reply. "Come on." He motioned to his men to follow him.

"Getting cosy with Millie I see." Jamie laughed.

"Is that a problem?" Paul snapped as he clenched his fists. He felt his temper build but swallowed it down. Now wasn't the time for an argument.

"No, it's good to see your heart isn't made of granite like everyone thinks." Jamie replied. "She's a pretty girl."

"And she's mine, so hands off. Now can we concentrate on business now that I have your approval." Paul pulled open the door and marched to his motor. His scar was itching, but he didn't know if it was because of Jamie or the gipsies. Probably both he decided.

"You do know they're not gonna admit it, the fire." Jamie said as he jumped in the passenger side.

"I'm not expecting them to." Paul turned on the ignition and sparked the engine to life. Tonight, he decided, would be the end of it, one way or another. He shoved the motor into gear and then pulled out of the car park with his men following.

Seven minutes later Paul pulled up outside the woodman public house and looked around the parked vehicles. "There's his truck. Come on." Paul entered the pub first and saw Duke standing at the bar with six other gipsies. As he made his way over, he noticed Duke turn when he spotted him, he stood with a smug smile spread across his face, he wouldn't be smiling for much longer, Paul reasoned.

"Paul, have ya come to confess?" Duke placed his beer glass on the bar.

"I couldn't give a shit about some dead pikey, but what I do care about is you setting fire to one of my pubs." Paul noticed the puzzled look on Duke's face.

"You here to make up more stories?" Duke replied.

"You gonna tell me it wasn't you or one of your lot?" Paul bawled his fists ready to take down Duke.

"I'm not gonna tell you anything. You've come here for a fight so we should...." Paul's fist crashed into Duke's face before he had finished the sentence. He was pleased to see Duke fall back against the bar; his face bloodied. Duke soon righted himself and Paul felt Duke's fist connect with the side of his head, as he countered with a punch to the stomach.

Paul sat on the floor wiping his own blood from his cheek, his shirt had been ripped and his gold tie pin had flown off in the fight. He looked around the pub. More damage had been done, all the punters had left, and Paul had seen the landlord grab the barmaid, then he had locked themselves in the back. Paul looked over to Duke who sat opposite him holding his ribs. "We can't go on like this."

"Agreed. Just tell me where Rueben is." Duke pulled out a cigarette and lit it, before handing the packet to Paul.

Paul shook his head. "I told you; I don't know who Rueben is and I don't know where he is.... Why did you set fire to the pub?"

Duke blew out the smoke slowly. "It wasn't me. That's not my style, I would want you to see me, see what I'd done. I'm not a coward."

"So, you reckon you didn't firebomb the pub, I'm not sure I believe you." Paul said as he re-focussed on Duke.

"I don't believe you either, so where does that leave us?" Duke replied as he stubbed out his fag.

Paul screwed his nose up, he hated smoking, just the smell made him feel sick. It amazed him that people would breathe smoke into their lungs for pleasure, and then there was the smell. Paul waved away the smoke before addressing Duke. "I don't know, but what I do know is this has to stop." Paul motioned to the pub. "We're causing too much damage."

"My lot will want justice before they stop." Duke looked over to Paul. "We could have a boxing match, just the two of us. That way it will pacify everyone and there'll be no need for retaliation."

Paul nodded. "You and me?"

"Yep. You and me. What do you say?" Duke held out his hand to Paul after spitting on it.

Paul shook and then wiped his hand on his jacket. "Deal. One month from now, you pick the venue."

"Well, being a traveller I think it would be fitting to hold it at the camp. There'll be no trouble from the gavers." Duke laughed. "That's police to you."

"I know what a gaver is. They smell the same whatever you call them." Paul stood and made his way to the bar. He slapped some pound notes down and called out to the landlord. "That should cover the damages." As Paul turned, he noticed Jamie slip out of the door.

Chapter Twenty-Five

It was early evening, and the pub was busier than it had been since the feud with the gipsies had begun. News of the fight had spread, and it had had the desired effect. It had reassured the punters. Millie wasn't happy though, but what could she do? Nothing. She caught her reflection in the mirror and admired the gold chain that hung around her neck. Another present from Paul. Despite the fight she felt good in herself. Confident. That was a feeling that had been taken away from her by Levi and his mother Flo. Millie wondered why Flo hadn't retaliated and why there was no retaliation for Billy. It didn't make sense. Millie felt Paul's hand on her leg and looked up at him, his words ringing in her ears, did she hear him right?

"An answer would be good Mil." Paul smiled.

"We've known each other five minutes Paul, don't you think it's a bit too soon to be moving in together?" Millie watched as his smile dropped. Her heart dropped too, just at the thought of hurting him.

"No, I don't. If I did, I wouldn't have asked.... Look you've been staying at mine a lot anyway. I don't see what the difference is." Paul grabbed his glass and took a sip.

"The difference is, it would be permanent and what happens when you've had enough of me, I can't expect Finn to just give me my old room back." Millie sighed. "Why can't we just carry on as we are for now, there's no rush is there?"

"If that's what you want but let's make one thing clear, I will never have enough of you." Paul replied.

Millie noticed Paul's shoulders slump; she really didn't want to hurt him. "You know how I feel about you..." Millie was interrupted when one of Paul's men barged in.

"Sorry Paul, there's trouble at the house." The man looked between Paul and Millie. "I couldn't find Jamie, so I came here."

Millie watched as Paul blew out slowly, he always did that when he was getting annoyed. "You go, I'll wait here for you."

"I won't be long." Paul replied before he kissed Millie on the lips.

Millie watched him leave, feeling puzzled.

"Where's Paul gone?" Finn asked as he walked through to the bar.

"There's trouble at his house. I didn't know he had a house, did you?" Finn turned away before he answered, making Millie suspicious.

"Don't know, you best ask Paul. Now are you having another drink?" Finn reached for the wine.

"I suppose so, as I'm left on my own." Millie turned as the door opened and Jamie walked in. "I think one of your men was looking for you, something to do with trouble at Paul's house?"

"Oh, you mean the brothel. I'm sure Paul can sort it." Jamie nodded to Finn.

"Brothel. He has a brothel?" Millie felt her insides go as she fought the feeling of being sick. Before she could stop herself, she was back in Flo's front room....

Flo nodded to the man 'don't mark her or we'll both be in trouble' and then grinned at Millie, 'Behave yaself girl,' then she left the room. Millie had her back pressed against the wall as the man approached.

She closed her eyes as she heard him undo his belt and the thud it made when it hit the floor. She let out a scream when he grabbed her hair and dragged her to the sofa....

"Excuse me, I need to go upstairs." Walking through to the back, Millie wondered if Finn knew. He looked shady when she had asked. So, Paul Kelly sold women for money. He was no different to Flo, he just had a nice suit to hide behind. Millie packed her overnight things and let herself out of the back door. As she walked across the road towards Rosie's she felt the first tear fall. She banged on the door and heard Rosie's footsteps coming down the stairs. Rosie opened the door, and Millie followed her in and up the stairs grateful that she hadn't questioned her on the doorstep.

"Take a seat. Bobby, can you give us a minute." When Bobby left Rosie continued. "Well. What's happened?"

"Did you know Paul owned a brothel?" Millie asked.

"Not exactly, I mean I thought he may have, but I wasn't certain. All the gangsters seem to own brothels. He hasn't asked you to work there, has he?" Rosie replied.

"No." Millie held her head in her hands. How could she tell Rosie, how could she tell anyone. Millie wanted to scrub her body clean, just like she had every time Flo had forced her to.... Millie squeezed her eyes shut.

"Does it change things between you and him?" Rosie asked.

"Yes." Millie didn't bother looking up. "Don't you think it's a big deal?"

"You knew what he was when you met him, I warned you about his business dealings. So, the question is, can you accept that side of him?"

"No.... I don't accept a man making money from selling women. It's sick." Millie looked Rosie in the eye. "Would you?"

Rosie knelt in front of Millie. "Only you can decide what you are willing to accept.... You know he's gonna come looking for you."

"I know." Millie sighed. "I don't suppose you've got any wine?"

Rosie left the room and returned with two glasses and a bottle. "I always keep a bottle for emergencies."

Millie held her glass as Rosie poured. "Thanks." She took a long gulp then jumped as a loud bang came from the front door. "That'll be him. I'll get it." Millie made her way slowly down the stairs, her heart rate had increased, and the beginning of a headache was starting to build in her temple. She pulled the front door open. "Paul." She greeted, annoyed with herself because her heart still did a little flutter when she looked at him.

"Mil. What's the matter?" Paul asked.

"Where have you been?" Millie made sure to keep eye contact, she wanted to see how honest he would be with her.

"I had a problem at work, you know that."

"No, you had a problem at your house, what house Paul, you live in a flat." Millie pressed.

"It's a business, we call it the house." He replied.

"Is that so people don't know you're a pimp?" Millie noticed a flicker of recognition flash through his eyes.

"It's not like that. I was asked to help, I'm not gonna do it for nothing" Paul sighed before continuing. "The girls needed somewhere safe to work, I bought a house, and they live there and work there. They get protection as well as a roof over their heads and in return I get a percentage.... I'm not even sure why I'm telling you this."

"Am I not worth the explanation?" Millie asked, her whole body deflated, she had been a fool to think she was. "I think we're done Paul." Millie attempted to push the door shut but Paul shoulder barged his way in.

"Oh no you don't. You can't burst into my life and then say we're done."

"I just did, and don't worry about your secrets, I won't tell anyone." Millie watched Paul's face harden.

"And I won't tell anyone you murdered your father-in-law." Paul closed his eyes. "I'm sorry Millie, I didn't mean that, you know I would never tell."

"Thank god I never slept with you.... Goodbye Paul." Millie noticed the hurt spread across his face. 1-0 to her, she thought, but it didn't make her happy, she would never trust anyone again. She waited for Paul to step outside and then she closed the door.

Millie leant back against the door. "Lesson learned." She whispered.

Chapter Twenty-Six

Millie was annoyed with herself; she couldn't get Paul out of her mind. It was made worse by the fact that no one else thought the brothel was an issue. Her mind wandered to Levi, there were warning signs there too, but she had ignored them, well she wouldn't ignore them this time. She wiped over the last of the pictures and then returned to the bar. She needed to keep busy. Millie looked around the pub, the holy table had a couple of Paul's men sitting at it, but no Paul. This annoyed her even more, not that he wasn't there but the fact she was thinking about him. She needed to get control over her life. She had a job and a real home for the first time in her life and she wasn't going to blow it. Her thoughts turned to Flo, why hadn't she come after her, and why hadn't there been any comeback from Billy's death. There were too many unanswered questions. Millie looked over to Finn when she heard him call her.

"Mil, are you sure you're okay to work?" Finn called.

"Yep. I'm sure." Millie kept her eyes on the door, on the one hand, she was dreading Paul coming in, but on the other she wanted him to. She wanted to face him, to see how strong she could be.

"Mil, Paul's not a bad man, I know Gladys the woman that runs the house. Her and the girls all seem happy there...You should speak with Paul, see if you can sort it out." Finn retreated into the back room.

She shook her head as she watched Finn leave, then sighed. How could she condone this, if she did it would make what Flo did be okay and it was anything but.

"Millie." Jamie called out as he walked in, breaking Millie from her thoughts. "Nice to see you back. How are you feeling?"

"I'm feeling fine. You're in a good mood." Millie noticed the roll of notes he was holding, there was a lot more than he normally had. "Had a win on the horses have ya?"

"No, it's a bigger win than that and I have you to thank. Have a drink with me, I'm celebrating." Jamie handed Millie the money and went and sat in Paul's seat.

"You thinking of taking over?" Millie slid into the seat opposite and smiled. She didn't like Jamie. There was something off about him.

"You'll find out in three weeks." Jamie laughed.

"That's if Paul doesn't kill you first." Millie noticed Jamie's smile drop.

"You've been his biggest downfall, Millie. Remember that." Jamie stood up and swapped chairs.

Millie's eyes narrowed. "I think you win that trophy." She turned and made her way back to the bar. That comment had hit her hard, but she wouldn't show Jamie that. Something didn't add up with him. The way he dropped the bombshell about the brothel, like he enjoyed it and knew it would cause trouble. But Jamie couldn't have known about Flo and what she had forced her to do. Millie continued to serve the regulars, but she couldn't shake the feeling that Jamie was up to no good and Paul was going to pay the price.

A little after 9pm Paul walked in. Millie's face dropped when she spotted the giant bouquet he was holding.

"Millie." Paul handed her the flowers. "Can we talk, in private?"

"Follow me." Millie walked through to the back room and nodded to Finn. "I need five minutes." She waited for Finn to leave before she continued. "The flowers are beautiful, Paul but why are you buying them for me?"

"Because I love you. Mil I'd do anything for you.... I'm closing the house down. I've given them a week to find somewhere else."

Millie thought back to the conversation with Jamie. "Who else knows you're selling it?"

"Only the girls and Jamie. It was his idea. He said it would show you how much you mean to me." Paul took a step closer. "And you do, mean a lot. Look, the truth is I've never had a proper relationship, I don't know how to show you what you mean to me, I'm hoping this will."

Millie sighed, Finn's words still ringing in her ears. What if Finn was right and then there was her suspicions about Jamie. Didn't she owe it to herself to gather all the information first? "I want you to take me to the house please. Now."

"What?" Paul frowned.

"You heard, but don't tell anyone, not even Jamie." Millie watched the confusion spread over Paul's face. To be honest she felt pretty confused too.

"Okay, come on." Paul turned and headed to the door.

"Finn, I need to pop out for a bit, is that okay?" Millie smiled at Finn's grumpy face.

"Sure, I wouldn't want your job to get in the way of your love life." Finn winked.

Millie smiled and followed Paul out. After she climbed into Paul's Range Rover, she waited for him to climb in. "What's happening in three weeks?"

"What, why three weeks." Paul shook his head.

"I don't know, why don't you tell me." Millie studied Paul's face closely. His jaw twitched. He was starting to get annoyed.

"I'm having a fight with Duke, you know that." Paul glanced at

Millie. "It's the only way to stop this tit for tat shit that's been going on."

"No, it isn't. The way to stop it is to find out who's behind the trouble." Millie looked out of the passenger window. "I think it's Jamie." Millie turned towards Paul when he burst out laughing.

"Jamie hasn't the money or the brain cells to pull off something like that."

"Then he's working with someone who has." Millie grabbed the dashboard as Paul slung his foot on the brake. "Christ Paul, you could 'av killed me."

"Will you stop being so over dramatic, and for god's sake stop getting involved. You don't understand this world."

Millie turned to face Paul; her nostrils flared; her jaw tight. "Don't you ever talk to me like that again. I may not know your world, and to be perfectly honest, I don't want to. What I do know is people, I can tell a wrong un a mile off, and Jamie is a wrong un." Millie folded her arms and glared out of the side window.

"Okay, I'm sorry." Paul pulled away slowly and continued along the road until he pulled up outside the house.

"Is this it?" Millie took in all the features. "It doesn't look like a brothel."

"And what does a brothel look like?" Paul asked as he unclipped his seatbelt.

Millie opened her mouth and then closed it. She had no idea what a brothel would look like. Maybe something sleazy or run down.

"Come on." Paul held out his hand which Millie ignored.

As Millie stood in front of the house, she felt her confidence leave her, but this was something she had to do. Things didn't add up. Jamie was celebrating something big. The way he sat in Paul's seat. The cockiness. "Okay, let's go."

Paul opened the front door and walked in; Millie noticed the blonde women as she came walking towards them. She had quite a presence about her, Millie decided it was a cross between a mother and a warrior. The woman patted her bleach blonde bouffant as she approached. Millie was amazed at the height of it, she thought they had gone out of style in the sixties.

"Paul, you haven't come to chuck us out today, have you?"

Millie picked up the sarcastic tone straight away. "Can I have a word please." Millie watched the women look her up and down.

"In the office." Gladys motioned to Millie. "Please, take a seat."

Paul stood behind Millie as she sat down. "Can I ask how you came to work here?" Millie noticed Gladys look at Paul. "I'm here miss?"

"Gladys... My name's Gladys. I asked Mr Kelly for help. I lost my old premises and couldn't afford a new one. Mr Kelly bought this house and became our landlord."

"Are any of the girls forced to work here?" Millie saw the surprise in Gladys's eyes.

"No, of course not.... Mr Kelly what is this?" Gladys stood up.

"Sit down Gladys. please." Millie instructed. Once Gladys was sitting Millie continued. "Paul's shutting this place down because of me."

"But why? We haven't done anything wrong?" Gladys pursed her lips and her eyes widened in surprise. "I can see it in your eyes, you feel disgusted, not because of us, but because of yourself. You think we are all forced. Well, you're wrong, for some of the girls here they have no choice, this is what they do. They have a safe and warm home. Do you hear what happens on the streets. How many girls get attacked or worse, killed." Gladys stood and placed her hands on the desk. She leaned towards Millie and glared. "That's what you've condemned these girls too, a life of fear."

"That's enough Gladys." Paul walked around the desk. "Be thankful you were given a week. Now get out."

"No." Millie looked at Paul. "I haven't finished.... Gladys has anyone approached you to work for them. I'm talking in the last few months?"

"No, but I did have one of your men looking through the accounts last week, I thought it odd." Gladys looked at Paul. "He told me to not say anything, and to be honest I didn't think anything of it, but now..."

Paul's face grew purple, the vein on the side of his neck started to pulsate and his scar turned red. "What fucking man?"

"Calm down Paul." Millie told him.

"This is calm." He growled.

Ignoring Paul Millie addressed Gladys. "Let me guess. Jamie Carter." Millie folded her arms and sat back as she watched Gladys nod. "What was it you said in the car.... I don't understand your world. Maybe next time you'll listen to me."

"So, there's gonna be a next time?" Paul asked.

Millie shrugged. "Dunno, anyway I would keep this quiet for now. Oh, and obviously the house won't be sold, but again I would keep that quiet too." Millie stood up. "Nice meeting you Gladys." Millie walked out of the door with a smile on her face. Made all the broader by the scowl she saw on Paul's.

"Wait. We need to talk." He said as he blocked her way.

"I'm not talking on the road Paul; can you open the door please." Millie climbed in and sat waiting for the question she knew was coming."

"What did Gladys mean, she could see it in your eyes?" Paul turned to face Millie.

"Isn't this about Jamie?" Millie sank down into the seat. "Because from where I'm sitting that's the most important thing."

"You're the most important thing to me. It's about time you realised that, now tell me. What did she mean?" Paul rubbed his scar.

"Flo owed a man money, she couldn't afford to pay him, so she offered him me. Millie squeezed her eyes shut as the memory returned.

Millie felt the man's breath on her neck, he was breathing much faster now which meant it would soon be over. The pain between her legs worsening with each violet thrust. She had tried fighting, but the man was too strong. She felt the weight of his body as he collapsed on top of her. The stinging sensation worsening. She didn't scream, she knew that would only make things worse.

"I tried to fight him, but he was too strong. He raped me." Millie looked at the floor, her body started to tremble, and her eyes watered. "I'm sorry." Millie felt Paul's hands as he wiped away her tears. As she looked up, she noticed he had turned a deeper shade of purple, he looked like his head was about to explode.

"What the fuck are you sorry for. Mil you've done nothing wrong.... I'm gonna kill that fucking bitch." Paul took a deep breath. "Why did you kill your father-in-law?"

"When I was in the hospital I had no clothes, so me and Rosie went to get them on the day of Levi's funeral. No one was supposed to be home. I let myself in with Levi's key and went up to get my stuff. While I was getting it the door opened and Elijah came back, I don't know why. Anyway, he caught me and tried to rape me, Rosie surprised him and while he was looking at her, I kicked him down the stairs. I didn't mean to kill him." Millie felt Paul's arms around her, she snuggled into him, feeling for the first time in her life, comfort.

"It's gonna be okay, no one will ever hurt you again." Paul kissed the top of Millie's head. "Let's get you home."

"Paul." Millie looked at him as he drove.

"Hmm."

"What about Jamie?" Millie watched as Paul sighed.

"You know a very clever man once said to me, never trust anyone 100%. No matter how well you may think you know them they are still capable of turning you over. I should have remembered that lesson.... Jamie will get what's coming."

Chapter Twenty-Seven

Millie and Rosie made their way to the council offices. It was a lovely spring day and despite all her troubles, Millie was excited, she walked with bright eyes and a broad smile. The offices were at the other end of the high street, so the two women walked and chatted excitedly. Before they knew it, they stood at the door. It was at that point Millie's excitedness turned to apprehension. She gripped her hands together tightly.

"Ready?" Rosie prompted.

"Ready." Mille confirmed after taking a deep breath.

After she had explained everything to the receptionist, a woman appeared at the counter and looked at her birth certificate. "I'm afraid we have no record of you." The woman told her.

Millie looked at the receptionist and frowned. "There must be some record of my birth, look, I'm here."

"I'm sorry there's nothing, the birth certificate you've got is a ...."

"We can try the hospital, Mil." Rosie cut in.

"They won't have any records." The woman snapped.

"How do you know that?" Millie asked, surprised. "You seem to know more than me."

"I don't know, I'm just surmising, now if you don't mind, I am extremely busy." The woman turned her back and walked away.

"Oh my god, I'm a fake, I don't exist Rose." Millie left the council office and walked to the bus stop. "How can I not exist?"

"Look we can still try the hospital, that woman looked shifty to me." Rosie jumped when Millie snapped.

"Didn't you hear her, there's no record of me. Wherever I came from, it wasn't a hospital.... Do you remember Mrs Webster from the children's home, she always told me I was found under a gooseberry bush, I thought it was a joke." Millie waved her hand for the bus to stop. "What if that was true?"

"Mrs Webster passed away a couple of years ago. Maybe someone else can help at the home, they must have records." Rosie replied.

Millie took a seat on the bus and shook her head. "What if no one knows. I should have asked when I lived there, why didn't I, why have I left it till now?"

"What, if only, and why, doesn't matter, what matters is that you are trying. Now let's go to the home and see if they know anything, you've nothing to lose." Rosie put her arm around Millie's shoulders. "There's got to be something they can tell you."

Millie jumped off the bus and looked at the pub. "I feel like I need a drink."

"No, you've been drinking too much lately, you need to keep a clear head. Come on, let's see what they know." Rosie linked arms with Millie as they made their way up the road.

Millie walked towards the front door of the children's home and climbed the three steps, she stood to one side and watched as Rosie knocked. "I hope they can help."

"Shh, someone's coming." Rosie whispered. "Hello Doug."

"Rosie and Millie, lovely to see you girls. How are you both?" Doug asked as he looked between the two.

"We're good thanks. We were wondering if you could help us, Millie is looking for her birth parents, unfortunately there's no record of her existence. Can you look in the records to see where she came from?" Rosie nudged Millie.

"Please Doug, I know nothing of where I came from, I..." Millie trailed off.

"I wasn't here when you came here, but I'm sure we can have a look and see if there's anything in your file." Doug smiled as he ushered the two girls in.

"I have a file?" Millie looked at Rosie and frowned.

"All the residents that live or lived here have files. Now let's go into the office and have a look." Doug replied, leading the way.

As they entered the large office, Millie scanned the shelves looking for files. All she could see though were books. "Where is it?"

Before Doug could reply the door flew open and in walked the head of the children's home. "What are you doing?"

Doug pointed to Millie. "I'm just looking for Millie's file, she wants to know if there's anything that might help her find her birth parents."

"I'm sorry but all files are confidential, now I must ask you to leave.... Now!" The woman stepped back from the doorway.

"But if it's a file on me, surely I have the right to read it." Millie planted both hands on her hips and glared at the woman.

"No, you don't, these are for our records only and if you don't leave, I will be forced to call the police." The woman replied frostily.

"Come on Rose." Millie looked at the woman as she walked past her. "This isn't over." As she made her way out she grabbed Rosies arm. "Don't you think she was a bit over the top. I mean threatening us with the police makes no sense." Millie whispered.

Rosie shrugged. "Maybe they have rules to follow, anyway I need to get home, are you gonna be okay?"

"Yeah, I'll catch you later." Millie watched Rosie walk away then turned back towards the home. If the old bag thought this was gonna stop her she was wrong. This was her life; didn't she deserve to know where she came from?

Millie made her way to the Artichoke, she said she needed a

drink so that's what she was going to do. Have one, two or three. Rosie had gone back to her flat, she was cooking Bobby a special dinner for their anniversary, Millie almost felt jealous, not that she begrudged Rosie celebrating, but she wished she had a normal life like Rose. Millie sighed as she reached for the wine bottle. Why couldn't life be easy? Millie spotted Paul as he entered, she tried to smile but judging by Paul's face she didn't succeed.

"What's wrong?" Paul asked as he slid his arm around her waist and kissed her.

Millie and Paul sat together at the bar while she told him all about the council and children's home. Millie watched Finn open up but stayed in her seat. She had lost interest in everything. The pub started to fill as the regulars made their way through the door. There was a buzz of chatter filling the bar.

"I should never have started looking for them, it was a stupid idea anyway." Millie declared.

"So, this woman just kicked you out, without telling you anything?" Paul asked in surprise. "I thought people like that were supposed to be caring."

"She said all files are private, only the staff can have access." Millie sniffed. "Doug obviously didn't get the memo." Millie's eye's started to mist up.

"How about we pay Doug a visit? He can read your file and tell you what's in it." Paul replied after a minute's silence.

"No, he could lose his job, I wouldn't want that." Millie sighed. "Let's just forget about it."

"Finn, can I have another whiskey please mate. Mil, do you want another one?" Paul asked. "Can you forget about it though, cos from where I'm standing it doesn't look like you can."

"I'll be okay." Millie smiled. She felt Paul's lips touch hers in a tender moment.

"I'll make sure of that.... Here comes your mate Rose, I'm gonna see the boys while you two talk." Paul slipped off the stool and sat at his table while Millie watched him.

She turned her head when she spotted Jamie. "Oh shit." Millie whispered under her breath. She watched Jamie as he slid into his seat. He looked even cockier than normal if that was even possible.

"Evening gentlemen." Jamie greeted. "Anything happening?"

Millie noticed all the men went quiet; Paul had obviously told them about Jamie. The atmosphere in the pub had changed too. The jovial chatting had now turned to whispers.

"No, it's been pretty quiet here." Paul replied.

Millie watched Paul closely, he looked angry, his jaw was set, and his eyes were narrowed. Rosie opened her mouth, but Millie shook her head. "Not now Rose."

"What about the pikeys? I can't see them staying quiet for long." Jamie asked, his cockiness slipping. "I'll have a whiskey, Finn."

Millie met Jamie's eyes; he grinned and then turned away from her. She knew he was up to something.

"Has princess forgiven you yet?" Jamie continued.

"You seem to be asking a lot of question's James' so here's one for you. Where do you keep disappearing to?" Paul asked.

Millie noticed a couple of the regulars leave; they hadn't even finished their pints. They simply got up and walked out, Millie knew more would follow.

"Gotta a little sort and she's very demanding if you know what I mean. Recon she's gonna ruin me." Jamie laughed.

"A lot of things can ruin a man, like taking money that don't belong to him." Paul replied.

Millie gripped her wine glass, her heart started to pound. "Shit."

"What's going on?" Rosie whispered.

"Shh." Millie put her finger to her lips.

"What are you talking about?" Jamie glared. "If you've got something to say then say it."

"I just did, and while we're on the subject, why are you looking at the house accounts. They have nothing to do with you.... You wouldn't be thinking of doing the dirty, would you?" Paul's voice grew louder.

"I looked at them cos I have a buyer, I didn't want to get your hopes up until I had spoken to him." Jamie smiled. "He wants to buy it, and for a good price."

Millie could see Jamie's brow glistening under the light. He was nervous. Another two punters walked out before Paul spoke. Millie knew what Paul was doing, he was giving Jamie enough rope to hang himself.

"Who is it?" Paul demanded.

"He wants to remain anonymous." Jamie sipped his drink.

Paul smiled. "You look a bit hot there James' are you feeling alright?"

"I feel just fine. Finn, another drink when you're ready." Jamie motioned to his empty glass.

"I'm not selling to anyone who's to shit scared to face me. You can tell them it's not for sale." Paul replied.

Millie met Paul's eyes and smiled as he winked at her. She was impressed at seeing him in action. Not one punch had been thrown and not one tabled broken, thank god.

"I'll be keeping the house until further notice, and while we're on the subject.... You looked at the accounts before I said anything about selling, so no more games. Oh, and I want the £150 you stole from the safe."

"I didn't steal anything, and this is the last time I try to help you." Jamie stood up so fast his chair tipped back. Without picking it up he turned and left.

"That was impressive." Millie said as she walked over to Paul. "No violence."

Paul grabbed Millie and pulled her to the side of the room. "I'm glad you approved. Look I've got a bit of business to take care of, I'll see you in the morning."

"You don't want me to stay at yours?" Millie asked.

"I wanted you to move in, but you said no, remember." Paul replied.

"So, you're punishing me?" Millie asked despondently. She felt like a bride being jilted at the altar. This feeling was all too familiar.

"No, It's just business, I'm not sure how long I'll be. I can wake you up when I'm done if you want?" Paul slipped his hands around Millie's waist. "It'll be about 2 or 3am."

"It's fine, I'm sure you will be grateful to have your bed back, it can't be fun sleeping on your sofa every night. I'll see you tomorrow." Millie slid off of the bar stool. "I'll lock up behind you."

Paul stopped at the door. "I'll see you first thing tomorrow." He pulled Millie against him and kissed her. "And just for your information, I will sleep on the sofa every night until you're ready to share a bed with me."

Millie smiled at his words, but one thing worried her. Where was Paul Kelly going at this time of night?

Chapter Twenty-Eight

Duke stood at the bone fire holding a can of beer with his son Jess. The weather had warmed up and the evenings were now lighter. He surveyed the camp; the trailers were all neatly in a row. Everything was tidy, as it should be. He remembered stopping here as a child. The farmer that owned this lane had always allowed them to stay. For a bit of money and a promise to clean their rubbish up he allowed them a few weeks a year. They had been here longer than that this time and the farmer had taken a bit of persuasion to let them back here so soon. But he had come good in the end. Duke listened to the men all chatting. He didn't join in, he just wanted to savour the moment, standing here with one of his son's, teaching him the Romany life. Just like his father had taught him. Duke turned when he heard Connie call his name. "Looks like me scrags ready. I'll catch ya later, Jess come on." Duke made his way back to his trailer, kissing Connie on the lips as he entered. "Smell's kushti Connie."

"Eat up while it's hot. Where's Aron?" Connie asked.

"Recon he's courting, you can tell he's my son, got a good eye for a pretty face." Duke ducked as the tea towel flew over his head.

"Duke Lee, if I catch you looking at another woman..."

"What do I need another woman for when I've got you. You know you're the love of my life. We been together since we were fourteen. Come and give us a kiss." Duke grabbed Connie's hand and pulled her onto his lap.

"Get off. Now eat up while the foods hot, I'll heat Aron's up when he gets in." Connie slid off of Duke's lap and busied herself at the stove, while Duke and Jess tucked into their grub.

"I heard you was in town today." Duke watched Connie as she potted about. "You seem to be going out a lot lately. Should I be worried?"

"I go to the shops. You know that." Connie put her head down. "I like to get fresh food every day, it's not like we live in a house with storage."

Duke glanced uncomfortably at Connie; he felt a pang of guilt. "Would you rather live in a house? I know it's a different way of life for you, not being a traveller, but you are happy, aren't you?" Duke placed his fork down and walked over to Connie. "You've been quiet lately, like you're somewhere else."

"I want to be wherever you are, Duke. You know that." Connie slipped her arms around Duke's neck. "You are my world, you and the boy's."

Duke smiled. "And you are mine, now come and eat with me." Duke watched as Connie sat opposite him. There was something she wasn't telling him.

* * *

After dinner Duke returned to the fire, he wanted to reflect on his life. Had he given his wife the best of everything? No, probably not. Did she ever ask for anything? No, never. In truth Connie had sacrificed everything for him, and what did he sacrifice? Nothing.

"Alright boy?" Nelson, Duke's father, called as he joined him at the fire.

"All good dad." Duke replied. He could feel his father's eyes on him.

"You looked deep in thought. Wondered if there was a problem." Nelson pulled at his braces. "How's Connie?"

"She's okay.... Do you remember when we used to stay here when I was a kid." Duke asked.

"It was different back then, boy, fields everywhere. Ten- or twenty-years' time this will all be houses. They call it progress, but it's not." Nelson replied glumly. "The time of the traveller will come to an end; they'll be no open road or fields to stop in."

Duke listened to his father, he may not be able to read or write but he was wise in other ways. Ways that mattered. "I'm gonna hit the sack, I'll see you in the morning."

"Night boy." Nelson called as Duke walked away.

Duke slid into bed and wrapped his arms around Connie, she was warm and soft. It didn't take long for his eyes to close. He dreamt of the open road. Driving through the country lanes of Kent, on their way to the horse fair. Duke looked at the passenger seat, expecting to see Connie, instead he was met with an empty seat.

Duke woke in a sweat and rolled over in the bed. Connie wasn't there. He looked at the end of the trailer and there she was, just staring into space. "What's the time?" He called over to her, but she didn't hear. Instead of calling again he climbed out of bed and joined her. "What's wrong Con, you've been like this for a while now.... Are you ill?"

Connie smiled up at Duke. "No, I'm not ill. I just couldn't sleep. I'll put the kettle on."

"Sit still, I'll do it." Duke lit the gas and placed the kettle on the stove. "You know if there's a problem you should tell me, I am your husband."

Duke watched as Connie stood up and busied herself getting the cups. "I'm fine, honestly. Now you stop worrying."

Duke sat back down but kept his eyes on Connie. "I feel like there's something you're not telling me."

"Duke everything is fine, now here, drink your tea." Connie sat next to him and continued to stare out of the window. "I recon we'll have a good summer."

"That's what my mother said. Reckon we'll go down to Kent for the summer after the derby. You always liked, show out Sunday." Duke sipped his tea while he studied Connie's face. "Might be able to pick up a bargain, get you a bit more crown Derby to go with the set you've got."

"I like it here." Connie replied.

"You know we never stay in one place for long." Duke pulled Connie round to face him. "If there were something wrong you would tell me?"

Connie nodded. "Of course."

Duke sighed. "It's too early to get up, come on let's go back to bed, I'll see if I can take your mind off of whatever's bothering you."

"Okay, but can we go out tonight, for a drink?" Connie asked.

"If you want, I know a nice little pub just outside town." Duke wrapped his arms around Connie's waist. "We can get some of the others to come too."

"No. I want it to be just you and me.... And I want to go to the Artichoke."

Duke stared down at Connie. "How do you know that pub?"

"I passed it the other day when I was shopping, why, is there a problem?" Connie held Duke's stare.

"No, no problem." He followed Connie back to bed, more confused now than when he got up. Why would his wife want to go to a pub she's never been to? Why on their own. He knew there was something she wasn't telling him, but what, he hadn't a clue.

Chapter Twenty-Nine

Millie woke to the sound of birds singing, and the sun was shining through a slit in the curtains which hit Millie directly in the eyes. She rubbed her eyes and stretched her arms over her head. She hadn't slept particularly well. The thought of what Paul had been up to had kept her awake. Was he okay? She wondered as she pushed the covers off of her. She swung her legs over the side of the bed and stretched once more. Millie made her way to the bathroom, on the way she caught the delicious aroma of bacon, Finn obviously had that sizzling away in a pan. Millie quickly washed and dressed and made her way down the stairs, she smiled when she spotted Paul sitting at the table with Finn. They were both sipping steaming cups of tea. "You're an early bird. What's that you're holding?"

"It's a present for you. Come and sit down." Paul placed the file down onto the table.

"Is this?" Millie stopped when she looked at the front cover. "Paul.... How?" Millie ran her hand over it and then looked at Paul. "Was this your business last night, why didn't you tell me?"

"Because you would have said no." Paul replied.

"Of course, I would have said no. What if you'd been caught?" Millie sat down next to Paul and looked at Finn. "Was you in on this?"

Finn stood up and made his way out as he called over his shoulder. "No, I had no idea, but I'm glad he got it, now don't go telling him off woman."

Millie looked back when she heard Paul laugh. "It's theft." Millie replied as she tried to hide her smile. How could she be angry when he had done this for her. It was more than anyone else had done. She could really count on this man when it mattered.

"Mil this is about you, your life. If any ones a thief, it's them for keeping it from you. Now please, read it." Paul stood. "I'll go and make you a cup of tea."

Millie sat and stared at the folder until Paul returned. "Now I've got it, I'm too scared to look at it. What if there's bad stuff in here?"

"Well, you won't know until you read it. Here drink this, do you want me to go?" Paul asked.

"No.... Sit with me." Millie pulled at the cover and looked at the first page as it fell open. "It says I was left on the step.... wrapped in a towel with a white bunny rabbit." Millie thought of the bunny that had been with her all her life. "Why would they leave the rabbit, if they can discard me like that, like rubbish."

"Before you start putting yourself down, I want you to remember one thing. I love you, Rosie loves you and I'm sure Finn does, although he probably would never admit it. We are your family, we are the ones that matter, not a couple of strangers.... I love you enough to steal confidential files for you and risk getting nicked." Paul laughed.

"That's not funny Paul Kelly so you can stop laughing." Millie smiled as Paul's eyes twinkled with mischief. "I know what you're saying and yes, you are the ones that are important to me, and I love you too."

"Give us a kiss then." Paul lent in but Millie pushed him away.

"Not yet, I want to see if there's anything else in here. I just want to know where I came from." Millie flicked through the pages while Paul went to chat with Finn in the bar. The file was detailed, it had her weight, 6lb 10oz. Millie read further.

The new baby found is believed to be no more than 24 hours old. After being checked over by a doctor she has passed all health checks adequately. While the police have been informed, it is unlikely that the mother will be found, therefore the baby will reside at the children's home.

Millie sat back and sighed; her shoulders slumped. She never realised this would be so painful. This was her life, well the beginning of her life. This was also a baby, a newborn baby that no one wanted. Why did they leave the rabbit? Was that to remind her she wasn't wanted, a reminder she would have until she destroyed it. Closing the file, Millie made her way up the stairs. She grabbed the rabbit and ran back down. She pulled out the kitchen drawer and rummaged through it until she found what she was looking for. Next, she walked through the bar and outside. She noticed Paul behind her as she took a match from the box and struck it.

"Mil what are you doing?" Paul asked as he looked at the white bunny on the ground.

"What does it look like?" Millie jumped up as Paul swooped down and grabbed the bunny.

"I can't let you do that; you'll end up regretting it." He replied.

"I have too, it's a reminder, that's why they gave it to me. To remind me I was never wanted." Millie sobbed. She felt Paul's arms around her and let him lead her back into the pub.

"I don't believe that for one minute.... Look you don't know why they left you, she could have been a young girl, not married. Struggling to survive, she may have thought it was the best for you." Paul reasoned. "I don't know, but what I do know is you will regret burning this." Paul held up the bunny and shook it. "You once told me this was what comforted you, when anything went wrong, when you were scared or lonely, this." He shook the bunny again and handed it to Millie. "Don't let bad thoughts take that from you now."

Millie threw her arms around Paul and hugged him. "Just so you know, you comfort me too."

"Good, now go and put that back on your bed, where it belongs." Paul ordered.

Millie placed the bunny back where it belonged and made her way back down to Paul and Finn "What are you two plotting now?" Her voice was low. She couldn't shake the feeling of rejection as easily as she had wished.

"Nothing. How did you get on with the file, anything at all in there?" Paul asked.

Millie frowned as he sharply changed the subject, but then another thought hit her. "Not really, although one thing I find puzzling. The woman in the registry office said my birth certificate was a fake, but in the file it says I was issued a birth certificate." Millie shook the thought from her head. "Anyway, you changed the subject. What are you two up too?" Millie caught Paul as he winked at Finn. "I saw that."

"It's a surprise, I will tell you tonight when I've finalised all the details. So do I get that kiss now?"

Finn stood and mumbled under his breath. "I feel like an intruder in my own fecking pub."

Millie laughed as Paul grabbed her. "Tonight you and me will be celebrating, now give us a kiss."

Chapter Thirty

Duke stood outside the trailer while he waited for Connie. It was a lovely spring evening, not light but not dark either. The lights were coming on in the trailers now most people were having their dinner, and the chavies would be getting washed ready for bed. It was peaceful when the chavies went in, no screaming or running around. He thought back to Aron and Jess when they were little. They could cause a commotion with their screams too. Duke looked up when Connie came out, she looked stunning. "You know you get more beautiful every day." He told her, and he meant every word of it. He often wondered what she saw in him. He may act cocky and carefree but when it came to Connie and his boys, he did worry about them. He worried that he wasn't good enough. "Right then, shall we go?"

Duke opened the door of his pickup and watched Connie get in safely. Before he closed the door, he asked her one more time. "Con, you sure you don't want to go to a different boozer, there's a lovely little pub just out of town?"

"No Duke, I want to go to the Artichoke." She replied. "Please."

"Okay Con, your wish is my command." Duke jumped in and

started the motor. It didn't take long to get there, Duke kept an eye on Connie, who had a distant smile on her face. "You are sure you're okay?"

"I'm with you, of course I'm okay.... It's nice to just be us. I miss this." Connie replied.

Duke felt another pang of guilt. Had he been neglecting her. He was always out, drinking, fighting, making money, but Connie was left cleaning and cooking. Did she feel trapped, he wondered. "We will have to do this more often then. If it makes you happy."

"But what makes you happy Duke?" Connie asked.

"You make me happy Con, you and the boys." Duke sighed. "Just being with you makes me happy."

Duke parked outside the pub and helped Connie out. "Are you sure you want to go in here, there's plenty of better pubs in the area."

"I want to go in here." Connie replied.

Duke watched Connie look at the pub, her eyes darted over the sign and then she looked at the door. "Come on then, but if there's any trouble we leave." Duke told her.

"Why would there be trouble?" Connie looked at Duke. "What have you done now?"

"I haven't done anything, not yet anyway. I've got a fight fixed tomorrow night with a man that drinks in here." Duke held his hand out to Connie. "Shall we?" As they entered the pub everyone went quiet. Duke spotted Paul at the bar and made his way over to him. "I've come for a quiet drink with my wife, I don't want no trouble."

Paul glanced at Connie and nodded. "As long as you don't cause none there won't be none."

Duke ordered their drinks and found a table to sit at. He kept his eyes on Connie as she looked around the room.

"That's the girl that came to see you, who's the man she's with?"

"That's who I'm having the fight with, Paul Kelly."

"The one you're having a fight with?" Connie queried. "Why are you fighting him?"

"Because of Rueben, I need justice and so do the others. Can we talk about something else, like why you've been so distant the last few months. Are you ill?"

"No. I'm not ill Duke, where did you get that idea from?" Connie asked.

"There's something different about you." Duke grabbed Connie's hand. "You know you can tell me anything."

"I...." Connie was cut off when Millie shrieked.

Paul shouted over to Finn. "Drinks all round Finn. We're celebrating."

Duke watched the display quietly as he sipped his beer. He also kept one eye on his wife.

"I need to spend a penny." Connie told him as she excused herself.

As Duke looked up, he noticed Millie had gone so he made his way over to Paul. "I hear congratulations are in order."

"You heard right." Paul replied. "Have a drink with me to celebrate my new nightclub."

"Okay, I'll have a beer, Connie will have a white wine." Duke smiled. "This is all very civilised."

"This is how we live; you know the people that live in houses, I guess that's why it's called civilization." Paul let the jibe hang in the air.

Duke tensed. "You think because we live in trailers were not civilised?"

"I've seen the state of the camps your lot leave behind, fucking shit and rubbish everywhere." Paul stopped when he noticed Millie approaching with Connie.

"I'll bet any one of yous in this pub my trailer is cleaner than any of your houses." Duke felt Connie grab his arm.

"Maybe we should go Duke." Connie begged. "Before someone says something they'll regret."

"I'll not have some gorja looking down his nose at us." Duke shook her off.

"Stop. Both of you. It's like dealing with children. Paul please, we are supposed to be celebrating the club. Duke, please finish your drinks in peace." Millie pleaded.

Duke nodded towards Millie. "Come on Connie, I've lost the taste for the beer." He grabbed Connie's hand and lead her out of the pub. His temper at boiling point. "When I get in the ring with him tomorrow night, I'm gonna kill him."

Chapter Thirty-One

The wimpy bar was busy. As Millie entered, she looked around trying to locate Rosie. The smell of the food hit her immediately, which made her mouth water and her stomach rumble. The waitress rushed around with plates of food while the pinging of the till rang out in the air. She spotted Rosie who had stood up to obviously get her attention. Millie made her way over and dropped into her seat. Before Millie had time to take a breath, Rosie had started with the questions.

"So he's bought the old picture house. Just how much money does Paul Kelly have?" Rosie asked in awe.

"I haven't a clue.... A lot I guess." Millie smiled as Rosie's mouth dropped open. "Have you ordered?"

"Yes, and don't change the subject." Rosie replied.

"I wasn't.... I wish you'd have been in the pub last night; it was weird." Millie frowned.

"Weird as in your boyfriend's bought the picture house and he's turning into a nightclub or weird that he's making you a partner?" Rosie asked dryly.

"No not that, although that is a little weird, I mean why would he make me a partner. What's he gonna achieve other than tying me to the business?" Millie smiled up at the waitress as she placed the two plates in front of them. "I love a wimpy grill, the way they make the frankfurters curl around. Pass the ketchup Rose."

"You love food girl, anyway back to the nightclub, you could be on to something. Do you think he's making you a partner so he can control you?" Rosie asked. "I mean it does seem a bit obsessive now you mention it."

"I don't know, maybe I should tell him I don't want to be a partner. After all, I've now got my life back on track. Anyway that wasn't what I wanted to talk about. It was what happened after that." Millie shoved a large forkful of frankfurter and egg into her mouth. She closed her eyes as she savoured the taste. "This is good grub Rose."

Rosie nodded in agreement. "It is indeed, so come on, what happened after. Oh my god Mil, he didn't propose?"

Millie almost choked on her mouthful of food. "No." Taking a mouthful of her tea she sat back and thought of the conversation she had had with Connie. "I went to the ladies after Paul announced the whole nightclub thing and as I came out of the cubicle, Connie was standing there. She looked odd, almost guilty. I can't put my finger on it."

"Other women are allowed in the loo you know." Rosie replied. "It's not odd, maybe she needed a poo."

"Rose! People are eating." Millie looked around the packed restaurant to check no one had heard. "Honestly, the things you come out with." Annoyed when she heard Rosie laugh, Millie refocused on her dinner.

"So do you think something else was on her mind?"

"No, I don't think she knew I was in there. I think I caught her by surprise...I took the opportunity to tell her we didn't kill Billy, and do you know what she said..." Millie paused for maximum effect as she watched Rosie's eyes grow wider. "I know!" Millie grabbed her cup and took a sip of tea. "I asked how she knew but she wouldn't answer, she just said I wouldn't have to worry about Billy or Flo anymore."

"Does that mean Flo's dead too?" Rosie asked.

"I don't know, but as she left the toilets she turned and smiled at me and said, 'we take care of our own'."

"Well now you can relax girl, you've no Billy or Flo to worry about, life is on the up."

Millie smiled at Rosie; she wasn't convinced. Something wasn't quite right with the way Connie looked at her, she just couldn't put her finger on it. Millie looked over to the waitress and waved. "You having a pudding, Rose?"

"Of course. I'll have a banana split."

"Two banana splits please." Millie sat back in her seat. She looked around the restaurant, people chatted and laughed like they hadn't a care in the world. Her thoughts turned to Paul. Last night they had finally spent the night together. He was gentle and caring; it was something Millie wasn't used to. The way he held her afterwards and whispered I love you into her ear. It was perfect. Millie picked at her banana split, the thought of tonight playing on her mind. "I need to make tracks soon, Rose. Paul's fighting Duke later and I need to get ready."

"You make it sound like you're fighting and I'm surprised Paul's letting you go." Rosie chuckled.

"He's not, but I'm going anyway. He can hardly stop me." Millie replied bluntly.

"Are you sure you're okay? You've gone very pale Mil and you've hardly touched your pud."

"I'm fine. Are you ready?" Millie stood ready to leave and stared down at Rosie's concerned face. "I'm worried about Paul; I don't want him to fight.... What if he gets hurt?" Millie sighed. "Come on, let's go."

"I need the loo first. I'll meet you outside." Rosie replied as she nodded towards the ladies toilet.

"Okay, don't clog up the toilet." Millie laughed as Rosie rolled her eyes. She made her way to the front of the Wimpy and opened the door. As she walked out onto the path she looked up and down the street, feeling uneasy. Shaking her head she sighed, maybe Rosie was right. Too much happening in such a short space of time had left her freaked out. As she looked across the road she spotted the woman from the town hall, the same one she had spoken to about her birth certificate being a fake. Millie took a double glance at the woman she was standing talking to. It was the same woman that ran the children's home. "Well that's odd."

"What's odd?" Rose asked as she appeared next to her.

"Rose, look over there, the woman who said my birth certificate was a fake and just look who she's talking to." Millie watched as the two-woman chatted like they were old friend's.

"Mil it could just be a coincidence." Rosie shrugged.

"You don't believe that for one second and neither do I. Do you think she's the one that's been watching me? Come on." Millie walked to the edge of the path, her eyes on the two women. "Come on Rose, this way." Before Millie reached the road she was thrown into darkness. Her throat tightened and she found it difficult to breath. She felt heavy hands drag her away. "ROSE!" Millie screamed as her body collided with a cold hard floor. Pain immediately ripped through her as her body trembled. She heard the doors as they slammed shut and then then she felt movement, she was in a motor.

* * *

Paul left the flat and made his way to the pub. He was finding it difficult to concentrate. Millie was firmly stuck in his mind. Last night had been amazing. Perfect. Perfect just like her. Her smell. The softness of her skin. The way she looked into his eyes as they made love. Paul smiled; this was what life was all about. Contentment. He wanted to take the next step, but what was that? She had already turned him down at the idea of living together. A house. He decided. He would buy a house and surprise her. Paul reached the pub and parked up. The sun was high in the sky and the trees that lined the road were in full bloom. Paul's smile widened. Today was going to be a good day. He made his way into the pub just as Finn was locking up.

"Good afternoon, Finn, lovely day." Paul beamed. He noticed the look of confusion on Finn's face and laughed.

"I suppose it is. Your men are all here. Whiskey?" Finn asked in reply.

Paul nodded and made his way to his table. He noticed the wary look in his men's eyes. They weren't used to seeing Paul smile, which only made him smile more. Today, Paul decided, was going to be better than good. It was going to be great.

Paul took a seat and placed his hands behind his head as he leant back in his chair. The pub was now closed, and his men sat around the table, all waiting for their orders. Paul watched Finn as he replaced one of the optics. He refocused on his men. These six men were his most trusted. Not that he trusted them completely, but close enough to trust them to collect his monies and fight with him if he needed them too. "So all collections are in?" He asked them, making sure to make eye contact with each and every one.

"Yes boss."

"And the girls are okay at the house?" Paul looked at his watch, he had expected Millie back by now.

"Yes boss. And the warehouse has been cleaned like you asked."

Paul nodded his approval. "I've also got a bit of good news.... If you weren't in here last night, you wouldn't have heard my offer on the old picture house has been accepted." Paul paused while his men offered their congratulations. "There's a lot to do before it will be ready to open which means we are all gonna be busy. And on that point has anyone seen Jamie?" Paul asked as he felt the irritation surge through him.

"No, no one's seen him around here, but I heard on the grapevine he's been over in Ronnie Taylor's territory."

"What, that doesn't make sense.... I'll have a word with Ronnie later after the fight. Right you lot." Paul stopped when there was a loud bang on the door. Paul jumped up and unbolted it, he clenched his fist as he yanked it open, annoyed at the intrusion. He looked at Rosie's tear-stained face and felt his blood run cold.

"Paul." Rosie panted.

"Where's Millie?" Paul grabbed Rosie by the arm and pulled her inside. He could see she was in a state. "Where is she?"

"A van.... Men.....They took her." Rosie gasped.

"What men?" Paul's chest tightened. "Rose what men?"

"We had just left the Wimpy when a van pulled up and two men jumped out. They grabbed Millie and dragged her into the back of the van. It drove off before I could do anything." Rosie wiped the tears from her cheeks. "They had black masks on, I couldn't see their faces."

Paul's eyes widened; a film of perspiration covered his body. "I need more details, Rose. Think." Paul swallowed down his fear.

"It was a green Ford. I managed to get the end of the number plate. It was 5E."

"Baz, get on to the old bill that we have on the payroll. Give them those details and tell them to run a plate match. I reckon they've used false plates but it's worth a try. Also ask them if any motors fitting this description have been stolen. Rose, are there any other details you can think of that might help. Anything at all?" Paul watched the concentration on Rosie's face.

"When the van slowed down before it stopped, I noticed it had lucky heather hanging from the rear-view mirror, ya know like the old gypsy women sell." Rosie shook her head.

"Well it's the first place I'm gonna start. I'll pay Duke a visit. Finn, keep an ear out for the phone, they may contact here if there's something they want. You four come with me." Paul made his way out of the pub; his heart was beating faster than it ever had and his body was full of dread. He vowed to himself there and then if anyone had hurt a hair on Millie's head he would end them in the worst possible way.

"You three go in that car, you wait at the end of the lane if I'm not out in 30 minutes come in and blow the fucking place sky high. Now go and get what you need to do the job. I'll meet you outside the pub just before the camp?" Paul slid into his motor and checked the glove box. He pulled out his gun and checked the chamber to make sure it was full. Once he had completed his task he set off for the pub. His thoughts firmly on Millie he contemplated phoning Ronnie, but figured there wasn't time. He should have realised, there were never good days in his line of work.

Chapter Thirty-Two

Duke climbed into the trailer and noticed one of his son's sitting on the bunk. "What's up with you boy? I've seen happier undertakers."

"Aron's gone off with Sherry. Again." Jess replied grumpily.

"He's in love boy, it'll happen to you soon before you know it." Duke watched the horror on his son's face and did the best to stifle his laughter.

"He's sixteen dad, sixteen is too young to find love."

"I was fourteen when I met ya mother, I knew straight away she was the one for me, and even though her parents tried to stop us being together, we made it work." Duke smiled as he recalled their first meeting.

"Where did you meet?" Jess asked, sounding a little disgusted.

"It was at the fair; I'd took a job for the summer. We travelled around from town to town. When I first lay eyes on Connie I was blown away by her beauty. She had the best smile, it made me feel warm inside.... Anyway, after that I quit the fair and spent every minute I could with her, that was until her mother caught us." Duke's smile fell. He would always hate that woman.

"Didn't granddad mind you being with a Gorga?"

"No boy, love is love. When it hits ya, you can't stop it. Now stop moping and...." Duke stopped when he heard a motor screech to a halt. "Who the fuck is that." He stood and peered through the window just in time to see Paul Kelly getting out of his motor, and he did not look happy. Duke made his way outside to Paul. "What the fuck are you doing here, the fight ain't until tonight?"

"Where is she?" Paul growled as he marched towards Duke.

"Who?" Duke frowned. Movement caught his eye as he spotted Connie coming towards him. "Connie, go inside." When Connie had done as he had asked, Duke then continued. "I don't appreciate you coming here, accusing me of something I know nothing about. So who are you talking about Paul, what is it I'm supposed to have done this time?" Duke held his hands up as the other travellers started to gather around the two men. "Can you give us some space?"

"I don't need space; I need to know where Millie is." Paul continued. "We had an agreement; we fight and keep everyone else out of it."

Duke rubbed the back of his neck. He was more than a little pissed off. "Come inside." Duke turned and walked to his trailer, he could see the others getting angry and he didn't fancy more trouble. "We can talk in here." Duke ushered Paul inside after he opened the door. "Now can you explain yourself? Coming here making accusations. I don't know where Millie is, and why would I take her, when we are fighting in a few hours?" Duke's head turned when Connie dropped a cup.

"What do you mean Millie's been taken?" Connie asked.

"Paul here recons I've taken Millie, only I haven't, and I don't know who did." Duke replied.

"The van that stopped and took her had lucky heather hanging from the rear-view mirror. Is that a coincidence?" Paul sneered.

"Duke Lee if you have anything to do with this you tell him now." Connie insisted. "Or you'll be sleeping on your own. Now take an oath."

"Hold on a minute woman, I just told you I've nothing to do with it." Turning his attention back to Paul, Duke sighed. "I swear an oath on my boys lives, I didn't do it and I don't know who did."

"Well I don't fucking believe you." Paul replied through gritted teeth.

"That's enough!" Connie stood in front of Paul. "He took an oath; he would not swear on our boys' lives if he were lying. You said the van had lucky heather in it, I've never known anyone here to hang that in their motors. Are you sure it wasn't done to make you think it was a traveller?" Connie asked Paul. "Only it sounds to me like someone's done it to cause a war."

"That would make sense. Millie said Rueben had never been in the Artichoke, and yet someone has put a rumour around that he had. I think there's more to this than meets the eye. Look Paul I wish I could help. I like Millie, she's a sweet kid, but I know nothing." Duke sighed as Connie interrupted again.

"You can help Duke, in fact you can both work together to find her. She's just a child.... She must be frightened." The last four words Connie whispered.

Duke watched as Connie held her hand to her chest. "Jesus woman, I've a fight tonight." Duke looked at Connie's face as it turned to anger.

"Well Paul won't be fighting if Millie is missing, Will he!" Connie turned to Paul. "And you. You should be concentrating on finding Millie, not picking a fight with my husband. Now both of you get out and find the child... And don't come back until she's safe."

Duke shook his head. "Fine. But this changes nothing.... Where do we start?"

Chapter Thirty-Three

Millie lay on her side on a cold rough floor. Her hands and feet had been bound and she had a sack over her head and a gag around her mouth. Her tears had dried making her cheeks feel tight, and her heart rate had slowed. She could now think straight, and the only thought she had was how to escape. She had tried to listen out for the men that had snatched her, but she had been on her own for a couple of hours, she had assumed. Although there was really no way of telling. Millie curled into a ball and attempted to move her arms, so she could put her legs through them. If she could get her hands in front of her, she would be able to pull off the sack. It was more difficult than she had anticipated, but eventually she succeeded. Once she had pulled the sack off, she pulled the gag down from her mouth. As she looked around for something sharp to cut the rope that bound her hands, she noticed piles of boxes stacked around the room. It made the place feel confined. Along with there being no windows and very little light coming through the doorway it had a creepy feel to the place. This didn't scare Millie though; she was used to the dark. She crawled to the edge of the room and felt around for anything she could use to free herself. After a few minutes Millie gave up as curiosity crept in. She crawled over to one of the piles of boxes and stood, she reached over to try and open it. It was sealed with parcel tape. Carefully she picked at the end and ripped the box opened. Millie's eyes popped out when she felt a small packet of pills. Pulling it out of the box she knew straight away what they were. They were known as disco biscuits, made from an antidepressant called Quaaludes. Party goers had been taking these for a while now. Placing the packet inside her bra she hopped to another stack of boxes and repeated the process of opening the box. This time she found a white powdery substance. Cocaine. Again Millie placed it inside her bra. As she was about to continue her search for something to cut the rope that bound her arms she stopped when she heard voices. They were too quiet for her to hear what they were saying. She hopped back to her spot and placed the sack back over her head and placed her legs through her arms before laying back down.

"She hasn't moved, what time did .....? Ouch what did you do that for?" One of the men asked.

"Don't say his name you prick, come on, grab a couple of boxes, we need to get them delivered." The other man replied. "We'll be back soon sweetheart. Then we can have some fun." The two men laughed as they made their way out.

Millie's breathing became erratic once more as the thought of what they would do to her. She calmed herself and focused on her mission. She listened until everything went quiet. Bringing her arms to the front of her once more she slipped off the sack and sighed. "You won't be having any fun with me." She whispered. Continuing her search she found a table behind a pile of boxes. It had parcel tape and a knife on it. She grabbed the knife then placed the handle in her mouth to cut away the rope. It was a slow process. She could feel the sweat dripping from her forehead as she did so. Once her hands were free, she hacked away at the rope holding her feet together. Millie made her way out of the room slowly as she checked for any signs of life. Going up a flight of stairs she realised she had been kept in a basement. She slowly peaked around the door to the hallway, the place seemed deserted. As she got to the front of the house Millie stopped, she turned and made her way to the kitchen and searched for a box of matches. There next to the gas stove she spotted a box and quickly grabbed them before making her way back to the basement. As she struck the match she smiled. "This is gonna cost ya." She dropped it onto a box and watched as it sprang to life. Slowly at first and then everything seemed to light up. As the flames danced from box to box, Millie's pulse quickened. She needed to get out before the fumes hit her. She made her way out of the house and along the street, checking around for signs of life. She hadn't a clue as to where she was. She walked to the corner of the road and found a street sign, then she headed off to find a phone box. She kept to the hedgerow in case the men returned. Millie turned the corner and there up ahead was a phone box, she sprinted the last few yards and grabbed the door. Once inside she dialled Finn's number. Her heartbeat quickened as she listened to the phone ringing. "Pick up." She demanded.

"Hello"

Finn's voice drifted down the phone and almost made Millie cry. "Finn, I need help."

"Millie! What happened, are you okay, where are you?" Finn gabbled.

"Listen, I don't know where I am. I've got a street name, that's all, Linnet Drive. Send Paul, I've found...." Millie stopped when the phone went dead. She looked at the receiver and sighed before replacing it. Now she needed a hiding place. Millie made her way back to the corner and stood across the road, the flames had burst from the windows of the house. She could hear the sirens as the fire engine approached and kept out of sight, just in case the two thugs returned. The fire engine pulled up outside and the firefighters got to work. Millie sank back further, this time behind a bush. Suddenly her eyes were drawn to a flash motor as it crawled along the road. Millie noticed the passenger. It was Jamie Carter. She didn't see the driver.

The car sped away leaving Millie alone watching the firefighters. Who was that man with Jamie and were they responsible for her kidnapping? While Millie was trying to put the pieces of the puzzle together, she spotted Paul's motor turn into the road. She leapt out of her hiding place and waved frantically as Paul screeched to a halt. Millie broke down as she watched Paul, he jumped out and grabbed her. She felt his arms wrap around her as she sobbed into his chest.

"Baby. I was so worried. Let me look at you. Did they hurt you?" Paul Asked.

Millie looked up at him and shook her head. She couldn't speak, she just wanted to be held.

"Are you sure you're, okay?" Paul pressed.

"I'm fine." Millie replied softly. "We need to go." She nodded towards the burning house.

"What the fuck happened there?" Paul asked.

"Can we get out of here please, and I'll explain on the way?" Millie replied.

"Sure, let's get you home." Paul opened the back door and helped Millie in. "You are never going out on your own again."

"Don't be ridiculous." Millie caught his stare in the rear-view mirror. He may be scary to other people but not to her. "Anyway, we've got things to discuss."

"We can discuss whatever when we are home." Paul snapped.

"Hello Duke, I'm glad you're here, as this concerns you also." Millie saw the confusion on Duke's face as he spun around in the seat.

"I had nothing to do with this Millie. How does it concern me?" Duke sounded irritated.

"Maybe you should pull over Paul. I've something to show you both." Millie waited until Paul had parked and both men turned to look at her. She reached into her bra and pulled out the two packets of drugs. "I was tied up in the basement. Once I got myself free, I discovered a load of boxes, there must have been forty at least, so I opened a couple and found these." Millie handed the packets to Paul.

"Drugs?" Duke asked.

"Cocaine and disco biscuits." Paul replied. "Did you see who took you?"

"No. But the weird thing is, as I was hiding in the bushes waiting for you, Jamie Carter drove by, he was in the car with someone, but I couldn't see who." Millie noticed Paul's jaw twitch. "Stay calm Paul, please."

"Calm. I'll give him fucking calm when I get hold of him. He's a dead man." Paul rubbed his scar as he turned and started the engine.

"I still don't see how this has anything to do with me." Duke stated.

"Your cousin was selling coke, just the same as Levi. This here could be the person that supplied them. It also could be the same person that killed him and set up Paul. Don't you want to get to the bottom of it and take your revenge?" Millie shook her head as Duke tried to process the information. "Fine, you two continue to fight each other while I find out who's responsible." Millie turned and looked out of the window.

"One thing Mil, what happened to the house back there?" Paul nodded behind him.

"I burnt it down." Millie held her face neutral despite wanting to laugh at the two shocked faces looking back at her.

As they neared the Artichoke another thought popped into Millie's head. What was the woman from the council office doing with the woman that ran the children's home.

Chapter Thirty-Four

Millie sat on the bed and leaned against the headboard. She had a pillow behind her back, courtesy of Paul who had been fussing over her for the last hour. Millie was pleased when he finally announced he was going out on business. Rosie sat next to her on Paul's request, probably to stand guard, Millie thought. She sat and sipped the tea Finn had made her and stared at the plate of chocolate digestives. She couldn't stomach even a biscuit for fear of bringing it back up.

"So not only did you save yourself you also torched the place?" Rosie asked in awe.

"Yep the whole lot went up in smoke." Millie replied proudly. She wouldn't let on to anyone how much this had shaken her. But it had. Now she had time to think about it, she realised how close she had come to being killed. If Jamie was involved and it looked increasingly like he was. There would be no way she would have been released. "Rose..." Before she could continue, she spotted Paul standing in the doorway. He still looked worried, worried and cross. His brow was creased, and he was watching her.

"And she won't be doing it again." Paul snapped.

"Paul, I am not going to be a prisoner." Millie rolled her eyes. "Anyway, I thought you had work to do?"

"I'm going now. You are not to go out on your own, Rose I expect you to keep guard." Paul ordered.

Millie watched as Rosie stood up and saluted Paul.

"Yes sir." Rosie replied. "I won't even let her pee."

Millie laughed as Paul's face started to turn purple. "I'm not going out, Finns just downstairs, I'm sure he would grass me up."

"It's not a matter to joke about Mil, you could have been hurt." Paul looked worried as he walked towards her. He leant down and gave her a kiss on the forehead. "It's my job to protect you, never forget that." Paul turned and left.

"Wow, he seems more shaken than you Mil." Rosie commented.

"He feels like it's all his fault." Millie sighed.

"I agree with him Mil. It is his fault; if you had never met him, you wouldn't have been kidnapped." Rosie replied. "I warned you about his business dealings."

"And if I were still with Levi I could be laying in a grave. Life is an uncertainty, Rose. You can't know the future." Millie rubbed her head; it was starting to ache. "No. it's not his fault, but he should've listened to me when I tried to warn him about Jamie."

Rosie shrugged. "Maybe."

"Do me a favour. Go and get me a Brandy please." Millie asked.

"Okay, but you won't solve your problems with drink." Rosie replied.

Millie watched her leave the room. The peace and quiet was what she needed; not lectures. Millie thought about Levi, how he had changed the minute that ring was on her finger.

Millie gushed over her wedding ring. She was now Mr's Cooper. She looked at Levi as he started the motor. Before he pulled away, he stopped and turned to her. She couldn't read the expression on his face. It was different. Millie's smile fell as he leaned over towards her. "You belong to me now. You do as I say."

Millie closed her eyes and rested her head back. She had never shared the full extent of the abuse with anyone. She had been made to believe it was her fault. That she deserved everything that had happened to her. The foul words, the beatings, even the cigarette burns. She deserved it all. The only thing she knew she didn't deserve were the rapes. Would Levi have punished Flo for those? Maybe. If he had believed Millie. But Millie knew she couldn't risk it, if he had believed Flo, then she wouldn't be here today.

"Here Mil. A Brandy for you and a glass of wine for me." Rosie said.

"Thanks Rose." Millie smiled as she took the glass and sipped the liquid. She felt the burn on her throat and savoured the feeling. "Rose, I want to tell you something, but you must promise you will never tell another living soul."

"Of course, I wouldn't. What's wrong Mil?" Rosie asked.

Millie could hear the concern in Rosie's voice. Was she doing the right thing? Probably not. "When I was with Levi, Flo forced me to sleep with this man..."

"WHAT!" Rosie bellowed.

"Shhh Rose, Finn will think there's something wrong." Millie warned her.

"There is something wrong. Fucking hell Mil......Why didn't you say something sooner?" Rosie jumped up and started pacing the bedroom as Millie watched. "Does anyone else know?"

"Paul knows.... He found out when I went to the house. Brothel." Millie stood up and grabbed Rosie's hands. "It's okay Rose, come and sit down." Millie led Rosie to the bed and sat next to her. "I need to start healing and the only way that will happen is with honesty. I don't want secrets between us, we've been friends forever."

"How can I help?" Rosie asked.

"You help just by being here." Millie replied. "Please don't cry." Millie wiped away Rosie's tears, she hadn't expected Rosie to cry, but then what reaction did she expect. Anger. Shock. Revulsion. Millie walked to the window and looked out. "You know I feel stronger all ready."

"It's gonna take me a while to get my head around this." Rosie told her.

"I know. But I need to focus on something else.... I want to focus on finding my parents. Starting with the woman from the council office and the woman from the children's home." Millie turned and faced a tearstained Rosie. "Will you help?"

"Of course, I will.... I think we should go and see them again. That is if Paul lets you out." Rosie sighed.

"He can't stop me from going out. Well he might think he can, I'll just have to show him otherwise." Millie laughed. She sat back on the bed and gulped down the last mouthful of Brandy then leant back against the headboard. She didn't lie when she said she felt stronger. She did, she felt in control. Tonight when those demons came for her, in her sleep, she was ready to fight back.

Chapter Thirty-Five

Paul watched the pub from a distance, he had been told Jamie was in there but had no way of checking. Duke sat next to him, and he had another two men in a car opposite. Paul was surprised that Jamie would be this far from home. It was a run-down area. The pub itself looked like it had seen better days. There were a couple of women hanging around outside, looking for business.

"I could go in there; he doesn't know we are working together." Duke offered.

"No, we can't risk it. Who knows who he's working with, they may have men watching." Paul checked his watch. "It's nearly closing time; we'll follow him to see where he goes and then grab him.... Remember I want him to die slowly after we get the info."

"Understood." Duke shifted in his seat for the third time, much to the annoyance of Paul.

"Have you got piles or something, you can't sit still." Paul sighed.

"Did you ask that because I'm a traveller or is that how you treat all the people you work with?" Duke snapped. "Because it's not." Duke stopped when Paul pointed.

"There he is. Get ready to follow him, but don't get too close." Paul looked over to the other car and waved.

Duke started the old car he had borrowed, and slowly pulled out, following Jamie, down the road. "He's stopping."

"Pull over here, let the other car go first." Paul watched as Jamie knocked on the door of a run-down house. It reminded him of a druggies squat. The windows had rags covering them with one window boarded up. "What the fuck would he be here for?"

"Picking up money. If he's been selling drugs and his men are dead maybe, he needs to collect himself?" Duke suggested.

"Maybe." Paul continued to watch the door until Jamie came out. "Ready. Don't let him spot you."

"Can you stop with the orders?" Duke started the car and pulled away.

Finally, they pulled up outside a small block of flats. Both men watched as Jamie made his way in. They both looked up at the window when a light went on, Paul smiled. "Come on." He motioned to his men then walked to the front door with Duke while the other two went around the back. Paul nodded to Duke to knock while he stood back out of sight. As the door opened a petite redhead stood staring at Duke.

"Can I help you?" She asked.

Paul rushed forward and pushed her out of the way then made his way to the bedroom. The flat was clean and tidy, which pleased Paul. He hated dirt and mess of any kind. When Paul pushed open the bedroom door Jamie was making himself comfortable.

"Paul. What the fuck is this?" Jamie threw the covers back and reached for his clothes.

Before he grabbed them Paul was on him. One punch was enough to knock him back onto the bed. "You shouldn't have involved Millie."

"What the fuck are you talking about?" Jamie's eyes betrayed his mouth. Paul could see it.

Duke entered the room as Paul raised a gun to Jamie's head. "Wait. Paul, you want answers first, remember."

Paul nodded slightly and watched as his men walked in. "Tie him up and take him to the warehouse."

An hour later Paul stared at the bloodied body of Jamie as it hung from a beam. He had to give it to him, he hadn't grassed his partner up, instead he had taken the blame for the drugs and kidnapping. Even when he had drilled his kneecaps, he had still kept quiet, apart from the screams. Finally Paul had tipped acid down his throat and watched him writhe in agony until he died.

"Well that's it then." Duke stood next to Paul and stared at Jamie's corpse. "We know who provided the pill's, but I still don't know what happened to Rueben."

"I think it's safe to say he was responsible. I'm more concerned about his partner though. Jamie didn't have the money or connections to produce the amount of drugs Millie said that there were in that basement. It's got to be a big player." Paul wiped his hands on an old rag.

"What did he mean when he said the threat was closer than you think?" Duke asked. "Could the other man he was working with be another of your men?"

"No. Impossible. It's someone with money. I'm betting he'll show his hand soon enough." Paul wasn't a sentimental man and Jamie often got on his nerves, but he never thought for one minute Jamie would turn on him. Just goes to show. Never trust anyone 100%.

Chapter Thirty-Six

Millie and Rosie walked in silence to the council offices. Millie knew Rosie was still struggling with the news of the rape. She had spoken to her again the night before. But Millie had drawn a line under it. There was nothing else to tell. The sun was shining, and Millie held her face towards it, enjoying the warmth it gave her. It was the simple things in life she enjoyed. Good friends, good weather and the great outdoors. And none of them cost a penny. Millie stopped and stood outside the council office looking at the sign for births, deaths, and marriages. "Well here we go again only this time I'm not taking no for an answer." She grabbed Rosie's arm, and the pair made their way inside.

"Look there she is. Excuse me madam, we came in here a little while ago to get my friend's birth certificate, but for some reason you said she didn't have one. Can you please check again as we've been told she was definitely registered." Rosie winked at Millie. "Oh and if there's any problem, we can ask the police to look into it."

Millie's mouth dropped open as she watched Rosie in action. She turned her attention to the woman behind the counter and noticed the colour drain from her face. "Is there a problem?" Millie added.

"No. No problem. Hold on one moment and I'll recheck for you." The woman disappeared into the back for a few minutes and reappeared with a large ledger. "Here we are, you were born 19th November 1951."

Millie frowned as she looked at the entry. "How did you know where to look, my name, date of birth. We didn't tell you?"

"I remembered you from before." The woman replied.

"That's quite some memory you've got. Is there something you want to tell us?" Rosie asked suspiciously.

The woman shifted on her feet and kept her head down. "Look ladies I've given you all the information you asked for now please leave or I'll be the one to call the Police." The woman slammed the ledger shut and walked through to the back office.

"Come on Rose, something doesn't add up." Millie grabbed Rosie and pulled her out of the building. "There's something she's not telling us. I mean I can barely remember what I had to eat three days ago, but for her to remember my name and date of birth, she must know something. Maybe she knows who my mother is?"

"We need to go to the children's home and see that other old bag. Or you could tell Paul and he could torture them." Rosie laughed.

"Rose! Shh. You shouldn't joke about things like that.... He probably would." Millie stopped when she got that same strange feeling of being watched. She turned and looked up and down the high street, but no one was there.

"What's wrong Mil?" Rosie asked in concern.

"Nothing. I'm being paranoid. Come on, let's get to the children's home before Paul comes looking for me." Millie kept looking behind her as she made her way down the road. The feeling of being watched stayed with her the whole journey.

"Right, I'll do the talking. You just stand there looking pretty." Rosie ordered.

"I have questions, Rose." Millie replied.

"I'm sure you do, but if you want answers then you need to make threats first." Rosie knocked on the door while Millie watched. It took a few minutes before the door was answered. Millie took a quick look behind her and wondered if it was Paul. She didn't know what she would do if he turned up now.

"Hello again. Look if you've come back for the file, I'm afraid I can't give it to you. I got a right telling off last time." Doug informed them.

"No Doug, we wouldn't want to get you into any trouble, we're here to see the boss lady." Rosie replied.

"Come on in." Doug ushered Millie and Rosie in. "Follow me girls."

Doug disappeared into the office returning a minute later shaking his head. "I'm sorry, she's too busy to see you at the moment. Can you come back another time?"

Millie felt her temper rise and walked towards the office door. Doug jumped in front of her and held his hand up. Without thinking Millie shoulder barged him out of the way and made her way into the office. "You know we saw you. Chatting away with the woman from the council, just like old friends." Millie noticed the look of shock on the woman's face. "Yeah, I thought so, there's more to this than you're letting on." Millie felt Doug's hand on her arm and shook him off. "Get off me."

"Doug, it's fine. As I've already been disturbed, I'll see Millie now. Not you young lady, you can wait outside." The woman ordered Rosie.

Millie nodded to Rose and watched as her and Doug left the room. "You know why I'm here?"

The woman nodded. "But I don't know what help you think I can be."

"I know you know more than you're telling me, so start talking." Millie pulled out a chair and sat opposite the woman.

"I think you will find that all my paperwork is in order, Millie." The woman replied.

"You know who my mother is." Millie sat forward and pointed at the woman. "All I need is a name." Millie watched the mean smile spread across the woman's face. She was tempted to punch her, but she managed to keep her temper in check.

"My dear child, what I do and do not know is none of your concern." The woman placed her elbows on the desk and leant forward, clasping her hands together. "Sometimes things are better left in the past, where they belong."

"But I'm not in the past, I'm right here. Sitting in front of you. Please, give me a name." Millie almost begged. She noticed the woman's face soften slightly.

"I'm sorry, I don't know anything. DOUG." The door opened and Doug popped his head in. "See Millie out please."

Millie stood and walked towards the door but paused briefly to address the woman. "If you're gonna play games, games with my life, I'm gonna play games with yours. I didn't want it this way.... Consider that your final warning."

Chapter Thirty-Seven

Duke sat with his sons Aron and Jess in the café on Bethnal Green high street. He watched the traffic go by as he thought of what he would say. He didn't want to worry his boy's, but he had no other choice. He turned his attention to them as they both tucked into a bacon roll. "Have you noticed anything strange about your mother lately?"

"Like what?" Aron asked as he took another bite of his roll. Duke watched the melted butter drip from his chin. He grabbed a serviette and threw it at him.

"I don't know.... Anything a bit odd?" Duke took a sip of his tea and watched Jess nod.

"Caught her crying the other day." Jess replied.

"Did you ask her what was wrong?" Duke felt his stomach tighten. He knew something wasn't quite right.

"She said she was being sentimental and not to worry." Jess looked at Duke. "Is she alright dad?"

"I think ya mother wants to settle down, maybe get a house." Before Duke had finished, Aron jumped in.

"I'm not living like a gorja in a heap of bricks."

"Calm down boy, I don't know for sure. I'll talk to her later. Right yous two pigs finished cos I need to get back." Duke stood and looked at his sons. They were only sixteen but already had the look of fighting men. "And boys, don't say anything to ya mother."

"We won't, will we Jess." Arron replied.

The drive back to camp was pleasant. The sun was shining, the trees were budding and everywhere looked green and wholesome. Just as he liked it. He wound the window down and breathed in the fresh air. As he pulled up the lane, he stopped so that Jess could jump out and open the gate. Once he drove through, Jess jumped back into the motor, and they continued up the track. Duke pulled up between his two trailers. He had one that he and Connie slept in, which was the family home, and he had a small tourer that the boys slept in. Now they were older, Duke felt they needed their own space. Duke jumped out of the motor and stuck his head in the trailer. "Connie?" Looking up and down he shook his head. His wife was always out lately. Heading back out he walked over to the bonfire and returned the greetings he received from the other travellers standing there. He stopped next to his dad and watched the flames.

"It's gonna be a dry ole summer boy." Nelson informed him.

"I know dad, you've been saying that for the last few weeks." Duke muttered.

"OK what's up?" Nelson nodded towards his trailer. "Come on, I've got a bottle stashed away from ya mother. Let's go and open it."

Duke followed his dad into his trailer and looked around. "Where's mum?"

"Who knows, she'll be in someone's place, tongue wagging. You know what these women are like, son. Love gossip, the lot of 'em. Anyway, what's on ya mind?"

Duke sighed. "It's Connie, I think she wants to live in a house."

"She tell you that, did she?" Nelson handed Duke a glass. "Drink up, it'll make ya feel better."

"No she didn't say that, but when I said about us moving on soon, she said she likes it here."

"I see.... Have you asked her?"

"No. I'm gonna ask her when I find her. That's another thing, she's always out. She says she's shopping but how much shopping does she need?" Duke took a sip of the golden liquid and felt the warmth hit his throat. "What if she does want to stay here, what then?"

"I would ask her first, before you jump to conclusions, then you can get a plan together." Nelson refilled Dukes glass.

"I don't want to live in a house, neither do my boys. We are called travellers for a reason. It's in our blood." Duke trailed off at the thought of losing his wife.

"You won't be happy in a house boy, but in a marriage you sometimes have to compromise. You have money. Why not buy a bit of ground and stick a mobile on there. You could keep ya trailer and still go away travelling in the summer months. You both get what you want, and as a bonus, me and ya mother can come and stay during the winter." Nelson laughed.

"That's not a bad idea. I'll speak to her when she's back. Right, you gonna pour us another drink?" Duke looked out the window as a car pulled up. Connie got out with a large bag. Duke jumped up and headed out to greet her. "Don't worry about the drink." He called over his shoulder.

"Duke. You're back early." Connie remarked.

"It's 5 o'clock Connie. You haven't even done dinner, what's going on?" Duke noticed Connie's cheeks colour up.

"I fancy a bit of fish and chips.... thought you could go and get it." Connie headed towards their trailer while Duke followed. He kept his eye on her. Even her body language looked different.

"Connie what's wrong. You've been acting weird since we got here. What is it?" Duke led Connie to the bunk and sat down with her. "Have you had enough of me?" Duke noticed the look of hurt on her face and immediately felt guilty.

"What! No. Duke, I love you, why would you think I've had enough of you?" Connie gasped as she threw the bag down.

"Because you've been distant, you keep disappearing and you won't talk to me. Do you want to live in a house?" Duke grabbed Connie's hand and gave it a little squeeze. "Be honest."

"No. I don't want to live in a house, but honestly, I'd like to stay here, even if only for a while."

"What if we buy a bit of ground, we can make a home here and still go away when we want. Would you be happy then?" Duke watched the smile light up Connie's face as she flung her arms around his neck.

"That would be perfect. Duke Lee, I love you." Connie laughed.

Duke smiled. "I love you too Con." He walked to the door and called Jess. "Go chippy for ya mother boy." Duke turned back to Connie. "I know someone selling a mobile, we can take a look after dinner if you want."

"I'd like that." Connie replied.

After dinner, Duke took Connie to where the mobile was for sale. It was someone he had done business with many times. As he pulled up at the man's yard, he watched Connie's smile broaden. "Come on Con, let's have a look." Duke walked around the outside of the mobile with Connie. "What do ya think Con?" Duke asked as he ducked down and studied the underside.

"It's perfect." Connie replied.

"It's only a couple of years old and in mint condition. Looks tidy from the outside, let's see what the insides like." Duke smiled as he watched Connie's eyes light up.

"And it's three bedrooms?" She asked as they made their way to the door.

"Three bedrooms, living room, bathroom, and kitchen. Come on." Duke motioned for Connie to go in first. He wanted her to be the first to see it.

"It's perfect." Connie gasped in delight. "And the boys will have their own room each."

"You sure this is the one you want?" Duke looked around the living room. He wasn't used to having this much space. He laughed when Connie nodded her head so hard, he thought it would drop off. "Fine, we'll have it."

"When will we be able to move in?" Connie called to Duke as she made her way into the main bedroom.

"As soon as we find a bit of land and can get it moved. Will need the base concreted and electric done. Should be able to move in by June, all being well. Go and get in the motor while I make a deal." Duke motioned to the man that was selling it. "Okay mate, let's talk."

The drive home was like old times. Duke smiled as he listened to Connie's excited chatter. The one thing that surprised him was the fact she wanted a Christmas tree. Even though she always decorated the trailer each Christmas, he had never given that a thought.

By the time they reached the traveller camp it had started to get dark. "Go inside Con, I'm just gonna get some fresh air." He watched her close the door behind her and then he sat on the step and watched the camp site. People were standing around chatting. He could see at the end, the children feeding the horses, the lights from the trailers and bonfire illuminated the place. One of the chavies attempted to ride bareback. Duke smiled; he loved this life. But his smile soon dropped. How would he manage in one place for more than a few weeks? Would Connie still be willing to travel? Duke sighed; did she really know what she wanted? But he wondered more than anything if this would solve the problem. In his experience, if something was wrong, it didn't matter where you lived. Your problems would always be with you.

Chapter Thirty-Eight

Millie stood inside the old picture house and looked around. It had been stripped of all the usual furniture that a picture house would hold. Instead, it had bare walls with plaster missing. The floor didn't look much better. There were holes in that too where the seating had been screwed to it. And the smell matched the surroundings. It smelt damp and dirty. Millie shook her head. "Paul this is going to take a miracle to get it ready for opening in four weeks, and just so you know, I don't believe in miracles." Millie planted both hands on her hips and stared at the chaos filled room. Her head flicked towards Paul as he laughed. "How is this funny or more to the point, how is it even possible?"

"Oh ye of little faith.... Trust me Mil, it will be. The work starts tomorrow, you'll see the difference by the end of the week. Now shall we go for dinner, I'm bloody starving." Paul replied.

"Fine, but don't moan to me when you realise you've given yourself an unrealistic deadline.... Where are we eating?" Millie asked.

"Indian?" Paul replied as he grabbed her hand.

"Okay." Millie followed Paul out and climbed into his range

rover, annoyed when he grabbed a handful of her arse. "Do you always have to do that?"

"Yep. I do. You know I wouldn't mind you grabbing mine." Paul laughed.

"I'm a lady Paul, we don't do things like that." Millie looked out of the passenger window as her face coloured up.

"You weren't a lady in bed last night. In fact I felt like a piece of meat."

Millie spun around just in time to see the twinkle in Pauls eyes. "Are you complaining?"

"My only complaint is that you ain't like it every night. Now give us a kiss."

Millie pushed Paul away and laughed. "Can we be serious for a minute?"

"I was being serious." Paul puckered his lips.

Millie obliged before changing the subject. "Paul?"

"What, and that wasn't a kiss it was a peck." Paul complained.

"For Christ sake, I'm trying to discuss something important." Millie folded her arms and returned her gaze out of the passenger window.

"Okay. The kiss can wait until later. What's wrong?" Paul stopped the car and turned to Millie. "What's happened?"

"Just before I was kidnapped, I spotted the woman from the council offices. You know the one that said there was no record of my birth, well she was talking to the dragon that kicked me and Rose out of the children's home." Millie stopped when Paul cut in.

"And?"

"And I went back to visit them and this time the woman at the council found my details straight away."

Paul cut in again. "That's good, isn't it?"

"Will you let me finish?" Millie waited for Paul to nod then continued. "She got my details out before I reminded her of my name and date of birth, like she had prepared them."

"From the sounds of it she did, what about the children's home?" Paul asked, now sounding interested.

"When I went to see her, she said the past should be left in the past. She knows something Paul, I know she does, but I don't know how to find out what she knows."

"Do you want me to find out?" Paul replied.

"I don't want her tortured. I just want to know who my mum is." Millie looked down at her hands, they were shaking again.

"It sounds to me that after your first visit they were able to get all the paperwork in order." Paul sighed. "Do you want them to pay Mil?"

"I want to know what they know Paul and once I know that, then I'll decide what action to take." Millie felt the tears forming in her eyes and turned her head away from Paul.

"Mil, look at me.... It's going to be okay. We will get to the bottom of this."

"I know, it's just frustrating. I have so many questions that run through my head all the time. It's like I'm being haunted." Millie closed her eyes and rested her head back onto the head rest. A headache was forming just behind her eyes.

"While we are on the subject of parents, I want you to meet mine." Paul announced.

Millie opened her eyes and stared at Paul. Thoughts of Flo and Elijah filled her head and her insides tightened. She gave a tight smile and curt nod to Paul before she refocused on the road. She didn't want to meet his parents, she wanted to meet her own. She knew that was selfish and the chances of Paul's parents being anything like Levis were slim, but there was still a chance, right?

Chapter Thirty-Nine

Saturday, 8 May 1976

Millie entered the club with Paul. She was kitted out in a little black designer dress. Matching shoes and clutch bag, and her hair was piled high on her head, showing her slender neck. Paul had told her she looked stunning, which made her feel better than good. Millie fanned herself with her hand. The weather was unusually warm for this time of year. Paul told her it would be good for business and improve the bar sales. She laughed; he was always the businessman. Millie checked herself in the mirror that hung in the foyer and fiddled with her hair.

"You look perfect Mil, stop fretting." Paul reassured her, but she was fretting. Paul had arranged for a reporter to be there. This was big news apparently. Millie followed Paul through the double doors and looked around the massive room. She smiled. He had done it; four weeks and he had managed to get the place ready for the grand opening. "I love that glitter ball." Millie smiled as she pointed to the ceiling. As the DJ started to do his sound check he played 'Save All Your Kisses For Me' by Brotherhood of Man. It had won the Eurovision song contest and was a massive hit in the country. Millie started to sing along as the music belted out.

"The journalist should be here soon, here have a glass of wine, it'll relax you." Paul handed Millie a glass. "How's your nerves now?"

"I'm okay now I'm here. Will the journalist ask questions?" Millie took a quick gulp of her wine, while she focused on Paul.

"He'll ask a couple, I guess. It will mostly be taking photos and reporting on the opening night. I don't want you to worry about that, just enjoy the evening. I've got a few VIP's coming, Ronnie's one of them, it's about time you met him." Paul took Millie's empty glass and placed it on the bar.

"I wonder if I'll get his approval." Millie laughed.

"I don't need anyone's approval. You're mine and if anyone has a problem with that they can fuck off." Paul grabbed Millie's hand. "Come on, the journalist is here, we need a photo out the front."

Millie stood with Paul underneath the large sign that read Kelly's in neon lights. It would light up the whole front of the club when it was dark. As the journalist snapped away Millie's nerves disappeared, and she started to relax.

"Come on, the guests should be arriving soon." Paul led Millie back inside and up the stairs to a balcony. It had further seating, with part cordoned off for a VIP area. It was also perfect for spotting any trouble. Paul grabbed Millie by the waist and pulled her towards him, as he planted his lips on hers.

Millie smiled. "Paul. Stop it. I thought we were supposed to be professional."

"We are. That was a professional kiss.... We could always go and lock ourselves in the office." Paul winked.

She knew exactly what he was thinking. Before she could reprimand him, she stopped. An older gentleman was approaching their table.

"Ronnie, glad you could make it. Millie, this is Ronnie, Ronnie, Millie." Paul announced.

Millie stood and held out her hand as the older man stared. "It's nice to meet you, Ronnie." Millie stared back, he had cold eyes, even when he smiled. It was like they were dead. Millie pulled her hand away. She had formed her opinion of him in those brief seconds.

"It's lovely to meet you too. You were right Paul, she is beautiful." Ronnie replied.

Millie squirmed as Ronnie grabbed her hand once more and pulled her towards him, and without notice he planted a kiss on her cheek.

"Place looks great, gonna be a little gold mine, well done son. We need to have a chat about the other business sometime this week, let me know when you're free, give me a call and we'll set it up." Ronnie continued.

Millie felt like she had been dismissed. She felt more than a little let down. After all Paul had told her about the great Ronnie Taylor, his friend, confidant, and father figure. Millie decided there and then she didn't like him. She was taught to trust your own instincts and so far, they had never let her down.

"Is everything Okay Ron?" Paul asked.

"It will be fine, but there's a hitch, let's discuss it tomorrow, tonight is for celebrating. Right, is that bubbly I see?" Ronnie reached out and took the glass as Millie handed it to him.

Millie smiled as the stirring of unease continued to hit her. She continued to watch Ronnie from the corner of her eye. He was cocky, acted like everyone here belonged to him. Millie found herself getting more and more wound up as the evening went on. So much for a great night, she thought. "Rose, I need to get a drink of water." She shouted over the noise of the music and continual chatter. She made her way to the bar with Rosie. The drinks were flowing a little too freely for her. Every time she emptied her glass someone refilled it.

"You lightweight Mil. You should be knocking the free champagne back, mind you, I suppose this will be your lifestyle from now on." Rosie surmised.

"I never used to drink Rose. At this rate either my liver will be packing its bags, or I'll be in a clinic drying out." Millie replied. Once she had her water the two women stood at the side of the dance floor and watched the clubbers as they bopped around.

Millie grabbed Rosie's arm and bent her head towards Rosie's ear. "I need the loo."

"Me too!" Rosie shouted back.

After the quick toilet break, Millie followed Rosie out of the ladies' restrooms when she collided with a man. "I'm sorry."

"Not a problem sweetheart." He replied.

Millie watched as he walked away, she could have sworn she knew him.

"Shall we go then Mil?" Rosie asked. "Mil....MIL?"

"Sorry, what?" Millie looked at Rosie with a frown.

"Are you okay?" Rosie pressed. "You seem miles away. What's wrong?"

"Nothing.... I'm fine. Come on, let's get a drink, this is a celebration after all." Millie followed Rosie along the corridor, but she stopped and turned back to where the man had been. There was something familiar about him. Millie shook her head and climbed the stairs as she reached the VIP area she stood overlooking the bar. "I love this song." She announced to Rosie.

"Everyone loves a bit of Abba." Rosie laughed. "Shall we go down and dance?"

"You go, I need to stay up here and entertain the freeloaders, I mean VIP's." Millie winked. She watched Rosie go down and head into the crowded dance floor, then turned towards Paul who was now in full conversation with another man.

"Mil, this is Eddie, Eddie meet Millie." Paul grabbed hold of Millie's hand and pulled her towards him.

"Nice to meet you, Eddie." Millie smiled.

"Lovely to meet you too darling. I was just saying what a little goldmine you have here." Eddie pointed around the club. "Very impressive."

Before Millie answered Ronnie appeared and cemented himself into the conversation. "Think I'll get myself a little club. Always fancied owning one. I'll have another drop of that champagne Millie if there's any more going?"

"Of course, Ronnie, I'll get another bottle and top you up." Millie spotted Paul's face as he frowned. "Would you like a top up too Paul?"

"No, and it's not your place to fill up glasses, WE, have staff for that." Paul pointed.

"Of course darling, just keeping your guest happy." Millie turned and made her way down to the dance floor, only stopping when Paul grabbed her arm.

"What's wrong Mil?" Paul asked.

"Nothing, I'm just gonna dance with Rose. You should get back to your VIP's." Millie shrugged him off and headed through the crowd of sweaty bodies.

"Hey, you've come to dance." Rosie shouted over the music.

"How could I let you have all the fun?" Millie shouted back.

"What?" Rosie cupped her ear. "I can't hear you."

Millie shook her head and joined in the dancing, the only time she stopped was when a slow song came on. "I'm going back up." Millie mouthed to Rosie. She pointed to the balcony for good measure. Satisfied when Rosie did a thumbs up, she made her way back to Paul.

She felt hot and sweaty after exerting herself on the dance floor and grabbed a glass of champagne to quench her thirst. As she placed the glass down, she felt Paul's arms slip around her waist.

"Are you enjoying yourself babe?" He asked her.

Millie spun around to face him and smiled. "I am. Are you?"

"I am now." He replied. "So how about we go and christen the desk?"

"Later, if your lucks in." Millie laughed. "You still have guests to entertain."

"We have guests to entertain, and just for the record. My lucks always in." Paul winked.

Millie looked over to Ronnie as he called for Paul. Like he was there solely to wait hand and foot on him. The wanker! She wondered how many other people thought the same. That brought a smile to her face. There were probably hundreds. Millie turned her attention back to the dance floor. Rosie was in Bobby's arms gently rocking from side to side as the slow song came to an end. Millie was glad it was time to wrap things up. It had been a long day. All she wanted now was to climb into bed with Paul and sleep. Millie was brought out of her thoughts when Ronnie approached her.

"I'm off now Mil. Got to say, you've certainly landed on ya feet with Paul. Bet you've never had it so good." Ronnie laughed. "But on a serious note, I want to say how sorry I was to hear about the kidnapping. Must have been a very traumatic experience."

Millie frowned and gave him a curt nod. She didn't realise the kidnapping was common knowledge. Millie turned and made her way downstairs to the ladies' restroom. As she approached the door, she stopped dead. A tight knot formed in her stomach, and she had to lean against the wall to keep herself upright. The man earlier. It wasn't him she recognised; it was his voice. He was one of the kidnappers.

Chapter Forty

Millie sat on the sofa and stared out of the window. It was another nice day. The sun shone through the window, illuminating the whole room as the birds chirped away. Summer was well and truly here. Millie loved the summer. The freedom of the great outdoors. She thought back to the mischief Rosie, Scott, and herself, got into, all those years ago in the children's home. She smiled to herself as she pictured the memories in her mind, until Paul spoke and brought her back to her surroundings.

"You not eating that toast? Paul asked.

"I'm not hungry." She replied, annoyed when he grabbed it and stuffed it in his mouth. Her thoughts returned to the previous night. "Who did you tell about the kidnapping?" Millie turned to look at him, she couldn't decide if he looked shocked or angry."

"No one, only those involved. Why?" Paul asked.

"Did you tell Ronnie?" Millie pressed.

"I don't think so. Mil what's this all about?" Paul's body stiffened as he spoke.

"He mentioned it to me last night." Before Millie had finished speaking Paul jumped in.

"Well then, I must have told him. Why do you have a problem with Ron?"

"I find it strange that you can't remember, it was a big deal, well to me it was." Millie stood and took the empty plate to the sink. She heard Paul huff behind her.

"I've got a lot on my plate at the moment, things slip my mind Mil."

"Are you sure you can trust him?" Millie flinched when Paul pulled her around to face him. His eyes were full of something she had never seen directed at her before. Malice.

"Can I do anything right?" Paul asked. "I've bought you a fucking nightclub, you should be happy, not picking holes in my friends."

Millie looked at Paul and shook her head. "I am happy, I'm just saying you shouldn't put all your trust in Ronnie."

"Why?" Paul answered abruptly. "I've known him years, he's like a second dad to me. Do you think he's gonna turn me over?"

"Jamie did." Millie jumped when Paul snapped.

"Ronnie Taylor is nothing like Jamie.... I don't want to hear another word on the subject. Now drop it." Paul blew out as if trying to contain his anger, Millie found it intimidating, but she wouldn't give up.

"For your information, just in case you're interested, one of my kidnappers was at the club opening." Millie replied.

"I thought you didn't see them?"

"No I didn't but I heard them. It was the same voice, Paul." Millie watched Paul's face harden.

"Is this the same as the mysterious person that keeps following you? Could you be imagining it? Or maybe your attention seeking?" Paul snapped.

Millie wasn't sure if she was more hurt or humiliated by Paul's comments, but she knew one thing. He could see the hurt he had just caused her, and he didn't care.

"You almost cost me one business, are you trying to ruin the docks too, before it's up and running.... Now drop it." Paul added.

"Fine. Let's drop everything, the club, the relationship. Everything." Millie stood up to leave Paul's flat, amazed when he opened the door for her, and handed her a five-pound note.

"Here. Get yourself a cab home."

Millie threw the money at Paul's feet. "I'm capable of getting home myself."

"Off you go then." Paul stood back to let her pass.

Millie walked out without looking back. She felt the tears building, but there was no way she would cry, not here. As she walked to the end of the road, she felt a familiar pain inside. He didn't believe her. She had trusted him, and he didn't believe a word she said.

Millie made her way along the road to the high street. She didn't need a taxi; she didn't need his money and she certainly didn't need him. As she made her way into the pub; the smell of the beer hops filled the air. It was a welcomed smell. She was home. Finn stood behind the bar, laughing with one of the regulars. His eyes creased as he laughed. Millie made her way through the pub and smiled at Finn.

"Mil, what's wrong?" He asked.

Finn's voice made Millie feel worse. She didn't want people's concern or pity. "Nothing." She replied as she headed up to her bedroom. She closed the door and locked it. As she fell onto the bed, her tears then flowed freely, each sob stealing her breath until she finally cried herself to sleep.

* * *

Millie opened her eyes and sat up abruptly when a loud knock woke her, followed by Rosie's voice as it drifted through the door.

"Millie, open up, it's me."

Millie climbed off the bed and unlocked the door, as she pulled it open, she noticed the sympathetic look on Rosie's face. "Don't just stand there, come in."

"Finn asked me to check on you. What's happened?"

"Me and Paul are finished." Millie plonked herself down on the edge of the bed and stared at the floor.

"What? You must have this all-wrong Mil, he idolises you." Rosie replied.

Millie took the tissue Rosie was holding out and blew her nose. "At the club opening last night I saw a man, it was one of my kidnappers. I recognised the voice. I told Paul this morning, but he didn't believe me. This was after I had questioned him about his friendship with Ronnie." She felt Rosie's arm wrap around her and fought the urge to cry.

"Well it's his loss, and for the record I believe you.... I think you need to concentrate on finding your parents, forget about Paul Kelly, he's no good for you Mil."

"Why would I bother finding my parents, they didn't want me. I would just be setting myself up for more rejection and at the moment I don't think I could handle it." Millie wrapped her arms around herself as she pictured Paul's accusing face. "He didn't believe me, Rose. About the person following me or the kidnapping.... He's got more trust in Ronnie Taylor than he has in me. I'm done with him, and I'm done with the club, in fact I'm done with everything."

Chapter Forty-One

Millie hadn't slept, her thoughts wouldn't let her. She couldn't shake the image of Paul's accusing face from her mind. The way he had looked in her eyes when he questioned her about the kidnapper. The hurt she felt when he accused her of attention seeking. And the jibe about the nightclub, she had never asked him for anything, least of all a bloody nightclub. Millie shook the thoughts from her mind and carried on down the road. The sun was already warm, despite it only being 9am. She went over her plan one more time and consoled herself that once this was done, so was she. Millie marched into the solicitors and stood at the reception desk. "I wish to see Paul Kelly's Solicitor please. Mr Barrett, I believe."

"Do you have an appointment, Miss?"

"No, but it's important and I'm not going until I see him." Millie folded her arms and glared down at the woman.

"I'm sorry but that's not possible, he's very busy today."

Millie walked past the desk and straight into Mr Barrett's room. "I need a word please."

The receptionist rushed past her waving her arms in the air as if to shoo her away. Millie smiled; it was quite a sight.

"I'm sorry Mr Barrett, I told her she couldn't see you without an appointment." The Receptionist's face went a light pink.

"Don't worry Donna, I'll see Mrs Cooper now. Come in Millie and take a seat. Now what can I do for you?" Mr Barrett sat back and looked sternly at Millie. He reminded Millie of a headmaster.

"I want to sign my half of the club over to Mr Kelly." Millie felt the knot in her stomach tighten at the mention of his name.

"But the partnership has only just started.... Are you sure you want to do this?" Mr Barrett sat forward in his chair. Millie knew he was studying her.

"Yes, Paul, I mean Mr Kelly funded the project so it's only fair that he owns it all." Millie gave a small smile.

"I see.... You know the business is worth quite a bit, money wise..."

Millie cut him off before he could finish. "Look I don't want the business, I don't want the money, I just want out.... Please Mr Barrett."

"Okay. I should really contact Mr Kelly first."

"Look, sign me off of the club, I'm not asking for money I just want out. Surely you don't need to bother him with that?" Millie demanded.

"Very well. Give me half an hour and I'll get it done for you." Mr Barrett nodded towards the door. "If you wait in the reception, I will bring it out when I've completed it."

Millie nodded, then left the office. As she walked past the receptionist, she made sure to give her a hard look. No one was going to mess with her today. Millie sat waiting patiently, until Mr Barrett brought out the contract. "All you have to do is sign at the bottom of both copies and you will no longer be a partner with Mr Kelly."

Millie's heart broke a little bit more as she scribbled her signature. She realised how foolish she had been to even think that this would help her. No, it wouldn't but it would help him. Why did she always give her love so freely? First Levi and then Paul. Rosie was right, he had hurt her. That one look he had given her, that one vile look of contempt, hatred, blame. That had hurt her more than any of the punches Levi had thrown. It had hurt more than anything Flo had done to her. Millie dropped the pen and shook the solicitor's hand. "Thank you."

Next Millie made her way to the club, she jumped off the bus directly opposite and made her way across the road. She unlocked the door with her key and walked in, a couple of Paul's men greeted her. She could feel there was a bit of an atmosphere as she made her way to the office and wondered what he had told them. Once in she closed the door and took a seat in the large leather chair, breathing in the new leather smell that seemed to fill the room. As she placed the signed contract onto the desk, she noticed a pile of papers left on the side. Reading through them she noticed the dock contract placed on top. Scribbled at the top, she read down the list of things Paul needed to do. At the top was buying Millie out of the club. So, he had planned to get rid of her. She felt glad that she had beaten him to it. Next on the list was forcing the dock managers to sign the contract. And last was Ronnie Taylor's name, scribbled at the bottom. Millie found that odd.

She grabbed the dock paperwork and placed it into her bag along with the club contract. She would write a letter first before giving it to him, that way she would never have to see him again. Now she had her future planned she wouldn't see any of them.

Millie walked out into the sunshine and made her way over to the bus stop. Her next stop she was dreading but she needed their help.

Millie reached her last destination 45 minutes later, thanks to getting on the wrong bus. However, the scenery was nice, and she wanted one last look around town and the surrounding area. She made her way to the front door and knocked, holding her breath as the door opened. "Gladys."

"Millie.... You had better come in." Gladys held the door open and pointed to the office. Millie noticed the dark-haired woman watching her from the stairs as she walked in.

Gladys pulled the office door too and motioned towards the chair. "Take a seat."

"I need to clear the air and explain myself." Millie stopped when the office door opened, and the dark-haired woman walked in.

"This is Maggie." Gladys motioned to the woman and then sat behind the desk.

Millie nodded and turned her attention back to Gladys. "Look, the place closing was my idea. I had it in my head that you were all forced to do this." Millie explained apologetically. "It was nothing to do with Paul.... Mr Kelly."

Maggie was the first to speak. "Why did you think Mr Kelly forced us?"

Gladys answered before Millie had opened her mouth. "Because of her past. Am I right?" Gladys replied.

Millie put her head down, as she felt her eyes water.

"Mr Kelly's only ever helped us, okay so he makes money from what we do, but he also keeps us safe. We're like a little community. We have each other and we have someone to protect us." Maggie answered.

Millie felt Maggie's hand rest on her shoulder, she didn't want comfort from her though, she wanted comfort from Paul. She had wanted Paul to keep her safe. "All I can say is I'm sorry. I need to go." Millie stood up and wiped at her cheeks.

"No. You ain't going in that state. Maggie get a bottle of brandy; she looks like she needs a drink." Gladys ordered. "Look love, I'm sorry for whatever it is you've gone through. Mr Kelly is a good man, and like all men he does bad things, now have a drink, it will help."

Millie took the drink and gulped it down, feeling the warmth of the fluid gave her little comfort. "I guess I did need it after all. Look I'm trying to make everything right, I've one last thing left to do, I could do with your help?" Millie watched as Gladys refilled her glass before answering.

"I'll help if I can. Go on, I'm listening."

Chapter Forty-Two

Millie stood behind the head office of the docks. She could smell the salt air. It reminded her of a trip they had at the children's home. Every year they would go on a train to Southend on Sea. It was magical as a child. Millie smiled; those were her happy memories. She turned her attention to the river, it was the Thames estuary, wider here than in town. The waves lapped gently at the quayside; Millie found it mesmerising.

"Can you see any movement?" Maggie asked.

"All four men are in there, seated at their desks. Where's the camera?" Millie whispered.

"It's here." Gladys replied.

Millie studied the large professional camera as Gladys waved it in the air. "Where did you get that from, it looks professional?"

"I borrowed it from one of the brothel's clients, he didn't want to lend it, but after a bit of blackmail he had no choice. After all, he didn't think it would do his marriage or career any good if it came out, he liked bondage." Gladys grinned.

"Good. Wait for the girls to go in. I'll check through the window, when they all have their pants down you run in, get the pictures and leave. Do not stay, the photos are the most important thing. Right, is everyone ready?" Millie watched as the four girls nodded in unison. "I've got this." Millie held up Finn's shotgun. "So any trouble and I'll be in there, do not let them hurt you."

"Fucking hell Mil, you can't use that." Maggie gasped.

"I don't plan to use it. I don't even think it's loaded. But if they start it should deter them. Right, let's go." Millie watched as the four women entered the office. They were wearing very little and had all their goods on show. After waiting ten minutes Millie peered through the window and smiled. The four pathetic men, who had their pants down, so to speak, were partaking in sexual activities with the girls. Waving to Gladys, Millie quietly followed her in and watched as she snapped away, while the men were oblivious.

"Smile for the camera gentlemen." Millie laughed as the men turned towards her and the realisation of their situation hit them. "Gladys go and get three copies of each."

As the men scrambled for their clothes Millie ushered the girls out, while Maggie stood beside her. "I'm not leaving you on your own with them." Maggie told her.

"I'm not on my own. I've got this." Millie held up the shotgun and smiled. "Right, gentlemen. This is what's going to happen. You are going to sign the lease contract for Mr Kelly and Mr Taylor. Or.... Your wives will be getting some beautiful colour photos of your exploits. As you are aware, we know where you all live. Any questions?"

She watched as they all shook their heads, then handed Maggie the paperwork so she could hand it to the men. After they had signed, Millie checked the signatures and nodded. "Thank you. It's been a pleasure doing business with you." Millie turned and left the office with Maggie following. As the two women walked back to Maggie's car Millie burst out laughing. "That was fun!"

"You looked happy doing it." Maggie replied with a smile.

"I'm not gonna lie, it was exciting. It's made me feel different."

Maggie looked at Millie and laughed. "You are different, you my love are now a gangster."

Millie enjoyed Maggie's company, she was fun, talked about anything and everything. And while they waited at the house for the photo's to be developed, she had lunch with her.

"We should do this more often." Maggie laughed.

"It's been fun." Millie conceded. "How much longer will the photos take?"

"They are here, he's just pulling up now." Gladys replied. "Come on, let's see our handywork."

Millie nodded and followed Gladys out, bumping into Scot as she went. "Scot, what are you doing here?

"Work Mil, protecting the girls. What are you doing here?" Scot asked.

"Just visiting, anyway I need to get on, I'll see you soon." Millie pecked him on the cheek and continued on her way. At least she now knew what he was up to. Rosie might not like that bit of information though. Putting thoughts of Scot and Rosie out of her head she grabbed the photos and left.

Millie made her way to the nightclub with Maggie in tow. She had that same strange feeling, like she was being watched. It unnerved her enough for her to stop and look around. She remembered what Paul had said. It was all in her mind. Maybe he was right after all. She turned to Maggie as they approached the night club. "I'm going to put the paperwork and photos on his desk and leave the letter for him, then we can go, okay?"

"Okay. I'm only here as a decoy, but don't be long. I can only talk for so long, and I don't fancy getting arrested for giving a blow job in the street!" Maggie stopped and checked her lipstick. "Right, let's go."

Millie watched Maggie knock on the door of the club, amazed when Maggie actually knew the man, whose name was Tony. As Maggie leaned against the wall with Tony almost on top of her, Millie slipped into the club, unnoticed. As she made her way down the dark hallway, she felt excited. Her heart was beating faster than normal as the adrenaline pumped through her body. When she reached the office door she slipped inside and closed it. Without wasting any time, she reached for the paperwork that she had stashed in her handbag. The only time she stopped was when she heard talking coming from outside the door. She ducked down underneath the desk and held her breath as the door opened. She recognised the voice; it was the bartender.

"Na, didn't leave it in here, it's in the storeroom mate, I'm sure of it."

As she heard the click of the door, Millie peeked her head up, to make sure the coast was clear. Once satisfied she took the contracts, photos, and letter that she had written for Paul and placed them on his desk. Millie sat back in the large leather chair and savoured the feeling she used to get, only a few days ago. The feeling of belonging. She ran her hands along the arms, as she breathed in the strong leather smell that came from it. "Well this is it girl. You won't be sitting in this again and it's your own fault." Taking one last look around the room, Millie stood. She felt a sadness she hadn't felt for a long time. It reminded her of all the shit she had lived through. The only difference being, now she was stronger. Stronger, but still alone.

She slipped back out of the entrance and winked at Maggie who was in full flirt mode with Tony.

"Right Tone. I've gotta go, come and see me soon, yeah."

Millie waited for Maggie to join her. "Okay?" Millie asked.

"Yeah, seems Mr Kelly has buggered off to Spain for a couple of days, Tony recons he was on his jolly's."

"What does jolly's mean? Women?" Millie swallowed down the sob that was building in her throat and started walking faster. Of course he would be with other women, why wouldn't he. He's a man.

"No Mil, I think it was to get over you." Maggie added.

"Well I guess going on ya jolly's will certainly do that.... Look. I've got a few errands to run so I'll catch you soon." Millie stopped and hugged Maggie. "Thank you for everything you've done, I will always remember your kindness."

"Anytime Mil." Maggie smiled.

Millie turned and set off home, enjoying the sunshine, taking time to look at everything. Everywhere she looked she spotted lady-birds. Not just one or two but thousands. On the news it said there had been an influx of the insect due to the dry weather. Whilst some people hated them, she thought they were pretty. She smiled at people as they passed by and offered them a greeting. She breathed in the warm summer air and contemplated her life. She pictured Rosie and Scott, playing over the park after school. The boys as they played football, which was where she had her first kiss. He was a good-looking boy from what she remembered. The kiss was disgusting. When he tried to put his tongue in her mouth, she could remember pushing him away and calling him a pervert. It didn't help when Rosie told her that's how you get pregnant. Millie smiled; those days were so much simpler. Millie stopped when she got that same feeling of someone watching her. The hairs on her arms stood up. She suddenly felt vulnerable. Millie tensed as she looked behind, but no one was there. Paul was right after all. She was imagining it. Millie continued on until she reached the pub, there she greeted Finn with a peck on the cheek and a hug, surprised when he laughed.

"And what did I do to deserve that?" Finn asked.

"You're kind Finn, and I'm grateful to you." Millie smiled at the giant then continued to her room, sighing when she looked at all the clothes she had bought. She wouldn't be able to take them all.

She placed the three letters on her dresser and then arranged them ready for Finn to find. Once she had her clothes packed, she grabbed her most precious position. Her white bunny. Millie then made her way out of the back entrance, she didn't want to see Finn again, not now, just the memory of the hug was enough. Millie made her way to the park and planted her bum on one of the swings. She pushed off with her feet and went higher and higher, until she could see the roof of her old school. The action caused a nice breeze against her face. Thoughts of Levi filled her mind. The bruises. The broken bones. The humiliation was all she remembered now. Nothing nice.

Nothing good. She finally allowed herself to think about Paul. The thought of all the women he had been sleeping with, made Millie's face crumple. Another piece of her heartbroken. She took a deep breath of the summer air and willed herself not to cry. He was on his jolly's while she, despite everything, still longed for him. Millie stopped the swing and stood, ready to leave. At least she had put her mistakes right.

Chapter Forty-Three

Paul headed towards the club. He had spent two nights in Spain before he returned home. All he could think about was Millie. Even the amount of whiskey he had devoured the night before didn't help. He wanted her, but Ronnie's words kept ringing in his ears, 'She's a gold digger son' but was she? She had never asked him for anything. As he pulled into the back of the club, he looked up at the building. It looked dirty compared to the front. That was something he needed to sort out.

Paul walked into his office and breathed in, he could smell Millie's perfume, or maybe it was wishful thinking? The first thing he did was reach into the filing cabinet for the Whiskey bottle. He stopped when the pile of papers on his desk caught his eye. He spotted the letter, the writing he knew was Millie's and that all too familiar feeling of guilt hit him again. He tore open the A4 envelope and pulled out the contents. He looked in amazement at the large glossy photos and the contract which had four signatures on it. Next, he grabbed Millie's letter, and ripped it open. He scanned the page. He read the first paragraph twice, she had got the contract signed by blackmailing the men. Gladys and the girls from the brothel had helped. Paul turned the page and learnt that Millie had signed the business over to him. "What the fuck Millie." Paul froze when he read the last paragraph. "NO!" He grabbed his keys and ran out of the club to his car. He could feel his heart, it felt like it was pumping in his ears. He screeched onto the high street and weaved in and out of the traffic hoping he wouldn't be too late. Finally, he reached the train station and pulled up directly outside. He jumped out of his motor and headed to the entrance.

"OI. YOU CAN'T LEAVE THAT MOTOR THERE." A ticket inspector called after him.

"I'M POLICE, I'M AFTER A SUSPECT." Paul called back as he jumped the barrier. He made his way onto the platform and looked around until he spotted Millie sitting on a bench on the opposite side. He headed for the stairs taking them three at a time. He could hear the train as it approached and cursed under his breath. As he reached the platform Paul made a dash for Millie as she stood up and walked towards the edge of the platform. "STOP THAT WOMAN." He watched as Millie turned towards him and then she started to run in the opposite direction. As Paul caught up with her, he grabbed her arm and spun her around to face him. "You're under arrest."

"Paul, get off.... HELP!" Millie screamed,

He watched her as she twisted and tugged her arm away, but Paul tightened his grip. "Stop fighting." His heart still beat wildly in his chest, and he took a few deep breaths as he tried to calm it.

As a train guard approached Paul, he pulled out his wallet and flashed it at the man. "I'm Police and this woman is a suspect in a robbery."

The guard nodded and stood back as Paul led Millie away. "Stop struggling."

"He's not old bill." Millie pleaded as Paul dragged her back through the station. "How dare you humiliate me like that. And what robbery?"

"You stole my fucking mind." Paul replied as he marched her past the ticket booth. "What the fuck were you thinking, just running away like that. I mean you've had some stupid ideas before but this. This is of fucking Olympian standards. Gold medal, there isn't a fucking medal big enough for this cock up!" Paul opened the door and pushed a shocked Millie into his motor before he climbed in the other side, Paul turned and looked at Millie. "Well.... Why?"

Paul watched her closely, she had gone a slight pink colour, he knew she would. She got embarrassed by the least little thing. He looked up as a passer-by stared into the window of the motor. Paul stuck his middle finger up. The man soon went on his way.

"I was putting all my mistakes right, taking accountability, and can you stop shouting." Millie answered.

"I'm not shouting. And can you stop looking at the entrance. You ain't fucking running away." Paul took a deep breath, to calm his temper. "Why would you even think it's a clever idea to run?" Paul waited for an explanation, but none came. "What, are you a mute now?" Paul started the motor and pulled away. "We'll continue this conversation at home."

"Why are you here Paul? Shouldn't you be shagging your way across Spain?"

"Jealous?" Paul snapped.

"No. I've experienced that side of you. Nothing to be jealous of there."

Paul felt like he had a red-hot poker plunged into his heart. He had never felt good enough for her, she was perfect, and he was nothing more than a wrong un. He took a deep breath, he had to make her see what she meant to him. "For your information I haven't touched another woman. My heads been full of you." Paul sighed. "I came back for you Millie, but as I don't live up to your bedroom standards maybe I shouldn't have bothered."

"This isn't the way home." Millie replied, totally ignoring him.

"It is to mine, and don't worry I won't touch you." Paul turned the corner and screeched to a halt outside his flat. He flung open the door and pulled Millie out. They walked to the front door in silence.

Paul only spoke when he had closed the front door of his flat. "I'll get us a drink, I'm going to need it more than you, once you start with the insults."

"You insulted me, Paul. You said I had made up the stalker for attention, but I didn't, so on that we can agree to disagree.... You need a shave." Millie added.

"Well excuse me if I'm not looking the best, only I had to rescue a fucking idiot that was about to do a runner." Paul took a sip of his drink and sat back on the sofa, unsure what to say next.

"How have you got a Police badge?" Millie asked.

"I haven't. I flashed my casino membership." Paul watched as Millie rolled her eyes. "They'll get stuck one day if you keep doing that."

"Why did you come back Paul?"

It wasn't a hard question; he knew the answer. It was how she would react that worried him. What if she didn't want to be with him anymore. Could he blame her after the way he had acted. Paul turned and faced Millie before he spoke. "I came back for you, and I'm glad I did." Paul sighed. "Millie, I told you before, you have an effect on me and to be honest I don't know if I like it, but one things for sure I can't fucking control it."

"I lied." Millie whispered.

"About?" Paul moved closer to Millie and took her drink; then placed it on the table with his own. He breathed in her scent and drank in her features. She looked like a scared little girl, but he knew better than that. She was a warrior. She had overcome things no woman should have to overcome. He could feel her eyes burning into his, like they could see deep inside his soul. "About Millie?" He repeated.

"I was jealous. The thought of you with another woman crucifies me." Millie swallowed down her tears. "Look. I know I've caused you problems. I've tried to put everything right. The last thing was to get out of your life, so you could carry on as normal without having to see me."

Paul continued to stare at Millie for a few minutes before he answered. "Seems the only way I can keep you out of trouble is to keep you with me."

"That is what started all this mess in the first place." Millie answered. "I think it's better if we go our separate ways."

"No." Paul, for the first time in his life knew what it was like to be afraid. "Give me another chance Mil, please?"

Chapter Forty-Four

Millie climbed out of Paul's motor and looked at the pub. It was strange being back here so soon. Especially after packing her bag and leaving only a couple of hours ago. But this was her home, and she needed to be here to think about her future. She had promised Paul she would after he had begged her not to give up on him. He had tears in his eyes, which was something she hadn't expected. Millie had never seen Paul so vulnerable. Millie put a big smile on her face and made her way into the pub. She spotted Finn at the bar, he looked anything but happy. Millie flinched when Finn smashed his glass down onto the bar. It splintered into pieces. "Finn, are you okay?" Millie asked as she rushed to his side.

"In the back. Now." He ordered.

Millie's face fell as she approached the back room. "What's wrong, has something happened?"

"I don't know, why don't you tell me?" In his temper Finn reached for the letter and threw it at Millie. "You know when I first met you, that night you asked for a job and wouldn't take no for an answer, I thought that kids got guts. Turns out I was wrong. I'm disappointed in you Millie."

"You seem more angry than disappointed." Millie reached down and swooped the letter off the floor.

"Oh, angry? You think I'm angry. Well I'll tell you something. I'm hurt Millie. Hurt that you wouldn't say goodbye. Hurt that you didn't trust me enough to tell me what you were going to do, and that also makes me angry." Finn told her.

Millie's heart dropped to the pit of her stomach as she swallowed down the shame. "That's not true." She placed her hand on Finn's arm and squeezed gently.

"Isn't it, so what's your excuse for being a coward then?" Finn shrugged her hand off and turned away. "I thought of you as family. And another thing, what did you expect me to tell Paul Kelly?"

"Someone mention my name?" Paul looked between Millie and Finn as he entered the room. "Now what?"

Finn turned his focus on Paul. "Did you know what she had planned?"

"Not until I read the letter, she left me." Paul paused.

Millie saw the realisation as it dawned on his face and waited for the next bollocking.

"Jesus Millie, how many other letters did you write?" Paul asked.

"Four in total." Millie pulled Finn's letter from her bag. "I also wrote one for Rosie and Scott."

"Where are the other letters, Finn? They need destroying." Paul grabbed the letter out of Millie's hand.

"They are on the side." Finn pointed. "Look, I need time on my own, can she stay with you for now."

"You're kicking me out? But Finn, please? I didn't mean to hurt you. I'm sorry." Millie watched as Finn stood and walked out, back into the bar without uttering another word.

"Go and pack your things, Millie. I'm sure he will calm down; he just needs time." Paul reassured her.

Millie cursed herself, every time she tried to do the right thing it backfired. When she reached her room, she grabbed an old case and started to pack. Paul walked in and handed her a couple of boxes.

Millie kept her head down as she emptied the wardrobe. Within half an hour the room was empty. She looked around the room, her old bedroom. With her bits packed up it was like she had never been there. The feeling of abandonment hit her again, only once again it was her own fault.

"Motors loaded. I can't believe you've got so much stuff; fuck knows where it's all gonna go. Recon we're gonna need a bigger place." Paul laughed. "It's gonna be okay."

"I don't understand why he's so angry, the letter explained everything. I even told him he's the father I never had, and how much he means to me." Millie blinked the tears away.

"He welcomed you into his home Mil, you became his family and then you just left, without so much as a goodbye or explanation. That's got to hurt. Anyway, come on, we need to go."

Millie followed Paul out through to the bar, where Finn was wiping down the side.

"Finn. I'm sorry, I wasn't thinking." Millie stood in front of Finn and watched as his face dropped.

"You never do, Millie. You get thoughts in your head and do things to make yourself feel better, with no thought to anyone else. How do you think Rosie would have felt getting a letter like that?"

"I don't know." Millie sobbed as the first tear fell. She felt Paul's hand as it wrapped around hers. Her eyes still on Finn. She could see he was angry by the way he snatched up the cloth and started wiping the bar, but there was something else in his eyes. Pain.

"That's enough Finn. Mil come on." Paul replied.

Millie felt him tug on her hand. It felt wrong to leave like this. She had never liked hurting the people she cared about, and she did care about him. Millie's legs felt heavy, too heavy to move, but then Finn spoke.

"Yes, it is enough, I've had enough.... Now if you don't mind, you need to leave, I'm busy."

Millie followed Paul out and sat in the motor. She could feel Paul's eyes on her. "Why are you staring at me?"

"I want to make sure you are okay. Here, dry your eyes."

Millie took the handkerchief from Paul and dabbed at her eyes. "Thanks." She looked back at the entrance of the pub. It felt wrong to just leave but then it also felt wrong to stay.

"It's gonna be okay Mil. My old nan always says things happen for a reason. You may not see it now, but eventually things will make sense." Paul told her.

"I've lost my home Paul and the reason it happened was because of me. My actions. But worse than that, I've hurt Finn, and I don't think he will ever forgive me, and for that, I'll never forgive myself."

Chapter Forty-Five

Millie walked towards Kelly's nightclub. It had been a couple of weeks since she had fallen out with Finn. She wanted to see him, but she was afraid. Afraid that he would reject her again. She shook her head as if to shake him from her mind. It was another beautiful day and she needed to be positive. She couldn't spend any more time moping around. She decided that last night when Paul had given her a pep talk. And that was why she was here.

Millie looked at her watch, it was 11.30am. As she walked towards the door she smiled; she didn't think she would be back here again. As she reached the entrance she stopped and looked around. The high street was busy with shoppers all going about their business. The sunshine seemed to make everyone happier.

"What are you doing, are you coming in or what?" Paul asked.

"Well?"

Millie smiled. "Okay, take me into your club." As she passed him, she planted a peck on his lips.

"I could get used to this." Paul mumbled back against her.

"Don't get too used to it. I need to find a job, why do you think I picked up the local paper." As Millie entered the office, she studied the job ads.

"You can work here." Paul snatched the paper away and threw it in the bin.

"I'm not working for you Paul, especially as I was once a partner. I'll be a laughingstock." Millie reached into the bin for the newspaper, then huffed as she tried to straighten it out.

"Would you like to be my partner again?" Paul asked.

As he went to snatch the paper once more Millie held it behind her back. "No. We already tried that, remember? It didn't work then, and it won't work now." Millie reached into her bag for a pen and then took a seat on the sofa. She looked up and watched Paul as he paced the floor. He looked nervous which unsettled her. Then he stopped dead in front of her. Millie's eyes widened.

"Why won't it? Things are different now Mil."

Millie returned to the job ads. "When you've had enough of me, I'll lose my job and my home. I can't risk it. Oh look, the Black Bull's looking for a barmaid." Millie circled the ad and sighed. She knew he had more to say.

"You ain't working in a fucking pub." Paul's voice rose.

Millie watched with her mouth open as Paul's anger grew, he snatched the paper and ripped it into pieces.

"May I remind you I was working in a pub when you met me." Millie looked at the shredded paper, covering the floor. "I paid for that!"

Paul handed Millie a crisp pound note. "That was different."

Millie grabbed the note and threw it back at him. "Why was it?"

"Because you weren't mine then. You are not going to work in a fucking pub." Paul shouted.

Millie laughed when he kicked out at the paper causing it to flutter up and land on his shoe. She laughed harder when he attempted to shake it off. "I will work where I want to work, stop dictating, and stop shouting." Millie stood and walked towards the door. "When you've calmed down, we can talk about this as adults."

Paul jumped in front of the door barring her way. "This is our club; you will work here as a partner and that is the end of it."

"It won't work." Millie stepped back; she kept her eyes on Paul as his temper grew. His scar had turned red, and he rubbed at it vigorously.

"YES. IT WILL BECAUSE YOU'LL BE MY WIFE!"

Millie dropped the pen as she looked at him, his face had turned purple, and his chest rose and fell as though he had run a marathon.

"Was that supposed to be a proposal, or a job offer. I'm confused?" Millie folded her arms and waited.

"You want a proper proposal. Okay, you can have a proper proposal."

Millie looked on as Paul reached into his pocket and pulled out a small box. He then opened it and knelt on one knee before he took Millie's hand. "Marry me."

Confused Millie continued to stare blankly. Where had this come from, and why now. They were supposed to be seeing how things went between them. Was he trying to trap her?

"Millie, Will you marry me?" Paul asked again. "Can you hurry up and say yes, I'm starting to get cramp."

Chapter Forty-Six

Duke was excited. Today they were off to Epsom for the Derby. They went every year without fail. His boys were happy. Connie was happy, and that made him happy. He wound up the draw bar on the trailer and called to his son. "Jess reverse the Transit back.... steady... whoa." He hitched it up onto the tow bar and grinned to himself. He loved the Derby. The atmosphere. The gambling and of course the fights. He made a pretty penny this time of year. The Epsom Derby was his favourite of all the race meets. The travelling community went there in their masses, staying on the racecourse grounds.

He looked over to Connie, who was busy loading the back of the Transit. She didn't seem as keen this year to go as in the past years, but she seemed happy to know they would be coming straight back to the piece of ground he had bought, even if they would still be living in the trailer until the groundwork had been done. "Right yous ready?" Duke listened to the chorus of yes's and walked to the Transit. Waiting for everyone to get in he wound down the window and shouted over to his dad. "WAGONS ROLL."

"You do that every time we move on dad." Jess replied from the back.

"Yeah, it's getting a bit old now." Aron chipped in.

"Just like dad." Jess laughed.

"Leave your father alone." Connie told them sternly. "Or he might make you walk."

Duke watched the smile spread across Connie's face; it was the first time she had smiled since they had planned to leave. "You okay Con?"

"I'm fine.... So we are coming back here after show out Sunday?" Connie asked.

"Yes darling, we'll be coming straight back. I need to check the bases have been concreted. Should be in the mobile by the end of June at the latest.... I'll get you one of them washing machines too." Duke glanced at Connie and was pleased to see her face light up.

"No more launderette for muvva." Jess laughed. "You'll have gran wanting to use it too."

"I reckon whoever stays will be using it. Dad are we gonna ave other travellers staying with us?" Aron chewed his nail as he waited for an answer.

"Ahh he's asking for Sherry's family. What's up bruv, are you missing her already?" Jess teased.

"Stop teasing your brother Jess, you'll be ready to run off before you know it. Now where's that Dean Martin cassette." Duke lent over and opened the glove box.

"Can you keep your eyes on the road. I'll find it." Connie ordered, Duke watched her as she rifled around in the glove compartment, until she grabbed the cassette and pushed it into the cassette player. Immediately 'Little Ole Wine Drinker' started blasting out of the speakers.

"That's more like it. Now sit back and enjoy the ride." Duke tapped the steering wheel in time to the music. Today, he decided, was going to be a good day.

* * *

The Epsom downs came into view as they travelled along the top road. Duke smiled, he could see the funfair on the right and the trailer with the Gypsy Rose Lee sign. He could never work out why gorja's fell for that and to be honest, why would anyone want to know their future. Life should be a mystery. He stopped at the edge of the turn off and waited patiently for the people to cross the road. In front of him for as far as the eye could see were trailers. This was what life was all about. The Romany community coming together. Dukes' chest swelled at the pride he felt. He was born a Romany, and he would die a Romany.

As he pulled onto Epsom Downs, Duke took a deep breath and smiled to himself. "Smell that boys, that's the smell of freedom."

"Smells more like cut grass to me." Aron mumbled.

"And that too boy. Now look out for ya Uncle Albert's trailer up on the hill. We'll camp near him." Duke slowed his motor while driving over the grass.

"Bit hard for us to see in the back, dad, we ain't got a window." Jess replied. "I don't know why we couldn't have driven the pickup. You let us drive around town."

"Because there's too many gavers up here, I ain't giving them a reason to spoil our time here." Duke explained.

"Over there, Duke." Connie said pointing.

Duke pulled up and jumped out of his motor. "Alright Albert, I'll get set up then we can head to the pub." Duke watched his brother nod in agreement before he headed to greet his parents. "You getting out then Con.... Con.... Connie?"

"What.... Oh yes, sorry." Connie took Duke's hand and slid out of the Transit.

"You looked miles away, what's wrong?" Duke asked as he studied her face. He had a sinking feeling but pushed it away.

"Nothing. Right, let's get this lot sorted out. Boys, come on, you can help before you think of disappearing." Connie pecked Duke on the lips and pointed to the trailer. "Once you've sorted that I'll do some dinner. You ain't going drinking on an empty stomach Duke Lee."

"Okay, the boss has spoken boys, let's get to it." Duke unhitched the draw bar and swung the trailer into place. After he had finished setting it up, he stood back and let the boys carry everything in from the back of the transit. "Right Connie, I'm gonna see Albert for a bit and have a mooch."

"Don't you go drinking Duke; I want you back here in an hour for dinner." Connie reminded him.

Duke nodded and then made his way over to his brother's trailer. "Albert, you coming for a mooch."

"About time. Thought you'd got lost." Albert stood and handed Duke a can of bitter. "Here, I bet you could do with this."

"Cheers brother." Duke opened the can and drank the beer straight down. "So, who's here this year?"

"One eye Ron's here, been giving it the biggen about his son-in-law. He reckons he can beat any man here in a fight. Can't see him wanting to take you on though." Albert grabbed two more cans and threw one to Duke.

"I'm sure they'll be queuing up Albert, anyway, let's go see the others." Duke walked with Albert towards a large group of men who were all shouting and laughing.

"Hello lad's, yous fancy ya luck?" Nelson asked as he tossed a penny towards a wall.

Duke watched as it landed a couple of inches away and grinned. "You're losing ya touch old man. Here." Duke handed over a five-pound note and pulled out a penny from his pocket. He flicked it firmly towards the wall, everyone watched as it landed quarter of an inch away. "And that gentleman is how you do it." He took his winnings and shoved the notes back into his pocket.

"Dad." Aron called. "Dinners ready."

"Tell ya mother to keep it warm, I'm on a winning streak." Duke replied before addressing the men. "Come on then, I'll give ya a chance to win ya money back.... Pass us another beer Albert."

Chapter Forty-Seven

Millie stood in front of Paul's parents' house and straightened her dress. "Do I look okay?" Her thoughts of Levi's parents in her mind. What if they hated her, worse than that what if they pretended to like her and then turned on her. Millie felt the perspiration on her body. Not only from the scorching temperature but also from the fear that had taken over her mind.

"You look beautiful, now stop worrying, my mums gonna love you." Paul replied.

Millie felt his hand tighten on hers and smiled. "Okay, let's do this." She followed Paul around the back and into a small kitchen.

"Hello mum." Paul greeted his mother with a kiss. "This is Millie, Millie my mum."

Millie stood in front of Paul's mum and smiled. "Hello Mrs Kelly." Paul's mum was petite like herself. Millie liked how her eyes creased when she smiled. It lit up her face that was otherwise stony.

"It's lovely to meet you Millie, and please, call me Bridie. Now come and meet the family." Paul's mum smiled.

Bridie Kelly's accent reminded Millie of Finn. A deep Southern

Irish that sounded more like singing, although Finns was gruff. She could never imagine him singing. The thought made Millie's smile broader.

* * *

After the greetings Millie sat on the sofa drinking a cup of tea. Her nerves had calmed, and she observed the family unit. It was clear to see they were all close. Paul had a brother, Rory. Paul had told her about him but didn't see him much as he had married and moved to Ireland. She paid particular attention to Paul's nan, she was also a petite woman with grey hair, wrapped up in a bun. She had a kind smile that lit up her eyes. Paul had enveloped her in a big hug. It was clear to see that she thought the world of her grandson.

"So, Millie, are you a Catholic girl?" Bridie asked as she sat forward in her seat.

"Leave the girl alone Bridie, we don't need to talk about religion." Paul's nan huffed. "You'll be asking for her full family history next."

Millie heard Paul laugh from the corner of the room as she turned her attention back to Bridie.

"Quiet down mum, it's important.... Millie?" Bridie pressed.

Paul had already warned her that his mum was big on the rosary beads. Apparently, religion was of immense importance to her, as it was to most Irish families.

"I'm not Christened, so I guess not." Millie watched Bridie's face drop.

"Oh, I see, I will make another cup of tea, Paul come and give me a hand."

Millie watched Bridie as she stood and motioned to Paul to follow her.

"Take no notice of my daughter Millie, I can see Paul's smitten with you." Nan told her.

Millie asked to use the bathroom to excuse herself, she now felt awkward. Closing the front room door behind her she walked towards the stairs when she overheard Paul's voice coming from the kitchen.

"Mum, this is 1976, not the dark ages. I'm Catholic and yet I don't go to church." Paul snapped.

"You need a good Catholic girl; you'll have to call the wedding off."

The more Millie listened, the more her temper grew. Was her lack of religion really cause to stop the wedding?

"What if I get her baptised?"

Millie burst through the door; she couldn't listen any longer. "I'm sorry I'm not good enough for your son Mrs Kelly." Millie threw her a look of disgust then turned her attention to Paul. "And as for you, if I have to get baptised for your family's approval, you can get stuffed, in fact I'll save you all the bother. Weddings off." Before allowing anyone to react, Millie was out of the door and marching down the street. As she neared the corner, she heard the familiar sound of Paul's car.

"Mil stop, please." Paul had slowed to a crawl, despite the car behind bibbing.

"Go away Paul." All the thoughts of how this relationship would turn out flashed through her mind. The disappointment on Bridie Kelly's face was all the warning signal Millie needed.

"Mil, please. Get in the car."

"Do ya know what Paul, all my life I've not been good enough. Well I'm done with people putting me down. I am good enough, and one day someone will see that, and until that day, I will stay single. Now please, go back to your family." Millie walked quicker when she realised Paul had stopped the motor and jumped out.

"You are good enough for me. You're all I want. If we go back now, we can fix this." Paul called as he ran to catch her up.

"Are you serious?" Millie asked as she spun around. "Your mother told you I'm not good enough to marry, and somehow, it's my fault? Unbelievable. You go back and tell her I'm happy the way I am, and you find a nice Catholic girl and make mummy happy." Millie turned to walk away but felt Paul's hand on her arm. He pulled her to a stop.

"I'm marrying you; I don't care what anyone thinks, get in the motor, we'll go and do it now."

"Don't be ridiculous." Millie tried to shake him off, but his grip was firm.

"Get in the motor. Now!" Paul swooped Millie into his arms and placed her in the passenger seat. "My mum was talking about a church wedding. I don't care if I marry you in a fucking bus stop. The point in all this is, I want to marry you, you said yes, eventually. So, we will be getting fucking married."

Chapter Forty-Eight

Millie sat in the café on the High Street, biting her nails. Her nerves were starting to get the better of her. She glanced at her watch and knew Rosie would be here soon. As the door pinged open, Millie looked up and saw Rosie's smiling face.

"Hey Mil." Rosie greeted.

Millie returned her smile as she watched her walk towards her before sliding into the seat opposite. "Two cups of tea please Mavis." Millie called to the owner. "How are you Rose?"

"I'm intrigued. So why the secrecy?" Rosie asked with narrowed eyes.

"I..." Millie trailed off as Rosie sat staring at her. "I got married."

"You got what?!" Rosie's mouth dropped open. "Without me?"

Millie sighed; She knew this was going to be a difficult conversation to have. "It was sudden..." Millie stopped when Rosie interrupted.

"You're damn right it was sudden. Mil, he dumped you, remember?"

"Actually I dumped him." Millie shrugged.

"As I remember it, you were the one that was left upset.... I just can't believe that you didn't tell me."

Millie watched as Rosie wrapped her arms tightly to her body. She was upset, and she had every right to be. "Look Rose, we did it on the spur of the moment, even Paul's mother doesn't know, well she's probably finding out about now. Paul's gone to tell her." Millie rung her hands at the thought.

"So how did that meeting go, wasn't it this morning you met her?" Rosie asked.

Millie didn't miss the sarcasm in her voice. "It didn't, which is why we got married, I guess. Look Rose I didn't want to upset you, you're my best friend."

"Exactly Mil, that's why I should have been there. Is there anything else I should know?" Rosie quizzed.

"Like what Rose?"

"Well the wedding was a bit quick.... Oh my god, you're pregnant!" Rosie shrieked.

Millie caught Mavis out of the corner of her eye as she headed towards the table.

"There you go girls, and here's a nice doughnut each. You've got to keep your strength up now you are eating for two. Congratulations Millie"

"NO!" Millie shrieked. "I'm not pregnant, Mavis." Millie returned her attention to Rosie. "That is one thing I'm not ready for."

"So?"

"Soooo?" Millie frowned.

"It just seems exceptionally quick, one minute you're not with him and then the next, you're married." Rosie sighed. "I'm supposed to be your best friend."

Millie put her head down, she couldn't look Rosie in the eye "I'm sorry Rose."

"You've been sorry a lot lately.... Millie, I love you, I really do, but you need to think about things before you do them. You need to think of the people you will hurt with your actions." Rosie replied.

"You're right, as usual." Millie conceded. Rosie didn't reply, they sat together in an awkward silence. Millie had never experienced tension like it. Things with Rosie had always been natural, easy. But then she guessed that was how it should be, when you are best friends.

"Paul's bought a house, it's over near the woods. The back garden leads to a paddock. Not sure who owns that but Paul said he will buy it so no one can build on it." Millie rambled to avoid the silence.

"Don't tell me he bought that today too. You certainly married the right villain this time." Rosie replied.

Millie felt her heart drop at the dig. But she carried on regardless. "He bought it a while ago but never told me. The sale was completed two weeks ago."

"Sounds great, that's your life sorted" Rosie sighed.

"Not really." Millie took a deep breath "I still want to find my parents." Millie watched Rosie closely. She was tapping her nails on the table, as if bored. "Will you help me?" Millie asked.

"No. In our friendship it's always been me helping you. Making sure you are okay. Standing by your side when your life is falling to pieces. I've had enough Millie. I'm sorry but I need time. This marriage business is one hurt to many. I've got to go; Bobby will be waiting."

Millie watched Rosie walk out of the café. Her shoulders were slumped, like she had all the stuffing knocked out of her. Millie reasoned she had. By her.

Chapter Forty-Nine

Saturday the fifth of June, Paul stood in front of the house with his hands covering Millie's eyes. "Ready?" He asked her. This was one surprise he had struggled to keep quiet. Although he had told her about the house, he wouldn't let her see it. Not until today. The day that they moved in.

"Yes." Millie squirmed. "Hurry up."

Paul took his hands away and waited for her reaction. He wasn't disappointed. He watched her mouth drop open as her eyes lit up.

"Oh Paul." She laughed. "It's beautiful."

Paul turned his attention to the large four-bedroom house. It had a double garage and spacious driveway. The large iron gates at the front would give maximum security and the trees would give privacy. "You like it then?"

"I love it." Millie replied.

He opened the door to their new home and picked Millie up then carried her over the fresh hold. "Some traditions need upholding, although my back probably wouldn't agree. Christ what did you have for breakfast?"

"Cheeky sod, I had bubble and squeak the same as you, only I had about a third of the amount as you had." Millie punched Paul's chest playfully. "Put me down, I don't need you ending up in traction."

"Not a chance Mrs Kelly." Paul carried Millie up the stairs. "We, my darling wife, need to consummate the bedroom."

"Paul." Millie giggled. "Put me down. We need to bring the stuff in."

Paul ignored Millie and carried her into the bedroom. He placed her gently on the bed before kicking off his shoes. He then climbed on top of her. "This is more important."

* * *

"That was fucking perfect." Paul whispered into Millie's ear as his orgasm subsided. "Only another three bedrooms to go."

"No. We need to unpack, and I want to look around." Millie replied.

Paul sighed. "I need a rest first.... Give us a kiss." He felt Millie's hands on his chest pushing him away. "Fine, but we are also going to consummate the garage, lounge, kitchen, dining room, study and garden, Mrs Kelly."

"You left out the bathroom." Millie giggled.

"And bathroom." Paul replied as he noticed her eyes twinkle. "It's good to see you smile Mil." He watched her face drop and wished he hadn't said anything. "Rosie will come around, and when she does, we will have a big housewarming."

"And what about Finn?" She reminded him.

"Him too." Paul replied after kissing her nose. "Come on, let's get sorted."

Paul dressed quickly and led Millie downstairs. He showed her each room, one by one until they finally arrived at the lounge. "So, what d'ya think?"

"It's bigger than it looks from outside.... Looks like I'm gonna spend all my time cleaning." Millie answered. "But I love it. Is that a real fireplace?"

"It is indeed. Just imagine on a cold winter's night, laying naked in front of the flames. We'll have to get one of them sheepskin rugs." Paul pictured it in his mind. His smile grew "Right Mrs Kelly, I think we should head to bedroom two." Paul stopped at the top of the stairs, when he heard a loud noise coming from behind the house. "What the fuck is that." He ran to the back bedroom before looking out of the window. There in the paddock at the end of the garden, was a digger, digging a large hole. "Stay here." Paul ordered as he made his way down the stairs, two steps at a time and out into the garden. Paul looked at the digger as he approached and cursed under his breath. "OI MATE." He called out as he waved to the digger driver.

"What can I do for you?" The man asked as he jumped out.

"What's going on?" Paul watched the man point to the hole.

"I'm digging a cesspit."

Paul turned and walked away without answering. He was not having a house built at the end of his garden. This was his dream house, and no one was spoiling it.

"What's going on?" Millie asked as Paul marched back into the house.

"Nothing for you to worry about. I need to pop out Mil, I won't be long." Paul grabbed his keys and marched to the front door.

"Don't forget we are going to the children's home later. You promised." Millie replied.

Paul waved his hand over his shoulder and jumped into his motor. First things first, he needed to know who had bought the land.

Chapter Fifty

Millie stood outside the children's home and stared up at the giant house, not that it seemed that giant anymore. Her house would now give it a run for its money. She walked towards the front door and knocked firmly. This time she would get what she came here for. Paul stood just behind her; his presence welcome. Not that she needed backup, this time she was determined.

"Millie, I'm afraid I can't let you in." Doug whispered. "Go before she sees you."

"I'm not asking for permission." Millie shoved past and marched straight to the office, while Paul stood over him. She pushed open the office door and made her way in, much to the annoyance of the woman.

"I told you..." The woman trailed off when she spotted Paul.

"This is my husband, now he doesn't like it when I'm upset. I've told him how you've declined to give me any answers and it's made him angry because I'm now upset. I say angry. I think that probably doesn't quite cut it, does it darling?" Millie turned to Paul and winked.

"No babe, it doesn't. So, shit bag, you are going to tell my wife everything you know or I'm going to have to take my anger out on you." Paul replied.

Millie heard the crack of Paul's knuckles and smiled as she watched the colour drain from the woman's face. "Now, tell me what you know."

The woman's shoulders slouched. "I don't know who your mother is, that's the truth."

"Then why shut me out?" Millie asked, confused.

"As you know I never worked here when you lived here. I've only been here the last two years."

"She's talking shit Mil. She knows something, let me break her arm, she'll talk then." Paul walked towards the desk.

"Paul, stop Please." Millie turned her attention to the now scared woman. "I can only control him for so long so if I were you, I would tell me everything you know. Like this woman's name and address."

"I met a woman, her name's Cathleen Brown. She never gave me any details, but she warned me not to give out any information about you. She said there would be repercussions."

"Where does she live?" Millie felt her heart rate increase. Was this woman her mother?

"She lives at 105 Vincent Street." The woman replied as she placed her head in her hands.

Millie placed both her hands on the desk and leaned over to the woman. "If I find you've lied to me, you will have worse to deal with than my husband." Millie turned and made her way out. Her head was starting to hurt with all the questions she had buzzing around. She climbed into the motor and stared into space. "What if she's my mum? She was so cold in the council offices. Maybe I shouldn't have bothered finding her."

"It's something you needed to do, it's been on your mind a long time and things like that don't go away." Paul replied.

She knew what he was saying was true, but that didn't make her feel any better. She continued to stare out of the window for the rest of the short journey. The sun was shining high in the sky and the hot weather made Millie feel clammy. There was talk of a drought on the news, everyone needed to do their bit to conserve water as the reservoirs were drying up. Millie squirmed in the leather seat, unsticking herself. The knot grew in her stomach as they got nearer.

"Keep an eye out for 105 babe, it should be up here on the left." Paul said as he slowed the motor to a crawl.

Millie smiled as Paul gave her knee a squeeze. "Here....105." She pointed. Millie waited for the motor to come to a halt and then climbed out. She studied the house while waiting for Paul to join her. "Here goes." Millie walked to the front door and watched Paul bang three times. "Mind you don't knock the door in." Millie laughed.

"Just making sure she hears." Paul winked.

"I can't hear any movement, can you?" Millie made her way to a window and peered in. "I don't think anyone's home."

Paul knocked loudly three more times as a man appeared from the house next door. "They're on holiday." He called.

Millie turned to the man and smiled. "Do you know when they will be back?"

"They went yesterday morning, down to Devon for two weeks. I'm looking after their cat. Can I help with anything?"

Millie looked at Paul and sighed. "Typical."

"No mate, we'll come back when they are home and I'd appreciate it if you don't tell them we called. It's a surprise visit." Paul replied to the man.

"My lips are sealed" The man placed a finger to his mouth and smiled.

"Thank you." Millie nodded and then turned and walked back towards the car. "Two bloody weeks."

"It'll soon go Mil, anyway, I need to get to the docks, gotta see Ronnie. I'll drop you home first." Paul opened the door for her.

"How's things been with him?" Millie asked. She still had her doubts about him. Something didn't add up.

"It's good Mil, the monies flooding in.... I'll only be a couple of hours then we can go out for dinner if you want."

"Why don't I come with you then, after all I should learn that side of the business too." Millie studied Paul's face as he turned towards her.

"I need to run it by Ronnie first, not sure he would like a woman involved in the docks. He's old fashioned." Paul replied.

Millie swallowed her temper down before she answered. "Okay, it was just a thought." She turned and looked out of the passenger window. She didn't like Ronnie and she certainly didn't trust him. She would bide her time and watch for now. Finding her mother was top of her priorities anyway.

Chapter Fifty-One

Millie walked into the Artichoke; it was time she made amends with Finn. The knot in her stomach tightened when she spotted him. He was standing at the bar serving one of the regulars. "Finn." She called as she made her way to the bar.

"I'm working, Millie." Finn turned his back to her.

"I see you're still angry with me." Millie jumped as Finn turned around sharply.

"What do you expect?" Finn walked to the end of the bar and motioned to Millie. "I told you my wife and child left me, and all I got was a note, and to this day I still don't know where they are. And you. You decided to do the same. I thought of you as family Millie, seems I was wrong."

"I'm sorry Finn, I didn't think...." Millie stopped as Finn cut in.

"No you didn't. Now, if you don't mind, I've a pub to run."

"I'm gonna make it up to you." Millie swiped at a tear as it ran down her cheek. "And for the record, you are my family."

"Is that why I didn't get an invite to the wedding because I'm family? You really need to treat people better, Millie."

"No one got an invite to the wedding because it was spur of the moment and maybe you need to get over yourself." Millie noticed the surprise on Finn's face as she continued her rant. "Leaving a note was cowardly, you're right....and if I could change it I would, but I can't, I can't go back and change the past, no matter how much I want to, and believe me, there's plenty I would change if I could. Like the beatings I got from Levi.... But then if I hadn't gone through that I wouldn't be here now, with you and Paul, so sometimes I guess, you have to go through bad things to get to the good things, and you Finn are one of the good things in my life.... I don't want to lose you." Millie ran into Finn's arms as he opened them.

"Promise me you will never run away again. If things are wrong, you come to me Millie." Finn replied.

"I promise.... does this mean I can have a drink?" Millie laughed as she wiped her tears away.

"You can pour it yourself and I'll have a medicinal whiskey." Finn replied as he made his way to a table.

Once seated Millie passed Finn his drink. "Who's the new barmaid?"

"That's Kate, she does a couple of lunch times and weekends. Anyway, I'm not here to talk about my staff, I want to know what's going on in your life."

"Same old. Still looking for my mum. Moved house. Actually Finn, do you know much about Ronnie Taylor?" Millie watched Finn's eyes narrow.

"Leave well alone child, he's not a man to be messed with."

"But Paul's gone into business with him. I don't trust him, there's something not right." Millie looked at her glass as she thought about the docks.

"Paul's a big boy, he can handle himself." Finn knocked back the rest of his drink.

"Paul's blindsided by him; he reckons he can do no wrong.... I get the strangest feeling when I'm in his company. It's like there's a jealousy hanging in the air...." Millie trailed off.

"Mark my words Millie, you will come off worse if you get in the way of business with those two men, now, leave it well alone. Do you want another drink?" Finn stood, ready to return to the bar.

"No. I best be going; I need to see Rosie.... Finn?"

"What?"

"I'm glad we're talking again." Millie hugged him and then made her way to the door. Her mind now full of Ronnie Taylor and the warning Finn had given.

* * *

Paul walked through the front door and threw his keys next to the telephone. "Mil, I'm home babe." He made his way into the lounge and was greeted with a hug and a kiss. "I could get used to this." He mumbled against her lips.

"Paul, I want you to stay calm." Millie replied as she pulled away.

"I'm calm." Paul noticed the worried expression on her face. "What's happened?"

"We've got new neighbours at the back.... Paul!" Millie called after him.

Paul turned and ran up the stairs, taking them three at a time. By the time he reached the back bedroom, the scowl on his face had spread. "YOU'VE GOT TO BE FUCKING JOKING!" He bellowed.

"You said you'd stay calm." Millie called out as she ran up behind him.

Paul turned and marched down the stairs and straight out into the garden. Ignoring Millie's plea, he continued to the fence and hopped over. As he approached the trailer, he could hear a familiar voice. He wasn't surprised when the door flew open, and he came face to face with Duke Lee. "This is private land. You can't stay here."

"You're right this is private land. Mine." Duke glared.

"Paul. This isn't going to solve anything." Millie called.

"I'm not having the view from my house tainted by a bunch of fucking pikey's. Now pack your shit up and fuck off." Paul noticed Connie appear and stand by Duke's side.

"Mr Kelly we've bought this land so it's you that's trespassing. Now please, can we speak about...." Connie stopped when she noticed Millie standing behind Paul.

Paul frowned when he saw the colour drain from Connie's face. "Millie go indoors."

"I'm not leaving you out here on your own." Millie argued.

"It's not up for discussion. Now go." Paul took a step forward and poked Duke in the chest. "I don't know what fucked up game you're playing, but it stops now. If you're still here when I wake up in the morning, I'll move you off myself."

"I'd like to see you try." Duke grinned. "Go stick the kettle on Con, I fancy a nice cuppa while I survey my ground."

Paul pushed Duke back and clenched his fist. "I'm not gonna tell you again."

"I'm not moving, if you don't like it you move. Connie, indoors, now." Duke turned and watched Connie shut the door. "Looks like we're at a stalemate."

Paul rubbed the back of his neck and focused on Duke. "I'll tell you what, we was gonna have a fight once before, but it never happened. How about this time we fight and if I win, I buy the ground off you."

"And when I win you move." Duke replied.

"If you win." Paul laughed. "I'm not liking your chances though." Paul turned and walked back towards the fence. "Saturday at 6." Paul shouted over his shoulder. As he climbed the fence, he heard Duke shout back.

"We'll hold it here."

Chapter Fifty-Two

Millie sat in the Wimpy on Stepney high street waiting for Rosie. It had taken a lot of phone calls and a lot of apologising to get Rosie to forgive her. The happiness that she had felt about the meeting soon dwindled after the argument with Paul that morning. He had turned into a total control freak. He had banned her from speaking to Connie as he didn't like the way she looked at her. His words were 'there's something going on with that woman' Millie rolled her eyes at the memory. Paul thought they had bought the land just so they could terrorise them.

"Hey Mil." Rosie called out as she clambered through the door. "Sorry I'm late, had to pick up a few bits."

"A few?" Millie laughed, as Rosie dropped the bags on the floor.

"Once I started, I couldn't stop. We're decorating the bedroom." Rosie sat and grabbed the menu. "I'm starving. What are you having?"

"What I normally have. A mixed grill and a cuppa." Millie reached over to one of the bags and looked in.

"So, how's things with you?" Rosie asked.

"Where do ya want me to start?" Millie sighed.

"Let's start with the mother front, found out anything else?"

"I've got the address of the woman from the council office, only she's on holiday for two weeks, so looks like that's on hold till then." Millie waved to the waitress to get her attention. "I'm bloody starving."

"How's the house, I bet its nice having all that room?"

"House is great but our new neighbours not so much." Millie shook her head. "Gypsies have moved into the paddock behind us, and not any old gypsies. It's Duke Lee and Connie."

"I thought you liked Connie?" Rosie asked as she frowned.

"I do.... I did.... It's complicated. Anyway, the upshot is, Paul and Duke are having a fight on Saturday night. The winner gets to stay, and the loser must go." Millie shook her head. "It's ridiculous, they need their heads banging together."

"Why don't you tell Paul you're not moving, whatever the outcome?"

"Don't you think I tried. I told him I didn't want him to fight, but it's his pride. He just can't let it go.... I'll have to stand by him. He's my husband." Millie added.

"You stood by Levi and look how that turned out." Rosie reminded her.

"Thanks for that Rose, I almost forgot I was once married to a wife beater." Millie sighed.

"I'm reminding you that you have your own opinion. You don't have to go along with things." Rosie explained.

"Here's the waitress." Millie nodded.

"Two Wimpy specials and two teas please." Rosie gave their order and placed the menu on the table. "Have you thought about what happens if you find your mum?"

"Not really.... I just wanna look her in the eye and tell her I never needed her anyway." Millie felt her heart sink. "Can we talk about something nice? What colour are you doing your bedroom?"

* * *

Paul stood on the dock side and watched his men unload the latest cargo. Usually, he would get a thrill watching the goods arrive but this time all he felt was anger. Anger at Duke Lee for ruining his dream home. He clenched his fists just at the thought.

"Penny for them son?"

Paul heard Ronnie call from behind him. He turned just in time to see Ronnie's grinning face. "Ron, good to see ya mate." Paul made his way into the office. He walked to the kettle and flicked it on. It was the best thirst quencher he knew. A nice cupper. "Fucking hot again, I feel like I'm melting." Paul wiped the back of his neck with his hanky.

"I don't mind the heat so much it's the fucking ladybirds I can't stand, the fuckers are everywhere." Ronnie replied as he hung his trilby up on the coat stand. "Anyway, what's up with you, you've got a face like a slapped arse?"

"I've got fucking pikey's living in the field behind me." Paul sat at his desk and opened the bottom draw. He pulled out a bottle of whisky and two glasses. He decided he needed something stronger than tea.

"What, at the end of your garden?" Ronnie asked.

"The very same." Paul sighed as he poured the drinks, then handed one to Ronnie. "I'm gonna fight him Saturday, the loser goes." Paul knocked his drink back in one and refilled his glass.

"Good. Make sure you win." Ronnie added.

"I intend to. Do you want a top up?" Paul refilled Ronnie's glass when he nodded and then slumped back into his seat.

"Just a thought, but won't the council move them on?" Ronnie asked.

"No.... He's bought the paddock." Paul replied through gritted teeth.

"He?" Ronnie frowned.

"Duke fucking Lee." Paul sighed.

"Isn't he bare knuckle..."

Before Ronnie could finish Paul butt in. "I don't care what he fucking is, or what he thinks he is. I'm going to annihilate him and if he don't go after that, I'm gonna burn the fuckers out."

Chapter Fifty-Three

Saturday came around far too quickly as far as Millie was concerned. Paul had been moody all week, and the atmosphere had been strained. "I don't want you to fight Paul, I have a bad feeling." She pleaded.

"Everything will be fine after tonight, just trust me, Mil. We won't have fucking pikey's living at the bottom of our garden." Paul grabbed his jogging bottoms and pulled them on while Millie watched him.

"Right, I'm meeting the boy's over there, so you stay here with Rosie, what time is she coming over?" Paul asked.

"She should be here soon." Millie replied as she watched Paul. He laced up his trainers then looked at the clock.

"I best be going.... you do not come over there. Understand."

"I don't see why I can't come...." Millie stopped when Paul cut in.

"Because I don't want you seeing this." Paul huffed. "Promise me Mil."

"Fine, I'll just sit here and worry." Millie replied sadly. A loud knock came from the front door. "That'll be her now."

"I'll get that. Now give us a kiss and I'll see you in a couple of hours, if not before." Paul turned and left.

Millie stood in the lounge as she listened to the door shut and Rosie's voice as she called out to Millie. "I'm in here Rose."

"Mil, I've brought wine and." Rosie rustled in her bag until she found what she was looking for. "Binoculars!"

Millie smiled. "You are the bestest best friend ever. I'll get the glasses; we can watch from the back bedroom."

* * *

Paul looked at the hay bales as he walked through the gate to Dukes land. They were arranged in a large square to mimic a boxing ring. He nodded to his men before he climbed over the bales and stood facing Duke.

"Right lads, bare knuckle, no rules. Are you both ready?" The old Romani man asked. Content when they both nodded, he stepped over the bale of hay and out of the makeshift ring.

Paul had cleared his mind of the day-to-day stuff that normally filled his head and replaced his thoughts with every man that had ever done him wrong. His temper was at exploding level. As he approached Duke, he let his fist fly straight into Duke's cheek bone. It had the desired effect as Duke staggered back a couple of steps before righting himself and lunged forward with a swift jab to Paul's ribs. Paul felt the crunch but disregarded it and continued with an upper-cut, smiling as blood trickled from Duke's nose. A bell rang and the old Traveller called for the end of the round. Paul returned to his corner where his men were standing watching. Paul sat on the bale of hay and studied Duke. Despite the blood, Duke smiled and raised his can of beer in a toast before swigging it back. It was at that point Paul realised this was going to be harder than he had at first thought.

* * *

"I'm going over there Rose, somethings wrong with Paul, he keeps holding his ribs." Millie walked away from the window and made her way down the stairs with Rosie following.

"He's going to be mad Mil if you turn up there." Rosie jumped in front of Millie and blocked her way. "Give it a bit longer. Please"

"My husbands in trouble and I'm going over there, you can either come with me or stay here, but you definitely ain't stopping me." Millie's tone was full of determination as she watched Rosie's shoulders sag.

"I'm not letting you go on your own." Rosie opened the back door and motioned for Millie to lead the way. "Paul's gonna be mad though."

"I'd rather him be mad than dead." Millie ran down the garden and hopped over the fence. "Thank God Paul hasn't put the 8-foot fence up yet; we'd need a ladder."

As Millie and Rosie approached the ring, Millie pushed her way through the shouting men until she reached the front. She noticed Paul's complexion had turned grey. "He's in trouble, Rose." Millie turned and spotted Connie standing at the edge of the ring. "Come on, I need to see Connie." Millie pushed her way around the crowd and grabbed Connie's arm. "You need to stop the fight.... Please."

Connie nodded and reached for a towel. She threw it into the centre of the ring as jeers went up from the spectators.

"What the fuck are you doing Connie?" Duke shouted angrily. Paul stood by his side still holding his ribs.

"Why are you here Mil. You promised me..." Before he had finished his sentence Paul stumbled and hit the ground. His breathing had become raspy.

Millie's pulse began to race. "Get an ambulance." She called out then turned her attention to Duke. Before she had a chance to speak, Duke did.

"It was Paul who asked for the fight, Millie, if you're gonna blame anyone, blame him." Then he turned and walked away while Millie knelt beside Paul. She held his hand as his breathing worsened. Her tears flowed freely, and she hoped the ambulance would soon be there. "It's okay Paul, you're gonna be okay." Millie heard the siren in the distance and hoped it wasn't too late.

"Stand back Mil, they're here." Rosie whispered. "You need to give them room to work."

"I'm not leaving him." Millie turned to Connie. "This is all your fault, you, and that thing you married. I don't ever want to see you again."

"Millie, I tried to stop the fight, if I could change this I would." Connie replied tearfully.

"Get away from me." Millie spat, she turned to Paul and stroked his face, only moving when Paul was loaded into the ambulance. He had an oxygen mask placed over his mouth and nose, but she could still hear the raspy breathing. "What's wrong with him?"

"From his breathing it looks like his lung has been punctured, the doctor will be able to tell you more. Sit back, miss, we need to go."

* * *

Millie sat in the hospital waiting room, she had kicked her shoes off and sat hugging her knees, rocking slightly, backwards, and forwards. She wiped at her tears as she heard a familiar voice.

"Hey Mil, how is he?" Rosie asked as she took a seat next to her.

"I don't know, they've took him down to operate. What if he doesn't make it Rose. What am I going to do without him?" Millie gripped her knees tighter as the panic set in.

"You mustn't think like that Mil, he's gonna be okay." Rosie slipped her arm around Millie's shoulders and gave a gentle squeeze. "He's fit, healthy and strong. Now let's have some positive vibes."

Millie closed her eyes, she wanted to believe Rosie, but she couldn't. Her life had never worked out that way, Whenever something good happened, something would always come along and ruin it. "If anything happens to Paul, I'm gonna kill those pikey's."

"Millie, Connie stopped the fight and from what I saw when you left, Duke was giving her a hard time."

"I don't care. I wish I'd never met them; I hate them, Rose. I hate them with a passion I never knew I had." Millie stopped when the doctor walked in.

"Mrs Kelly?"

"Is he going to be, okay?" Millie asked as she jumped up.

"He has broken a couple of ribs. One of these had punctured his lung. Now we have put a drain in and reinflated his lung. He will need to be monitored, most likely for a couple of weeks, at least, but I'm sure he will make a full recovery."

"Can I see him Doctor, please?" Millie asked hopefully.

"He's still in recovery Mrs Kelly, when he's taken to a ward, I'll send a nurse to get you. Now I must get on."

"Thank you, Doctor, thank you so much." Millie threw her arms around the doctor and hugged him.

* * *

Duke paced the trailer trying to contain his temper. Everyone had left, and his boys had made themselves scarce. He clenched and unclenched his fists trying, unsuccessfully, to unwind. "You've made me look fucking stupid.... My own wife throwing the towel in.... What was you thinking?"

"He has been rushed to hospital, Duke; how would it look if you had killed him?" Connie stayed sitting on the bunk and stared out of the window while Duke watched her. "I did you a favour."

Duke's temper flared and he smashed his fist through the cupboard door. What was wrong with her? Why couldn't she see what she had done? "What fucking planet are you living on.... We live by a different code. We fight, we don't ever throw in the towel. How am I supposed to face everyone now?"

"You don't understand..."

"No I don't because you won't tell me.... I can't deal with you right now. I'm going to the pub." Duke grabbed his keys and left. He loved Connie, really loved her, but he didn't want to stay and make things worse.

As he drove along the road, he tried to put all the pieces together. Everything had been fine until they moved to Stepney. They had the perfect marriage, that's not to say they didn't row, but it had been nothing like this. Everything seemed to change when they moved to Stepney.

* * *

Millie stroked Paul's forehead. "Hey sleepy head." She watched as his eyes flickered open. "I thought I'd lost you."

"You can't get rid of me that easily." Paul lifted his head slightly. "Ouch. What happened?"

"You had a couple of broken ribs, one of them punctured your lung, but you're gonna be okay." Millie smiled and kissed him gently on his lips.

"Where's my clothes, I need to get out of here." Paul replied.

Millie watched as Paul rolled onto his side. "Oh no you don't. You Paul Kelly are staying right here until the doctor says otherwise." Millie helped him onto his back. "And you will not give the nurses a hard time."

"I've got a club to run, and the house and let's not forget the docks." Paul winced.

"I'll be taking care of business while you recover, and I don't want any arguments." Millie smiled at last she had the chance to find out what Ronnie Taylor was up to.

Chapter Fifty-Four

Monday morning Millie walked into the office at the docks. "Good morning, Ronnie."

"Morning. I heard about Paul; tell him I'll take good care of the docks while he's out of action." Ronnie replied.

Millie smiled sweetly. She could hear the annoyance in his voice. "It's fine, Paul's asked me to keep an eye on things for him. He wants me to look over the accounts, I take it you're okay with that?" Straight away his body stiffened, Millie conceded he was more than annoyed, he was on the verge of anger.

"If that's what he wants.... anyone would think he doesn't trust me." Ronnie handed Millie a ledger and glared.

"Oh he trusts you 100 percent." Millie grabbed the ledger and took a seat at Paul's desk.

"And you?" Ronnie enquired.

"If Paul trusts you then so do I." Millie opened the ledger and scanned the rows of numbers. The one good thing she came out of school with was a head for numbers.

"So why the need to snoop?" Millie looked up as Ronnie placed both hands on Paul's desk and leaned over menacingly.

"My husbands in hospital, I need something to keep me busy, I thought as you and Paul are such good friends you wouldn't mind and to be honest, I think Paul wants you to keep an eye on me." Millie watched as Ronnie stood up, but was he convinced that she wasn't a threat? "Also I was hoping we could get to know each other a little better. You're such a big part of Paul's life, it would be nice if we got on. Don't you think?"

"Of course, sounds like a good idea to me." Ronnie walked back to his desk and took a seat.

Millie started at the previous week's entries. Whilst the columns added up, the outgoings seemed a little dubious. She could feel Ronnie's eyes on her. Watching her every move. "I don't know how you do this; maths has never been my strong point." Millie made eye contact with Ronnie and shrugged. "Just tell Paul I was a help. I don't want him worrying about me."

Ronnie laughed. "Your secret's safe with me. Now I've got a bit of business to take care of, will you be okay here on your own?"

"Yeah, I'll just pretend I know what I'm doing. Have you got a kettle? I could do with a cuppa?" Millie glanced around the office and spotted a table with a kettle. "Would you mind if I help myself?"

"Course not. You drink tea and put your feet up. I'll only be an hour or so." Ronnie grabbed his trilby and left, but Millie wasn't content that he thought she was clueless. She felt in her pocket for Paul's keys. She would get copies made of each for future use and come back one night.

As the door closed Millie jumped up and made herself a cup of tea. She wasn't going to drink it; it was just for her cover.

The door opened and in walked Ronnie a few minutes later. "Left my papers Mil. Enjoy your cuppa, see you in a while."

Millie smiled and nodded; she knew she would have to play the long game, both Paul and Ronnie thought she was stupid, well they were both going to find out otherwise. The fact Ronnie had come back so soon to check on her proved that. But more importantly what was Ronnie Taylor hiding?

Chapter Fifty-Five

Paul sat, propped up in his hospital bed. He was agitated by just being stuck here. The noise of the old man in the bed next to him was pissing him off to. Day and night he would call out for the nurses. 'I need the bathroom nurse. I need a drink nurse.' If he stopped fucking drinking, he wouldn't need to piss so much. He would've smothered him with a pillow if he'd had his way. Paul took a deep breath. He had to stay calm. When he spotted Ronnie approaching, he smiled, until he caught the stoney face. "Ron, what's happened?"

"Your wife, that's what. Why have you asked her to look over the books?" Ronnie asked.

Paul frowned at Ronnie. "What do you mean she's looking over the books?"

"She said you wanted her to keep an eye on the business, she's been in every morning for the last three days.... I've got to say Paul, I'm more than a little disappointed that you don't trust me." Ronnie sighed. "After all we've been through together."

"Ron, she decided to take care of business, I had just come out of the operating theatre and was in no fit state to argue. Pass me my clothes." Paul nodded to the locker next to his bed. "Nurse, I'm discharging myself."

"Mr Kelly, I really think you should speak with the doctor first..."

"No time, now discharge me or I'm walking out." Paul grabbed the clothes as Ronnie passed them to him and started to get dressed.

"That's the Paul Kelly I know." Ronnie laughed.

"Can you give me a lift home Ron; I'll sort out Millie then I'll come over to the docks." Paul added.

"No need for that son. Everything is under control there, I'll be able to get more done without that interfering wife of yours there anyway." Ronnie clocked the doctor as he approached. "Look out, incoming."

The doctor looked between the two men and shook his head. "Mr Kelly, can I remind you that you need constant supervision until I'm certain the hole has mended in your lung."

"Look doc, I've made up my mind, now if anything happens, I'll come back but as you can see, I feel fine." Paul slipped on his trainers and stood. "Now where do I sign?"

* * *

Millie sat at the dining room table. She had opened all the windows and patio doors, trying to get some air into the room. The heat was making it hard for her to concentrate. She rubbed her hand across her forehead. It was moist with sweat. She wasn't sure if it was from the heat or the apprehension she felt, as she studied the paperwork in front of her. Last night she had taken a copy of the paperwork in the filing cabinet of the docks. Ronnie had kept it locked and told her not to go in there. This had raised her suspicion, as well as him being jumpy around her. She flicked her hair back and read over the name again. T Royal Trading's. There was no signs of this company, pre the docks business opening. A lot of money had been syphoned off into this company. "T Royal, that's a weird name." Millie mumbled to herself as the front door opened. She jumped up, her heart thudded as she ran to the hall just in time to see Paul slipping his trainers off. "What the hell are you doing here?"

"I had a visit from Ronnie, seems you've been getting in the way." Paul brushed past Millie and made his way up the stairs.

"Paul.... Paul. Will you stop." Millie marched up the stairs behind him. "You should be in hospital."

"And I would be if you wasn't poking your nose into my business." Paul slid down his jogging bottoms and walked to the shower. "What have you got against Ronnie?"

"He's having you over Paul. You can't trust him." Millie's eyes went wide when Paul turned on her.

"I trust Ronnie where business is concerned, he's done more for me than anyone else and I won't have you interfering."

"So, you trust him more than me?" Millie asked but she already knew Paul's answer.

"Yes. Now if you don't mind, I want to get cleaned up before I see what damage you've done." And with that Paul slammed the door.

Millie walked back down the stairs, wondering why she even bothered. Her heart ached at the thought of Paul blaming her. When she heard his footsteps coming down the stairs she tensed.

"Look Mil I'm sorry, I didn't mean the things I said. Of course I trust you but you're wrong. This business at the docks is a right good earner. This is all because of Ronnie, he asked me to be his partner."

"Firstly, you meant every word you said. Secondly, all I did at the docks was look over the accounts, so how has that interfered with the business? If Ronnie fucking Taylor had nothing to hide, he wouldn't have minded. So maybe you should ask yourself why. Why did Ronnie have a problem with me looking over the accounts and why, if he's such a great friend, did it take him until today to see you in hospital?" Millie replied as she pointed her finger angrily.

"Fine, I'll think over what you've said. Now I need to get going, it's getting late, and I'd like to get home and spend the evening with my wife.... Do I get a kiss?" Paul stood and walked towards Millie.

"Wouldn't you rather kiss Ronnie?" Millie replied as she backed away.

"That's pretty childish Mil.... I need to pick up Tony on the way, so I'll see you later." Paul shook his head as he left the lounge.

Millie waited for the front door to close before returning to the table and her paperwork. "Now where was I.... T Royal Trading." Millie grabbed a pen and rearranged the letters. "Taylor!" She sat back and smiled. "Got ya."

After she hid the paperwork Millie called a cab and went to meet Rosie at the Artichoke. She needed someone to talk to, someone she could trust, and Paul was no longer on that list.

Making her way to the other end of the high street and the Artichoke, Millie spotted the Blue Lion pub. Fire had ripped through the front of it, leaving it almost a shell. "Can you stop here, please." She told the cab driver. She jumped out and headed across the road catching the eye of Billy Brown, the landlord. "What happened here?"

"Mrs Kelly, where's Mr Kelly?" Billy Brown looked broken, his face was still smoke stained, and his eyes looked weary.

"He's sorting business somewhere, but I'm here, so if you have a problem, you should tell me."

"Fine." Rubbing his dirty hand over his face Billy pointed to the shell of his pub. "There were four of them. First, they demanded protection money. Of course, I refused to pay, they then smashed a few glasses and pushed the fruit machines over. Minimal damage. I told them I was under Mr Kelly's protection, and they said he's out of the game. They reckoned if I didn't pay, they'd be back with a little surprise. I didn't realise that surprise would be a can of petrol and a match!"

Millie's complexion paled as she cursed Paul. Her mouth was dry which made it difficult to speak. She took a deep breath to control her dread. "Seems it's open season."

Billy shook his head and leaned nearer. "They could be from North London, by their accent."

Millie placed her hand on Billy's shoulder. "Don't worry, this will be sorted. Are your family okay?"

"Yeah, we managed to get out before the blaze took hold. Look Mrs Kelly, no disrespect but Paul needs to get his face seen, otherwise this is gonna happen to all the places he runs protection for." Billy turned and made his way back to the ruins of his pub, while Millie's heart sank. She turned and carried on down the street. Annoyed now that Paul was turning into Ronnie's lapdog and leaving his businesses open to anyone that fancied taking over. She calmed herself as the Artichoke came into sight. As she walked in the door she spotted Rosie sitting at a table with Bobby. "Hello. How's things with you two?" Millie greeted.

"Millie, lovely to see you again, I'm afraid I've got to make tracks, I'm in the middle of painting. Rose, I'll see you when you get home." Bobby left the two women to it.

"So, what's happened now, you sounded miserable on the phone." Rosie asked as she waved to Finn. "I've ordered you a drink."

"Thanks Rose." Millie sat down and kicked her shoes off. "It's 7.30 and still bloody hot."

"They've started putting standpipes in up the road. They reckon this is the driest summer on record...... Well, what's happened?"

"Nothing much. My husband has discharged himself from hospital. I've caught Ronnie fiddling the books, but Paul won't believe me and in two days' time I get to face that old bag from the council and possibly find out who my mother is. Everything is going wrong Rose." Millie placed her head in her hands. She decided to leave the Blue Lion out of it. That would be a discussion to have with Paul. If he could be bothered to listen to her.

"Woah, wind back a minute. Pauls discharged himself from hospital, so where is he?" Rosie asked.

"With Ronnie Taylor at the docks, Ronnie told him I've been interfering at work, so Pauls gone to see what damage I've done." Millie took a deep breath to stop herself from crying. "I told him all I'd done is look through the accounts, I also told him Ronnie was having one over on him, but he wouldn't believe me.... I also found something else out." Millie lent forward to Rosie and whispered. "I've seen the contract for the docks. If one of the partners die, the docks automatically transfer to the surviving partner." Millie was grateful that Paul had taken Tony with him. She didn't like the idea of Paul being alone with Ronnie, not as he was still healing.

"That's standard practice surely Mil?" Rosie whispered back.

"Maybe, but it would allow Ronnie to get rid of Paul and take everything.... I know Paul put a lot of money into the set up and let's not forget it was me that got the contracts signed." Millie chewed her nail.

"Yeah, why did you bother doing that, it doesn't make sense?" Rosie asked.

"Because I didn't want Paul getting into trouble. I knew Ronnie would get him to sort the men out, with force, and then he would hurt them or worse. He could have ended up in prison or Ronnie would have had another hold over him. I couldn't risk it. Even though Paul didn't believe me" Millie straightened her back and looked at Rosie. "Ronnie fucking Taylor needs to pay." Millie sat back and gave Rosie a knowing nod.

"So, what do you plan to do?" Rosie asked with a gasp.

"Simple, I'm going to get the evidence then kill him before he can touch Paul, even if Paul doesn't like it." Millie winked at an open-mouthed Rosie. "I just need to make it look like an accident."

Chapter Fifty-Six

Millie woke to the sound of chirping birds and opened her eyes slowly. She had spent the last two nights sleeping in the spare room, much to Paul's disgust. They hadn't rowed since Thursday but hadn't spoken either. Or rather Millie had refused to speak to him. The house was full of bouquets of flowers that Paul had bought for her, to apologise for his behaviour, but she wasn't going to let him off that easily. He never listened to her, he thought she didn't understand his world, but she did. She knew how people could manipulate situations to get what they want, and she knew Ronnie was doing just that. Millie climbed out of bed and pulled open the curtains. The heat outside was already stifling. Millie looked over to the Traveller site and rolled her eyes, there was a massive mobile home now in place. That was another problem that needed sorting, selling the house. Today wasn't that day though, today she was going to see the woman from the council offices. She would go after breakfast and wait all day if she had to.

"Morning Mil." Paul walked into the bedroom and sat on the

edge of the bed. "I missed you last night, it's not the same in bed without you to cuddle."

Millie looked at his sad face and almost gave in. "Paul.... For a marriage to work you need trust, you don't trust me and now I don't trust you, and I'm not sure where that leaves us."

"I never said I didn't trust you. Look Mil, I was just angry, you knew I didn't want you at the docks, not because I don't trust you, it's because I don't want you involved in that business. If we get raided it could be a long prison sentence, so I don't want you involved."

"You said the docks was legitimate, is that another lie?" Millie brushed past Paul and headed for the bathroom.

"Woah, wait up." Paul grabbed Millie by the arm and pulled her to a standstill. "I told you it appears legit, but you know the old bill, if they want to find something they will." Paul sighed. "You Mrs Kelly are my life, why can't you see that?"

"It's not that simple." Millie stood still as Paul slipped his arms around her.

"It's as simple as we want to make it.... Do you still love me?" Paul asked.

Millie felt his lips brush her cheek. "Of course I do." She felt her resolve weaken as Paul planted his lips on hers.

"That's what I want, my wife.... Mil, let's go back to bed." Paul smiled.

Millie placed her hands on his chest as he pulled her closer. She felt his throbbing body as he wrapped his arms around hers. Annoyed with herself, she gave in.

* * *

Millie sat on the bus, it was only a short journey through town to her destination, but the sun was already high in the sky and the heat was starting to become unbearable to walk any great distance in. She watched the shoppers hurrying into the shade as they made their way from store to store. Millie blinked when she spotted Ronnie Taylor going into the Green Dragon pub. She had heard rumours he had been spending a lot of time around here while Paul had been in hospital. Making himself known to the different drinking houses. Just what he was up to she couldn't work out. Not yet anyway. Millie sighed, she had bigger things to think about today and didn't expect to be making this journey on her own. Paul knew today was the day she was confronting that woman, but all he seemed to care about was getting to the docks and Ronnie bloody Taylor. Well Ronnie obviously wasn't with him, so who was he with? Another woman maybe? Millie shook her head as she stood up and rang the bell for her stop. She didn't think for one minute Paul would go with another woman, but then probably most wives think that. As the bus ground to a halt she jumped off and continued down the street. All the gardens were brown instead of green and a haze rose from the road, almost like a shimmer. She passed a standpipe, another reminder of the drought. A lot of streets now had these in place in the hopes to conserve the water supply. It wasn't much fun washing her hair in a bowl, she just didn't feel like it was clean. And then there were the strip washes she had morning and night. What she wouldn't give for a bath or shower right now. The sweat dripped down her back as she stopped opposite 105 Vincent road.

Millie stood there for over an hour, in the shade of a tree. It brought some welcome relief from the sun as it scorched the surroundings. Finally, Millie decided to give up. Her throat was dry, her feet ached, and she realised she didn't know if they would be back today. After all, they could always choose to stay another night, wherever they had gone. As she turned to walk away, she heard a car pull onto the drive of the house she had been watching. Her heart started to beat faster as she watched the woman climb out of the car. Without giving herself time to think, she marched across the road. As the woman spotted her, Millie noticed the colour drain from the woman's face. "I think we need a chat, don't you?"

"I have nothing to say to you. Now please, leave."

"I'm not going anywhere until you tell me what I want to know, so the question is, would you like all your neighbours to hear what you've done, or would you like this chat in private?"

Millie entered the house and was shown to the dining room. She looked around as she walked through, noticing all the ornaments adorning the sides. Her attention was drawn to a photograph of a small child with blonde hair in pigtails and big blue eyes, smiling at the camera.

"Please take a seat." Cathleen pulled out a chair and motioned for Millie to sit.

"Thank you. You know you've led me on a right merry dance.... Now start talking." Millie folded her arms and glared at Cathleen.

"I'll leave you ladies to it." Cathleen's husband announced.

"Not so fast. Who are you?" Millie called before he left the room.

"I'm Cathleen's husband, Peter." The man closed the door behind him.

Millie refocused on Cathleen. "So Cathleen, let's start at the beginning, shall we."

Cathleen nodded slightly and began. "You know I had put the memory out of my mind. Buried it for years, and then you showed up, out of the blue. Bringing it all up again.... Now it won't stay buried any longer."

Millie sat forward and studied the woman. Her grey hair set just right and her blue eyes that radiated sorrow. Sorrow for being caught? Millie wondered. "This is my life; I deserve to know. Now can you start at the beginning."

"My daughter was a good girl, always did as she was told. I'd never had a day's trouble from her." Cathleen shook her head. "It was when she was fourteen it all changed. She met a boy, not a nice respectable boy but a tearaway. Someone you wouldn't want your child to be in the company of. She started sneaking out at night, lying about where she was going, bunking off school to meet him. Her whole personality changed.... It wasn't until she was fifteen, I noticed her stomach growing, of course I knew she had ended up in the family way. I couldn't let her throw her life away."

Millie cut in as her anger grew. "She was having a baby, that's nothing to be ashamed of."

"But it was back then. It was frowned upon. Her life would have been ruined." Cathleen reached into her pocket and pulled out a hanky while Millie watched. She dabbed at her eyes and then blew her nose.

"So, you ruined mine instead." Millie snapped. "Didn't you have any thought for the baby.... for me?"

"My first thought was for my daughter, and I reasoned you would have a better chance in life with a loving family adopting you."

"But I never got adopted, I never got that chance of a loving family. You took that away from me." Millie felt her own eyes mist up and looked away. All the hurt was coming to the surface. The hurt, the loneliness and the not belonging. "Carry on." She snapped.

"I sent my daughter away to live at her aunts in Bow. That's where you were born, just after her sixteenth birthday."

"So, if I was born in Bow how did I end up in Stepney?" Millie asked, now confused.

"When you were born, my daughter named you. It was at that point I knew she would search for you, so instead of leaving you there I brought you back here and left you on the steps of the children's home. I left her white bunny with you. I knew if I gave it back to her, she would want to see you.... I thought she would never find you if you were so close, and to make doubly sure, I told her you had died not long after birth."

"You did what!" Millie fought the anger that had replaced the sadness. "You're evil, evil and twisted." Clenching her fist she smashed it onto the table. "Thank God I never had you in my life, you sick bitch."

"I'm not proud of what I've done Millie and trust me I've paid the price ever since."

"You've just been on holiday, that really looks like you're paying the price." Millie took a deep breath to steady her nerves. "So does my mother know I'm alive now. Have you told her?"

"No, that's just it. I lost her anyway." Cathleen blew into the hanky again and sighed.

"What, she's dead?" Millie asked wide eyed.

"No.... She ran off with that boy when she was sixteen.... I had no idea she had met him again." Cathleen stared into space, as if reminiscing.

"Sounds like she had a lucky escape if you ask me.... You can't dictate who someone falls in love with." Millie replied sarcastically. "It's probably the best thing she ever did."

"When you have children Millie you will understand. You will do whatever you have to give them a good life."

"Yes you're right, I will do whatever I have to do to give them a good life, which includes not taking away their child, because grandmother dearest, that child will also be a part of me." Millie stood up and pushed the chair back. "There's only one thing left I need to know. What's her name?" Millie was interrupted when there was a loud bang coming from the front door.

"Excuse me while I see who that is." Cathleen left the room and returned a minute later. "It seems it's a day for visitors. Millie...... This is your mum."

Millie's mouth dropped open, unable to speak; she stood there; the room swam around her. Darkness followed as she hit the floor.

Chapter Fifty-Seven

Paul slammed the ledger shut and pushed back in his chair. He walked to the door and looked out over the Themes. It was early evening and still the heat was unbearable. Paul undid his tie and pulled it off. He undid the top button of his shirt and ran his finger around the collar, to loosen it from his skin. He glanced at his watch, annoyed that Ronnie hadn't showed. As he was about to grab his keys and return home Ronnie walked in. "Ron. Thought you were gonna be here all day."

"I had a bit of business to take care of, anyway I'm here now. Is everything all right?"

"Yeah, I just had a look over the books. Everything seems healthy." Paul sat on the edge of his desk and studied Ronnie. He seemed on edge. "You alright mate, you look worried."

"All's good son, all's good.... I've got some paperwork that needs your signature." Ronnie riffled through his briefcase and handed Paul a pile of papers. "The usual stuff, just sign at the bottom."

"I'll take it home and do it, I need to get back to Millie, she's only just started talking to me again." Paul placed the papers on his desk and bent down to tie his shoelace.

"Why can't you do it here, you know I don't like business papers taken out of the office, she can wait. Never let a woman interfere with work, son." Ronnie ordered.

"I've been here all day waiting for you if it were that important you would have got here earlier. Now I'm going to see my wife, whom I chose not to keep waiting. I'll see you in the morning." Paul grabbed the papers and marched out. Ronnie had been acting strange the last couple of days. He would have even said Millie was right about him, he was acting shifty. He Put all thoughts of Ronnie out of his mind, as he started up his motor and made his way home.

* * *

Paul walked into the Artichoke and made his way to the bar. He had been home looking for Millie, but she wasn't there. He could curse himself for being so long. He promised her he would only be a couple of hours and not most of the day. So, this was his first port of call and next it would be Rosie's. "Alright Finn, have you seen Millie?"

"Paul, you lost that wife of yours, she hasn't been in here. You gonna have a drink?" Finn held a glass up and motioned to the whiskey.

"Just a quick one, I've got a feeling I'm in trouble, so a bit of Dutch courage won't hurt." Paul laughed.

"If I were you, I'd have a couple of doubles." Finn replied.

As Paul raised the glass to his mouth he heard a familiar voice.

"Paul, what did she find out?" Rosie stood at his side excitedly.

"What?" Paul frowned.

"What. You didn't go with her?" Rosie asked in astonishment. "Christ Paul, this was important to her. I can't believe you let her go on her own."

"Rosie. Go where?" Paul felt his chest tighten as he waited for Rosie to share the information.

"To find out who her mother is. You was with her when she got the address." Rosie snatched Paul's glass from his hand and pointed to the door. "Don't you think you should go and make sure she's okay?"

Paul froze on the spot. "I, I." He stuttered, as he looked at the ground.

"Paul, go!" Rosie screamed.

Paul jumped off the stool and walked to the door, cursing under his breath. Of course, he knew she was seeing that woman today, but he was busy, so why didn't Millie remind him. Was he supposed to remember everything?

Millie sat on the sofa with a glass of brandy. She had walked home the long way, to give herself time to think. She still had a slight headache from where she had hit the floor but at least it had stopped bleeding. She heard the door open, and keys clatter on the side.

"Mil, you in here?" Paul called as he walked into the lounge.

"Yep. I'm right here." Millie replied before draining her glass.

"Why didn't you tell me you were going to see that woman?" Paul's voice had an air of accusation in it, almost like she had done it on purpose.

"You knew I was going today, Paul; you was with me two weeks ago when we went there, remember?" Millie reached over to the coffee table and poured herself another large measure of brandy.

"I'm a man Mil, I don't remember yesterday, never mind two weeks' time." Paul took a seat next to her and placed his hand on her thigh. "I'm sorry baby. I should have been there."

"Yes you should have been, but, it's been dealt with, now can we talk about something else." Millie took a deep breath and willed herself not to cry. She wasn't sure what had upset her the most, finding out who her mum was or the fact her husband didn't care enough to accompany her.

"Don't you want to talk about it, or tell me who she is?" Paul asked in amazement. "I thought this would have been something you'd want to share with your husband."

"I would have done, if you were there, but you wasn't, you were with Ronnie. As usual." Millie took a large sip of the brandy and closed her eyes. She didn't want to row, not today. Her head was full of questions. Questions that she knew she would need answering.

"I said I'm sorry.... I wish I had been there with you; I've just been so caught up in the docks and what you said about Ronnie that it's been playing on my mind. I think you might be right, something's off with him."

"At least you've listened to something I've said.... So what are you going to do about him?"

"I'm not wasting time talking about him, not now Mil. You're all that matters. Why is there blood in your hair?"

* * *

Duke pulled up outside his mobile and jumped out of the pickup. He had been to the bookies and had a right result on the horses. He looked over to the mobile and saw Connie standing in the doorway.

"Sorry I'm late Con, business took a little longer than I thought. Didn't even get time to go round shit bag's and demand he moves." Duke was ready for the verbal battering, but none came. "Con, what's the matter?"

"Duke I've got something I need to tell you..... It's something that happened a long time ago."

"Spit it out woman, you're starting to scare me." Duke noticed her pale complexion. His heart dropped.

"Do you remember when we first met?" Connie smiled.

"Of course I do." Duke frowned. "You're not ill Con are ya?"

"No I'm not ill. Now please, just listen.... When my parents took me away, when I was fifteen, it was because they had found out I was pregnant." Connie paused.

Duke was momentarily stunned. His mouth couldn't keep up with his brain. "With my child?"

"Our child Duke." Connie replied sadly.. "I had a little girl; my mother took her away shortly after I had given birth and told me she had died."

Duke walked to the sofa and sat down on the edge. He ran his hand through his hair to push it back. Was this why she had been acting strange? He had a daughter that had died, and he never knew. How could she keep a secret like that? Duke looked at Connie with accusing eyes. "Why are you telling me this now?"

"Because I found out today, she didn't die. I had my suspicions when I first saw her. I asked around and everything seemed to fit, but I needed to be sure. I needed proof."

Duke looked at Connie's hands, they were shaking. "Who is she?" He asked through gritted teeth.

"Duke I...."

"I said who is she?" Duke stood and walked towards Connie. "What's her name?" Duke's voice got louder.

"Millie.... It's Millie, she's our daughter."

Duke rubbed his face. His heart was beating through his chest as he looked at Connie. "That's a pretty big secret for a wife to keep from her husband."

"I didn't mean to, I just wanted to bury the pain. By the time I had met you again it seemed best to keep it buried.... I'm sorry Duke." She pleaded.

"I need some time alone Con; I'm going to the pub." Duke grabbed his keys and walked to the door. He felt his eyes mist up but didn't know if it was in temper or sorrow.

Chapter Fifty-Eight

Paul placed the teacup on the bedside table and sat on the edge of the bed. "I'll be working from home today."

"I don't need a babysitter, Paul." Millie rolled her eyes and sat up. "I've got stuff to do anyway."

"Oh no you don't. You sit there and drink your tea.... How's your head this morning?" Paul twisted around and knelt on the bed, he studied the back of Millie's head, pulling her hair away from the small gash. "You should've let me take you to the hospital last night, just to be on the safe side."

"Will you stop poking me, it's fine." Millie replied.

"Mil, we need to talk about yesterday. You need to talk about yesterday." Paul propped himself up on his pillow and studied Millie's face. It was clear to him Millie had shut down; she had hardly spoken since she had shared the news of her parents.

"It's no big deal...."

"Yes it is babe. You now know who your parents are, so what now?" Paul sighed. "At least I now know why Connie acted strange around you.... Duke Lee of all people, I mean, I didn't see that one coming." Paul hid the irritation in his voice. He wasn't best thrilled at the prospect of a pikey being his father-in-law.

"Paul. I know you mean well but can we talk about something else. Please?"

"Okay, if that's what you want, but at some point, you're gonna have to face it." Paul sat up and reached for his cup. "Do you remember that day in the hospital, the very first time I lay eyes on you?"

"You laughed at me." Millie replied surprised at the choice of subject.

"You were wearing the most hideous clothes." Paul laughed as Millie rolled her eyes. "But straight away I felt it."

"Felt what?" Millie frowned.

"A feeling, it was like I'd been swept away by you, your beauty, your determination.... And that look you gave me." Paul started laughing so hard he had tears rolling down his face. "I mean seriously, you were dressed like a clown, and you had the cheek to look at me like I was the nutter."

"You grabbed me."

"You ran into me." Paul countered. "And I'm so glad you did. I couldn't imagine life without you."

"Is there a point to this conversation?" Millie asked as she started to giggle.

"The point is, I'm here for you. I know I fuck up from time to time, I'm a man but I'm here Mil, whenever you need me."

"Okay. I want to move." Millie replied bluntly. "I don't want to be reminded of them every time I look out of the window."

"I think you should give yourself some time before you make any rash decisions babe. You've had a shock. A fucking big shock. Look, give it a week and if you're still sure I'll phone the estate agent and get the ball rolling. Now drink your tea while I look over these papers Ron wants me to sign." Paul smiled as Millie placed her arm over him.

"What papers?" Millie asked.

"Something to do with a trading company we do business with, T Royal Trading Ltd, look don't worry about this. I'll be extra careful." Paul placed a small kiss on Millie's forehead and settled down to work.

* * *

Duke turned into the paddock and pulled the Transit to a halt. He spotted Connie sitting on the step of the mobile. Despite her smile he could see she had been crying, her eyes were red and sunken. He felt guilty at staying out all night, but he couldn't forgive her, not yet. They had never had secrets in their marriage from each other, or so he had thought. But now he wondered what else she wasn't telling him, like was the girl even his? He shook his head at the thought, Connie may have not told him, but she wasn't a liar. He jumped out of the motor and made his way over as she stood to greet him.

"Duke.... I've been so worried...."

"You don't need to worry about me Connie, I'm a grown man." Duke walked around her and went inside. He knew there was a conversation to be had but not now, his temper was still hanging by a thread, and he didn't want to say something he'd regret later.

"Where have you been all night?" Connie asked as she walked in behind him.

"Ain't I allowed secrets too Connie?" Duke called over his shoulder. He grabbed a bag and started to throw some clothes into it.

"You're leaving me, aren't you?" she said with a sob.

Duke spun around to face her, as he looked into her eyes he asked himself one question. Couldn't she see what she had done? "I need some time, it's not every day you learn your wife has lied to you for the last 20 years."

"It wasn't a lie; I just couldn't speak about it.... Look I know it's a shock..."

"A SHOCK! .... No Connie this isn't just a shock, I feel

betrayed." Duke slung the bag over his shoulder and pushed past Connie.

"BETRAYED.... YOU FEEL BETRAYED...TRY HAVING YOUR OWN MOTHER TAKE YOUR BABY AND TELL YOU SHE'S DEAD. THEN YOU'LL KNOW WHAT THE REAL MEANING OF BETRAYED IS." Connie walked towards Duke; her fists bawled as she quieted her voice. "This is your ground, Duke. This is your mobile, and this is your home. I'll go."

"Don't be stupid woman, the boys need you." Duke stared in disbelief as Connie grabbed her things.

"Like you said the boys are now men, they don't need me either." She grabbed her bag and headed for the door, pausing as she passed Duke. "There's one person you're forgetting in all this." Connie pointed to the house behind them. "A young woman has had her life turned upside down, and she just happens to be our daughter.... Goodbye Duke."

Duke watched her from the doorway as she walked towards the lane. He wanted to stop her, but his own stupid pride wouldn't allow it.

Chapter Fifty-Nine

A week had passed, and Millie was feeling more like her old self. Most of the time. She still had thoughts of Connie and Duke. Most nights in fact. A part of her wanted to know more about them, but then part of her wanted to just forget the whole sorry story. She reasoned she had lived 24 years without them, so why not the rest of her life. But then there was that little niggling voice in her head. 'You liked Connie before, why not get to know her.' Duke she wasn't so sure of, he seemed like a cocky shitbag. She put them to the back of her mind and instead focused on Ronnie. Three days she had researched T Royal Holdings Ltd. They had a P O box and no registered building. The bank account seemed to be associated with an offshore account, which immediately rang alarm bells. Millie made her way to the house to seek Gladys's help. She was one of the few people she knew she could trust, her and Maggie. After she let herself in, she made her way to the kitchen where all the girls were sitting eating breakfast and drinking tea.

"Millie." Maggie jumped up and gave Millie a hug. "It's good to see you. How's things?"

"Hi Mags, can I have a private word in the office?" Millie looked over to Gladys. "With you too?"

Gladys stood up and led the way. "Problem?"

"You could say that.... I need a bit of help." Millie entered the office first and took a seat behind the desk. "Firstly, if Paul asks, I was here looking over the accounts." Millie continued when both women nodded. "Ronnie Taylors setting Paul up. Now I don't know what for or why, but it looks like he wants him out of the way."

"Paul would have surely noticed?" Gladys reasoned. "I mean he hasn't got where he is today by being the trusting type."

"This is Ronnie Taylor we are talking about; Paul trusts him implicitly. He thinks of him as a second dad." Millie pulled her notes out and handed them to Gladys. "This holding company is dubious. It only appeared when the dock business was set up. It only has a P O box, and the banking details are offshore. Any money that has been paid into that will never be recovered."

"Paul must know who it belongs to?" Maggie scratched her head. "I mean, he wouldn't pay money to nobody."

"Ronnie's been taking care of that side of it. The trouble is, it's Paul's signature on all the paperwork that pertains to this company. If this company gets raided, Paul will go down for fraud." Millie pinched the bridge of her nose. She could feel the beginnings of a headache.

"Why haven't you shown this to Paul?" Gladys asked in amazement.

"I warned him about Ronnie, but he won't see no wrong in him. Even with proof he would still back him." Millie looked at Maggie as she opened her mouth to speak.

"But you're his wife, surely he'd listen to you?"

"Paul's old fashioned, he thinks women don't understand the business world. He also thinks women, me especially, need protecting from such things. So, ladies, you can see the dilemma in which I've been left. The question is, will you help me to fix it?"

* * *

Duke sat at the table with his head in his hands. Connie had been gone now a whole week. He had spent the last three days searching for her, but there was no trace.

"You can't just sit there dad." Jess reasoned. "She's got to be somewhere."

"I've searched everywhere boy, there's nowhere left to look." Duke stood and walked to the fridge, he pulled out a can of beer and cracked it open.

"So, you'd rather sit here drinking. A fine husband you've turned out to be." Aron added.

"I'm still ya father and you will show some respect." Duke took a long swig from the can before smashing it onto the table. He blamed himself, he knew he had fucked up. The way he dealt with problems had always been with violence. But how could he use violence against Connie or his daughter?

"What about Millie, she may know where mum is?" Jess asked.

"She's the one that caused this mess." Duke sighed. "I'll not be asking her." He felt his chest tighten. This all began with her and yet he had a strange feeling when he thought about her. He didn't want to dwell on it, it unnerved him.

"She's your daughter.... Our sister.... Doesn't she deserve a family dad?" Aron spoke softly. "She didn't cause anything. You let mum go. I'm gonna drive around a bit, you never know I might spot her."

"She's probably long gone, don't waste your time boy." Duke watched his son's as they walked to the door.

"I don't call looking for our mother a waste of time." Aron nodded to Jess and they both left.

Duke walked to the window and watched the pickup truck pull away. They were right, looking for Connie wasn't a waste of time. He thought about Millie, he didn't blame her, not really. He blamed himself. He should've stayed and faced it. Instead, he acted like an idiot and blamed Connie for something she had no control over. It was her mother he should've confronted. She was the cause of this. He decided to take his son's lead and left the mobile and walked down the lane. If there was the slightest chance Millie knew anything, then he should ask her.

He walked up the driveway and noticed the for-sale sign, sitting proudly at the end of the garden. He felt a tinge of sadness, but he wasn't sure why. As he stood at the wooden front door he knocked loudly, then stood back and waited. He had no idea what he was going to say. This was his daughter, a stranger, but still his daughter. He looked up as the door opened and he came face to face with a hostile Millie. "Look I haven't come to cause trouble. Connie's left me, if you have any idea where she might be, then please tell me."

"Why would I know where she is?" Millie asked. "I'm the last person that would have a clue, I don't know her."

Duke's shoulders sagged as he turned away. "Thanks anyway." He called over his shoulder.

"Wait." Millie called after him.

Duke turned and for the first time he noticed how alike Connie and Millie were. They had the same big blue eyes and button nose. She did however have his full lips. She reminded him of Connie in her younger days. Annoyed that he hadn't noticed it before he smiled sadly. "You look like her you know, I never took any notice before, but you do."

Millie gave a small nod. "You'd better come in."

Duke followed Millie into a large lounge, he could see now why Paul loved this house. It was splendid, in a lord of the manor type of way. It fitted Paul perfectly. All show and nobody. Even though it was grand, it was not his cup of tea, he liked the open road too much. "I see you're selling up."

"I thought it best under the circumstances." Millie replied. "Do you want a cuppa?"

"If it's not too much trouble." Duke followed Millie into the kitchen. "I can't believe only two people live in this house. It's massive."

"It was Paul's dream house, the dream's kind of turned into a nightmare though." Millie shrugged. "That's why we are selling up... A fresh start and all that."

"I'm sorry Millie, I really am." Duke took a seat at the breakfast table. He was finding this harder than he thought. Being so close to her now he knew she was his daughter made him feel nervous. He wanted to look at her, study her. Ask her questions, but now wasn't the time.

"Me too, Duke.... Anyway, what's this about Connie?" Millie asked.

"We had a row when she told me what had happened, I blamed her for not telling me. But thinking about it now, there was nothing I could have done, it was a dark time in her life, and she buried it." Duke took the cup and nodded his thanks. "Anyway, I was gonna leave for a couple of days to get my head straight, but she was the one that ended up going. I should've stopped her. Why didn't I stop her?" Duke shook his head and sighed. He was a man full of regret.

"When was this?" Millie asked out of curiosity.

"A week ago, now. Me and the boys have been driving around everywhere. No one's seen her."

"I doubt she'll go to another traveller, Duke, she's a gorja, she wouldn't trust them, and they are not her family, they are yours."

Duke felt the dig as if it had been physical and almost winced. "Then where would she go?" Duke pleaded.

"Have you tried her mother; I mean I doubt she'd go there but that's the first place I'd start." Millie raised an eyebrow. "She also works at the council. She may be able to see if Connie's applied for a council house. With a bit of blackmail."

Duke smiled. His daughter was clever, obviously took after himself. "Will you come with me?"

"Yeah, but this doesn't change anything, okay?"

"Fair enough." Duke agreed, but it was a start. She was talking to him.

Chapter Sixty

Millie looked at the house from the window of the transit and blinked away the tears. The last time she had been here, her life had come crashing down. A cat caught her eye as it rolled in the dry grass and then plonked itself in the shade of a tree. "Shall I wind the window up?" She asked Duke.

"No, it's hot enough with the windows open and I doubt anyone would pinch it." Duke laughed.

Millie agreed on that point, it was a rust bucket. She climbed out and straightened her dress. "Well, that was quite an experience, did you really have to drive so fast?"

"I thought you wanted to hurry?" Duke replied as he eagerly looked at the house.

"Listen, let me do all the talking, you just stand there looking mean." Millie noticed the determination in Duke's eyes and placed her hand on his chest. "I mean it, you don't touch either of them."

"What if they don't talk?" Duke cracked his knuckles and Millie's thoughts turned to Paul. He wouldn't like her being here especially with Duke.

"She'll talk, trust me." Ignoring him she made her way to the door and knocked. As the door opened Millie pushed her way in. "Hello grandma, remember me." Millie laughed as Cathleen's mouth dropped open. "You remember Duke, I take it."

"What is the meaning of this?" Cathleen looked between Millie and Duke. "I've told you everything."

"We've got a new problem that you are the cause of. You see your little lie has had a ripple effect and caused a lot of shit for a lot of people. Now. Connie has gone missing, and you are going to help us find her." Millie motioned to the lounge. "Maybe we should make ourselves comfortable while I explain."

Millie walked into the front room and took a seat. She waited for a shocked Cathleen to sit on the chair opposite before she continued. "Have you any idea where she may have gone?"

"How would I know; last week was the first time I had seen her in over 20 years." Cathleen glanced up at Duke who was looming over her.

"You work for the council; I want you to see if she's been given a council place." Millie waved her hand at Duke to step back.

"I work for births, deaths, and marriages, that's a totally different department. If I go snooping, I will lose my job." Cathleen reached for her hanky ready to dab at her eyes.

"Cathleen...Granny.... I'm not too sure how to address you." Millie laughed. "Anyway, surely it's better to lose your job helping your daughter than going to prison for stealing a baby and pretending she died. Oh and let's not forget about abandoning her on the steps of a children's home. I think that would be up there with murder, don't you Duke?"

Duke nodded then added. "Or better than being tortured to death."

Millie watched the remaining colour drain from Cathleen's face. "I want an answer by tomorrow at 10am. This is my phone number. Don't keep me waiting. Oh and if you're thinking of skipping town then I must warn you, we have gypsies watching the house, and they will kill you.... Right, I think that's everything, Duke, ready?" Once

Duke had nodded, Millie walked to the front door. It reminded her of the last time she had left here, with Connie fussing over her. Her hair was bloodied from when she had black out and Connie had begged her to let her take her to hospital. Just like a real mother would, she assumed. Millie shook the thought from her mind and instead opened the door. She looked at the old transit parked right outside and felt the urge to laugh. Cathleen would have some explaining to do once the neighbours started gossiping. She noticed a few curtains twitch from across the road and gathered they already had. She looked over to Duke who walked silently next to her. He had a big smile on his face. "Thanks Millie, I really appreciate what you've done."

"No need to thank me, it's a favour for a favour." Millie answered without any emotion in her voice.

"And what would that be?" Duke frowned.

"I want someone killed." Millie watched the shock spread across Duke's face and wanted to laugh.

"You shouldn't be involving yourself with things like that, you're a young woman." Duke's face was a picture of shock and concern, but Millie ignored him.

After she had climbed back into the transit she waited for Duke to get in. "Fine. If you won't do it, I'll do it myself."

10am the next morning Millie waited for the phone call. She could see Paul watching her from the kitchen doorway, while she dusted.

"Is something going on?" Paul asked.

"I'm cleaning." Millie replied, more than a little put out. "This isn't a self-cleaning house Paul, or did you think the dust fairy came in every day and waved her wand?"

"Jesus Mil, I was only asking. Anyway, I need to get going, I should be back about two." Paul kissed Millie on the lips and then let himself out.

Millie breathed a sigh of relief when the phone started to ring shortly after. "Hello."

"I have the address. It's 25 Edenside, now please, don't ever contact me again." Then the phone then went dead.

Millie listened to the dialling tone and then replaced the handset. "Rude woman." She mumbled. With no time to lose, Millie grabbed her bag, then made her way around to Duke's. She knew he would be waiting impatiently. The journey home yesterday had been strange. He wouldn't stop talking. He told her about his parents and then her brothers. She wasn't sure if he thought it was some kind of bonding session. The only good thing to come out of it was that he had agreed to kill for her. As she approached the ground, she could hear the dogs barking. Cautiously, she unlatched the gate, and let herself in. As she neared the mobile home, Duke came out to meet her.

"Did you get it?" He asked.

"Of course. She's at 25 Edenside, and Duke, don't mess it up." Millie turned to walk home until Duke called her back.

"Ain't you coming with me?"

He sounded nervous, but this wasn't her problem. "No Duke, this is a family matter." Millie turned once more until she heard a voice she didn't recognise.

"But you are family.... I'm Aron, your brother."

"And I'm Jess, your other brother."

Much to Millie's disgust they both looked her up and down.

"Mum might only listen to you." Aron added.

"Hardly. She doesn't know me." Millie replied indignantly.

"You're her daughter Millie, whether you like it or not, she will want to see you." Duke added.

"Fine." Millie sighed. "But I need to be quick, I have other matters to attend to."

"We can go in the pickup dad; Millie can sit on your lap." Aron pointed to a Toyota pickup that had seen better days.

"I am not sitting on anyone's lap." Millie informed him. "I'll get a taxi."

"No need for that, I'll take the transit." Duke laughed. "Come on, in case your mother goes out shopping."

The drive only took 8 minutes. Millie was amazed she was so close and yet they couldn't find her. Bit like herself, right there all the time and yet invisible. "Here it is, pull over up the road, you don't want her seeing you."

Millie jumped out and made her way back down the street. "I'll go in first, then call you when I'm done."

Millie knocked on the door and found herself holding her breath until the door opened and she came face to face with Connie. Millie stared at her as she stared back and swallowed; her throat felt like it had closed up. "Well, are you gonna invite me in?" She managed after a while. She followed Connie into the front room.

"Please, take a seat."

"Thanks." Millie sat next to the window in an old armchair that had seen better days.

"The place is a bit sparse I'm afraid, I need to get a job and then I can buy furniture and that...." Connie trailed off.

Millie could see the woman was embarrassed. "It's fine, you won't be here long anyway."

"Oh?"

"You have a husband Connie and two sons that miss you." Millie noticed the sadness in Connie's eyes.

"I also have a daughter." Connie replied.

Millie caught the hope in her voice, but she couldn't have that. She wasn't here to lead this woman on. "A daughter that you don't know." Millie reasoned.

"A daughter that I want very much to know.... Would you like a cup of tea, I have new cups." Connie added.

"Sure, I have time for a cuppa." Millie followed Connie out into the kitchen. "Why did you leave Duke?"

"Because he blamed me, just like everyone else. I understand I should have told him when we met again but I was 15 Millie, just a child...."

"Don't you think Duke needed time to get his head around it, I mean it is a big deal?" Millie listened to the sound of the kettle boiling as Connie placed the cups on the side. "I understand what you went through Connie, that woman is evil, but you've known about me all my life or death if you want to look at it like that. Duke didn't, this was totally out of the blue for him."

"I realise that, but I needed him, Millie. When I saw you in the hospital I rec..."

"What, that was you?" Millie asked, surprised.

"I was up the hospital taking some stuff up for Duke's mum. As I walked past your room, I spotted you sleeping. It's going to sound silly, but I knew it was you."

"Why didn't you tell me then?" Millie narrowed her eyes. "Just how long have you been stalking me?"

"Every possible chance I got. I needed to be sure before I said anything. Millie I'm sorry, I didn't mean to scare you."

"You should have told me." Millie took the cup from Connie and sat back. "Why was you at Cathleen's?"

"To find out the truth before I came to see you.... Millie I want to get to know you, I want my daughter in my life. Okay so I may have handled things the wrong way, but I didn't have an instruction manual, it's all new to me too."

"Look I know this situation is hard for everyone, but the truth is.... I don't know how I feel. It's confusing. I spent so long wanting my mum but also hating her. Hating her for abandoning me and making me feel like I'm not good enough to be loved, even by my own mother."

"That's not true Millie. I've loved you every day of your life..."

Connie stopped when there was a knock at the front door. "Excuse me."

Millie listened to the sound of Duke's voice and rolled her eyes. She had told him to wait until she called him. "I need to go." She told Connie as she walked towards the door. "You two need to talk, that's more important."

"Millie please, this is more important.." Connie begged.

"I've heard enough for one day. I'm sorry." Millie walked out into the bright sunshine and took a deep breath of the scorching summer air. She carried on along the street until a familiar sound caught her ear. Paul's motor, and it stopped next to her.

"Mind filling me in Mil?" Paul's voice sounded more than a little pissed off.

Chapter Sixty-One

Paul sat open mouthed as he listened to Millie as she pleaded with him to help her. "You don't need driving lessons Mil; I can get one of the men to drive you if I'm not about."

"I don't want one of your men to drive me, I want to learn for myself. What if there's an emergency and you're not about? I'd have to wait for someone to get here after I had phoned around finding someone to drive me. You know it makes sense.... You could teach me in your car."

Paul swallowed down his annoyance before answering. "I don't think it's a good idea but, I'll think about it. Now I need to get going, Ron will be waiting at the docks, and no more sneaking off to see Duke, there is still a feud going on, you know."

"Will you stop dictating, you know what had happened, I explained it in great detail last night when you interrogated me, remember?" Millie replied sarcastically.

"Not arguing Mil, Now give us a kiss." Paul grabbed Millie around the waist and pulled her against his body so she couldn't move. After giving her a long slow kiss, he released her and made his way out.

* * *

Paul stood on the dock an hour later waiting for Ronnie. He was mesmerised by the light on the waves of the water as they lapped the quayside. They glistened and twinkled with the water's movement. He turned his attention to his men as they unloaded the latest cargo. Never in his wildest dreams had he thought he could get drugs, fags, and alcohol into London, in a legal way. He should have been happy. He was. But he was still wound up from the conversation with Millie, earlier that morning.

He heard Ronnie call over to his boys, breaking Paul's trance. And watched as he approached him.

"What's she done now?" Ronnie asked.

"She wants to learn to drive, can you fucking believe it? I've told her she can have a driver to take her wherever she wants, but no. That's not good enough. I wouldn't mind but she's the clumsiest person I know and now she wants a fucking car, a four wheeled weapon! Can you imagine the fucking mass demolition of the East End. And on the news today, woman demolishes entire fucking high street doing a three-point turn." Paul shook his head at the thought.

"You didn't tell her that, did you?"

"Of course I didn't, I'm not that fucking brave. I told her I'd look into it." Paul plunged his hands into his pockets and hoped Millie would forget all about it by the time he returned home. He turned his head when he heard Ronnie laugh.

"Glad someone's enjoying my pain, anyway you said you needed a word, what's up?" Paul walked towards their office, breathing in the salt air from the river Themes, with Ronnie in tow. Once they were both inside, Ronnie locked the door.

The office was smaller than most on the dock due to a false wall they had put in. In case they needed to stash goods in an emergency. In front of the false wall, boxes were piled high, making the office look normal. A coat stand was placed in the corner, holding one of Ronnie's trilby hats. It had two desks, facing each other, and a row of filing cabinets on the side wall. The filing cabinets were full of legal transactions that they had both, over the years, made. The business appeared legitimate, or so Paul thought.

"Someone's approached me about a job. They want us to smuggle a man out of here and take him to Ireland. They have also offered us a lot of money to do so, and I mean a lot." Ronnie sat on the edge of Paul's desk and waited for his response.

"If we get caught that will be a long stretch, how much money?" Paul watched the pound note signs in Ronnie's eyes.

"The figures not finalised yet. We will ask for more than they are offering but you're looking at 50 grand."

"If they have offered that much, he's gotta be high profile. Sounds risky to me, I want no part of it." Paul shook his head, "Greed has got a lot of good men caught Ron, remember that."

"Yeah, you're right. I'll let them know we aren't interested." Ronnie agreed. "Shame really, we could have earnt a right little fortune. Anyway, I need to go away on a bit of business this weekend, can you manage the docks? You'll need to be here for the deliveries, I've got some specials coming in that will need your attention."

Paul tensed and narrowed his eyes. "Why can't your men handle it, I promised Millie we'd spend some time together before the club opens?" Paul studied Ronnie's face and frowned. Something didn't sit right with him.

"Look son, you either want this business to thrive or you don't. Millie can wait. Now I need to get going." Ronnie stood and grabbed his trilby from the coat stand.

"What's the rush, you've only just got here?" Paul asked.

"Things to do son. Now don't forget, I need you here 6am on Saturday morning."

"You're giving me orders now Ron, I thought we were business partners?" Paul saw the flash of anger cross Ronnie's face. "Is there something you're not telling me?"

"All will become clear Saturday son; it'll be a nice little surprise.

Trust me, you're gonna love it. Now I'll see you Monday." Ronnie's anger was replaced once again with his calm demure.

Paul watched Ronnie walk out and shook his head. Something seemed off with the man. Paul Walked to the piles of boxes and moved a stack of them out of the way. He knelt and pulled a panel from the wall and then lifted a loose floorboard. There just underneath rested a safe. Paul turned the dial and waited for the click, but it never came. Four times in all he tried and each time the safe never opened. Realising the code had been changed he replaced the floorboard, panel, and boxes. Next, he went to the filing cabinet and rifled through the paperwork that nestled there. Pulling out a handful that contained T Royal Holdings Ltd, he sat back down and started to read through them.

* * *

Millie perched on the arm of the chair, watching the car parked across the road. She sipped her tea as she studied it. She didn't recognise the driver or the car, but something didn't sit right with her. She was certain he was watching the house, or rather her. She placed her tea down and reached for her house keys and bag, then made her way out of the front door and walked along to the bus stop. When the car moved along the road slowly towards her, she rolled her eyes. She turned and marched back towards it and banged on the driver's window then waited for the startled man to wind the window down. "Why are you following me?"

The man, in his early twenties stuttered his reply, "I...I...I'm not miss...I'm waiting for someone."

"Christ I'm not stupid, I spotted you an hour ago. Who sent you?" Millie lent forward, almost sticking her head through the window. "It was that husband of mine, wasn't it?"

The young man sighed and slumped his shoulders. He gave a short sharp nod. "I'll get into trouble if he finds out you've spotted me."

"Well, you should've done your job a bit better then. Now piss off before I call the police." Millie stood back and waited for the car to leave. She stayed watching it until it drove out of sight. "You are in so much trouble Paul Kelly."

Millie returned home and spent the rest of the morning cleaning the kitchen. She was trying to keep her mind off Duke and Connie. She found herself wondering if Connie had returned home, even going upstairs to look out of the window. She watched the mobile for a good 20 minutes, waiting for signs of life, but none came. Hearing the front door slam, Millie made her way down the stairs just in time to see Paul as he walked into the kitchen. "Paul?" Millie stopped as he turned around. "Whatever is the matter, you look like someone's died."

"Nothing for you to worry about..." Paul reached for his expensive bottle of whiskey and poured himself a large measure.

Millie's eyes bulged as she watched him knock it back in one. "Nothing for me to worry about.... Just when Paul Kelly are you going to treat me as an equal?" Millie asked as she placed her hands on her hips. She listened to the long sigh that left his lips.

"Fine...I think Ron's up to something."

"I already told you that." Millie snapped. "So, what's happened?"

"He's changed the code on the safe without telling me and you were right, there's something dodgy with this T Royal Holdings. It's a firm that Ronnie hooked us up with and it's always me he gets to sign the paperwork." Paul refilled his glass and walked through to the lounge.

"I didn't know there was a safe in the office, where is it?" Millie's heart started to beat a little faster. Her plan would now have to change.

"It's behind the false wall, under a loose floorboard. We had it put in for emergency money." Paul sat on the sofa and rested his head back. "I don't want you worrying, Ron probably forgot to tell me and to be honest I'm more annoyed that he's going away for the weekend and wants me at the dock, like I'm his lackey."

Millie swallowed down her temper. Whatever Ronnie Taylor was up to it would go down on Saturday, she was certain. "Okay. I'm going to see Rose tonight, you'll be okay at the club, won't you?" Millie lied.

"Yeah, get Rose to come here though, I don't want you out on your own." Paul drained the rest of his drink and stood ready to leave. "I need to check on Gladys and the girls. I'll see you later."

Millie looked out of the window as Paul left before picking up the phone and dialling Gladys. "Gladys, it's me."

"Millie, how are you?"

"I've no time to chat, now listen. Paul's on his way over to see you, don't mention me at all and make sure the girls don't." Millie took a deep breath before continuing. "The plans come forward; it'll be tonight."

Chapter Sixty-Two

Millie made her way down the end of the garden. Her nerves were hanging by a thread. So much could go wrong with her plan, especially now there was a safe involved. She approached the fence and hopped over it. The dogs were the first thing to grab her attention. They always barked when she came here, probably as an alarm. Warning Duke of intruders. She certainly wouldn't miss them when she moves. Millie spotted an old car at the edge of the paddock. Paul would do his nut if he thought this place was turning into a scrap yard. As she rounded the mobile she called out. "Duke?"

"Millie?" Duke slurred.

"Are you drunk?" Millie looked Duke up and down and her chest tightened. "Christ man, sober yourself up, and quick."

"Connie won't come home...." Duke trailed off.

"Look we can sort out Connie later but first the plans come forward, we need to do it tonight." Millie tried to keep the urgency out of her voice, but she was now in full panic mode. Duke could hardly stand, never mind commit murder.

"Millie." Aron called as he stuck his head out of the door. "He's been like that the last couple of days, and what plan?"

"Get him inside and sober him up, I'll explain then." Millie watched as Jess joined Aron and they both man handled Duke back into the mobile.

"Coffee, where is it?" Millie pulled open the cupboards and riffled through. "Stick the kettle on.... oh here. Keep making them until I say." Millie knelt in front of Duke and held his face. "I need you to sober up."

"I have a daughter." Duke replied. "I have a daughter...."

"Duke, I need you, please." Millie begged. The knot in her stomach grew as she pleaded with him.

"He's not gonna sober up Mil. What's the urgency anyway?" Jess asked as he knelt next to Millie.

"Just sober him up." Millie stood and walked to the end of the mobile and started biting her nails.

"If you tell us, maybe we can help." Aron called. "Drink up dad."

"And maybe you can't. Duke owes me. It's his debt that needs paying." Millie replied.

Aron sighed. "We're your family as much as we are his Millie. Let us help."

Millie ignored him and turned as Duke gulped at the coffee before pushing the cup away. "I don't want that boy, where's my beer?"

"Oh Christ." Millie exclaimed as she threw her hands in the air. "I'll have to do it myself."

* * *

Millie stood back and watched as Jess and Aron lifted out the safe from underneath the floor. "You look like you're struggling boys."

"You could always give us a hand." Aron replied through gritted teeth.

"You need to put it in the Transit, and while you're at it, make sure Dukes okay, surely he should wake up soon?" Millie urged.

"He'll be fine when he wakes anyway, shouldn't you be phoning that man now. We don't want to hang around here too long?" Jess put the safe down on the sack barrow and grabbed the handles, while Millie watched him.

"I've got two calls to make, take that out while I make them." Millie picked up the phone and dialled Gladys. "I'm ready, phone Paul now and make sure he comes straight to you." She cut off the call then phoned Ronnie. "Ronnie, hello. Paul asked me to phone you, there's trouble at the docks. He's just left to go there with some of his men, but he thought you should be there too." Millie listened to the rant Ronnie threw at her and then placed the phone down. Her heart rate increased. So much could go wrong, but then she reasoned she had the element of surprise. Looking up when Aron and Jess both reappeared she smiled. "Now all we have to do is wait."

* * *

Millie clocked the headlights as they illuminated the quay side. "He's here and it looks like there's only one car. Wait around the corner. He will send his men to have a look around, so make sure you get them before they see you." Millie placed her feet up on Paul's desk and put her hands behind her head. She heard Ronnie's footsteps as he approached.

"WHAT IS THE FUCKING MEANING OF THIS?" Ronnie's voice bellowed as he stepped into the office.

"Ronnie. It's good to see you again." Millie greeted.

"Where's Paul?" Ronnie asked.

"Oh Paul's at work, he had some other business to take care of. You look a little shocked Ron, maybe you should sit down."

"I don't know what game you're playing Millie, but I can assure you Paul won't like it." Ronnie took a seat behind his desk. "In fact I reckon he will be heartbroken when he finds you dead."

Millie had remained focused on Ronnie as he spoke, her temper building. "Let's have a little chat, shall we?" Millie replied, almost cutting him off. She stood and walked towards Ronnie's desk and perched on the edge.

"We haven't got anything to chat about. My men are outside, as soon as I call them in, this." Ronnie pointed at Millie. "Will be over."

"Surely you want to know what this is about; I mean I would. Aren't you just a little curious?" Millie raised her brow.

"Fine, we'll play this little game of yours."

Millie eyed him carefully while he reached into his cigar box and pulled out a large cigar which he then lit and sat back. He blew the smoke directly at her while Millie waved it away. "You know those things are gonna kill ya, but I guess you don't need to worry about that now." Millie smiled as Ronnie's eyes narrowed. "Anyway, back to business. It all started at the club. You see, I watch people. I watch their body language, their movement, even the way they talk. I found you particularly interesting that night. The way you spoke down to people, especially me. I could tell straight away you didn't like me. You thought I was a threat. Paul loved me and you couldn't have that. You needed his full attention, so you could manipulate him. Paul always thought you were his mentor, but really you were using him. Paul was your scapegoat. Of course Paul didn't see it, why would he. His mentor could only do good in his eyes. You were like a second father to Paul." She knew her voice had a tinge of sadness to it, at the betrayal she felt on Paul's behalf.

"I've always thought of him as a son, you know that. So why has it come to this?" Ronnie shook his head. "I had such high hopes for Paul."

"Was that before you arranged to have Paul framed?" Millie saw the mild film of sweat break out on Ronnie's forehead.

"I have no idea what you're talking about, you silly girl."

"I warned Paul, but he believed you because he trusted you.... You know he told me the very first lesson you ever taught him. It was to never trust anyone. Not completely. Well, it got me thinking, you see when Paul realised something was wrong with this T Royal Holdings..."

"What?" Ronnie snapped.

"Yes, he noticed, you know, eventually. But I was already one step ahead. I had already worked out what you had planned" Millie paused and waited for Ronnie to reply.

"And what was that?" Ronnie wiped at his brow with his hanky.

"You feeling a bit hot there Ron?" Millie laughed, as she watched Ronnie's forehead glisten. She was enjoying this, maybe a little too much. "You had Paul sign all the dodgy paperwork; you were setting him up. Now I've got to admit, I scratched my head for a while. A man that's treated my husband like a son, a man that looked out for him inside, gave him direction. But that first lesson that you told him came back to me. Never. Trust. Anyone. Completely.... So, after the arson attack on one of Paul's pubs, I asked around. Seems you've been spending quite a bit of time on my manor while Paul had been in hospital. Throwing your weight around, acting like you owned the place. I've got to say, I'm extremely disappointed in you!"

"Millie. Dear sweet Millie. What do you plan to gain from this... My men are outside, you're already as good as dead." Ronnie grinned. "You can come in now." He called to his men.

The door opened and in walked Duke followed by Aron and Jess.

"Whoops, I forgot to tell you I have back up too." Millie turned to Duke. "Did you see Ronnie's men out there?"

Duke nodded. "They're a little tied up at the moment."

"So, what now, you gonna kill me, that will cause a war Millie, you know that." Ronnie half smirked. "And will Paul be happy with that?"

"Paul's weak when it comes to you purely because he feels he owes you, but I'm not. As for killing you. No, I'm not, but something else you probably missed. You remember Duke here, well, turns out he is my dad." Millie watched the colour leave Ronnie's face. "And we all know what those fucking gypsies are like for revenge. Fuck with one of their own and they will take the whole town out if they must.... Paul may have blinkers on when it comes to you, but I haven't." Millie glanced at her watch. "So now, as much as I want to kill you, I promised Duke he would get the honour." As Millie went to leave she stopped for a moment and turned to Ronnie. "Why Ron?"

"Paul was getting too successful. Too big, almost unstoppable. I had to bring him down a peg or two. It was never personal Millie, just business."

Millie walked outside and took a deep breath before she turned and nodded to Duke. "He's all yours."

Chapter Sixty-Three

Paul stood on the dock side and studied the burnt-out shell of his office. He was still in a state of shock that there had been a body found. It had been unrecognisable due to the fire, and he couldn't work out who would have been in there.

"Mr Kelly?" The police officer enquired.

"Yes." Paul turned his attention to the man.

"We've sent someone round to your business associate, Mr Taylor, to inform him." The police officer produced a notepad and pen. "Is there anyone you can think of that had a grudge against you?"

Paul blew out slowly. "No, not that I can think of, but in business you do make enemies.... I tried phoning Mr Taylor, but his wife said he had gone out in a hurry late last night."

The police officer took notes before asking. "Did you have anything of value on the premises?"

"No, just paperwork. Is there anything else officer, I need to get back to my wife, she will be worried." Paul looked at his watch, it was already 4.30 am.

"No Sir, we have your address if we need any more information."

With that Paul left and made his way home. His head throbbed at the thought of someone doing this to him. He knew Ronnie would have a fit at the pure audacity of the arsehole. He would turn London upside down and inside out, finding and punishing the scumbag.

The drive home was fast, as there was hardly any traffic and when he pulled up on his drive, he was grateful the house was in complete darkness. He let himself in, as quietly as he could, and tiptoed up the stairs to his bedroom. Millie lay there, asleep. He undressed quickly and climbed into bed then pulled Millie closer for a cuddle. He needed to feel the comfort he always got from holding her.

"Mmmm Paul?" Millie asked sleepily.

"Shhh, go back to sleep." Paul replied softly.

"What time is it?"

"It's late, now sleep." Paul stroked her face until he was sure she was asleep once more and then lay there till the morning, his head filled with thoughts of revenge.

* * *

Millie felt the bed move; she knew Paul was getting up. She glanced at the bedside clock. It was only 6.30am. She hadn't slept a wink either. After Duke and the boys had set the fire, they waited down the road for the fire engines to arrive. Once they had passed they made their way back home, with Millie jumping over the fence into her garden so she wouldn't be seen. She wondered how long it would be before they discovered the body was Ronnie's. She also wondered how Paul would take the news. Not well, she expected. Slowly getting up she made her way downstairs and into the kitchen. Paul was sitting there with his head in his hands. "Hey, are you okay?"

Paul looked up, his face a mixture between worry and anger. "The office at the docks was set fire to last night. They also found a fucking body. The police are gonna be all over this."

Millie did her best to look shocked as she made her way over to him. As she stood behind him she slipped her arms around his shoulders and squeezed. "Thank god you're okay. Have they any leads?"

Paul shook his head. "They don't even know who the body is, it was so badly burnt.... You know it could be the pikey's." Paul spun around and pulled Millie onto his lap.

"I doubt it Paul, what beef have they got with you now?"

"I don't know, but I'll find out. One thing I do know though, Ron's gonna do his fucking nut."

"Oh and we couldn't have that, could we." Millie bit her lip and wished she'd remained quiet.

"And what's that supposed to mean, you know Mil you seem awfully worried about the pikey's considering you want to move house to get away from them." Paul glared.

"And you seem awfully worried about what Ronnie fucking Taylor will think." Millie pushed his arms away and stood up. Annoyed, she walked to the window and stared out down the garden. She could see the roof of the mobile sticking over the fence. She wrapped her arms tightly around herself. "All I'm saying is don't cause another war with them. We don't need that, and you haven't got any proof it was them." Millie squirmed when she felt Paul's arms slip around her waist..

"Sorry I forgot your parents are pikeys, I'll mind what I say in future."

"Thanks for that Paul." Millie pushed him away. She knew this would be hard for him, but to make comments like that to her was unforgivable.

"I'll go and try Ronnie again; I would've thought he'd have rung me by now." Paul replied.

Millie put the kettle on then continued to stare out of the window. Would Paul turn on her when the truth came out. If it came out. Or would he turn on her one day because she was Duke Lees daughter. She knew how much he hated gypsy's, and here she was half of one. Millie poured the tea when Paul came rushing back into the kitchen. "I've gotta go babe. No one can find Ronnie, somethings not right."

The urgency in his voice annoyed her. "Where are you going?" Millie asked as Paul shoved one foot into his shoe.

"I'll go over to his place and then to the old bill station. I'll phone you when I know what's going on and I don't want you going out." Paul replied as he shoved the other foot in.

"I need to go out Paul, I need shopping..." Millie stopped when Paul grabbed her by the arm.

"I said I don't want you going out. Christ Mil, this fire's obviously personal."

"Paul you're hurting me." Millie shrugged Paul off and stared at him. "Maybe it was personal against Ronnie, he's the crook."

"We're both crooks you idiot, now do as you're fucking told. I've enough on my plate without having to babysit some gypsy lover." Paul replied and then stormed out.

Millie stood still; all she could see was the spiteful look on Paul's face. She knew he was worried, but even still he should not have spoken to her like that. "Idiot." She whispered. "Yeah, an idiot that saved your bacon." Millie ran upstairs and grabbed a case from the spare room. She threw in as much as she could before she headed back downstairs. Millie looked around the house that had become her home and felt the tears as they formed in her eyes. She wouldn't allow herself to cry. She had wasted enough tears on men that didn't deserve it. Instead, she slipped her wedding ring and engagement ring off and laid them next to the telephone with her door key. "I was treated like shit once before; I'll not be treated like it again." And with that Millie left the house.

* * *

After the short bus journey Millie stood in front of the house and just stared. She had no idea what she was doing here and felt her nerve falter. Just as she was about to turn around and leave, the door opened, and she saw Connie's concerned face looking back at her.

"Millie?" Connie asked.

"I had nowhere else...." Millie trailed off. She knew she was going to cry; she could feel the floodgates were at bursting point. "I need to go."

"Oh no you don't." Connie grabbed the case and led Millie in by the arm. "Come into the front room, I'll stick the kettle on and then you can tell me all about it."

Millie sat on the sofa and looked up at Connie in surprise. "You have a three-piece suite. It's nice."

"One of the neighbours gave it to me, when I told them I was looking for furniture. They also gave me a single bed that they were dumping. People can be nice." Connie smiled. "Sit there while I make the tea, do you take sugar?"

"One please." Millie replied. Her mind was still firmly on Paul and the way he had looked at her. She had never been frightened of him but this time she had flinched. Was it because she was scared or was it because she was guilty? That was something she would have to work out.

Connie came through with two cups of tea and placed them on an old wobbly coffee table. "The coffee table was a freebie too." She smiled.

"You've made the place homely." Millie pointed out. "But...don't you miss Duke and the boys?"

"Everyday." Connie replied sadly.

"Then why don't you go back to him?" Millie asked.

"I've always been someone's property Millie. First my parents and then Duke's. Don't get me wrong, I love Duke, more than he will ever know, but in all this mess, when I really needed him, he let me down." Connie reached for Millie's cup and passed it to her. "So, why have you packed your bags?"

"Truthfully. I'm sick of being the problem. He called me an idiot." Millie laughed bitterly. "Can you believe that, oh and let's not forget a gypsy lover that needs a babysitter.... But it was the look on his face when he said it, that was the last straw."

"I'm sure he loves you Millie, even if Paul and I haven't seen eye to eye, I can see it." Connie perched on the sofa next to Millie.

"If he loved me, he would never have made me feel like that, I've been there once before and I certainly ain't going back to that. Paul and I are finished." Millie felt the tears roll down her cheeks as Connie threw her arms around her.

Chapter Sixty-Four

Paul left the police station in a state of shock. The body they had found had been Ronnie's. They were certain of that as his dental records had been used to identify it. The old bill reckoned it was a burglary gone wrong. Ronnie had caught the assailants in the act and had been attacked and then set on fire. Paul climbed into his motor and started the ignition. There was only one place he wanted to be now and that was with Millie. He needed the comfort only she could give him. Would she though? He knew he had been bang out of order that morning. The look on her face had said it all. He blew out slowly as he started to pull away. His first stop would be the florist.

The journey home took longer than normal due to an accident on the A13. He had been diverted through Poplar and had taken an extra 45 minutes. Paul walked through the door with the large bouquet and headed straight into the living room. "Mil?" The house was silent as he waited for her reply. When none came, he ran up the stairs and searched the bedrooms then made his way back down, where he spotted Millie's front door key. His heart sank when he noticed her wedding and engagement rings nestled beside it. He turned and ran to the garden.

"DUKE." Paul screamed as he jumped the fence. "WHERE IS SHE?" He ran to the front of the mobile, his face set in anger. He spotted Duke as he came out of the door.

"Who?" Duke replied.

"My wife, where is she?" Paul clenched his fists as he neared Duke.

"She's not here." Duke stepped aside as Paul jumped up the step and searched the mobile. As he came back out he rounded on Duke. "Everything was fine until you turned up." Paul lunged at Duke and punched him in the side of the head. Duke blocked the second punch much to Paul's annoyance.

"Stop." Duke shouted as he held his hands against Paul's shoulders in an attempt to hold him back. "This isn't gonna solve anything.... What's happened with Millie?" Duke spat the blood from his mouth and wiped his chin on his wrist.

"She's left me." Was all Paul could say. The knot in his stomach tightened.

"Why?"

"We had a row this morning. If I can just find her, I can fix it." Paul looked at Duke. "If you know where she is, tell me."

"I don't know where she is for sure but maybe she's gone to Connie's."

"What. Wait, Connie doesn't live here anymore?" Paul asked, now confused. "I thought you went to get her back."

"I did, and I barged in and made it worse. Now I'm giving her time before I try again.... Paul, Millie's my daughter and..."

"She may be your daughter, but you don't know her, so save on the pep talk."

"I'm aware of that.... This whole things a fucking mess." Duke mumbled.

"I tried to speak to Millie, she shut it out, maybe that's how women deal with things." Paul sighed.

"I know she loves you.... She did something last night that more than proved that...You need to talk to her and let her explain."

Paul stood and looked down at Duke. "Okay. I'm going to get my wife back; I suggest you do the same."

* * *

Millie sat curled up on the sofa, the TV was on, but she paid no attention to it. Her mind was full of Paul. Paul and his hurtful words.

"Would you like another cup of tea Millie?" Connie asked.

"No thanks. I think three is more than enough, don't you." Millie replied. As she looked at Connie, she could see the worry lines etched into her face. "Why do you keep staring at me?"

"I can't believe I'm sitting here with my daughter.... It's what I've wanted since I first saw you."

"Oh yeah since you first started stalking me...." Millie trailed off when there was a knock at the door.

"I'll see who that is." Connie said, grateful for the interruption.

"I want to see my wife."

Millie heard Paul's voice drift into the front room. Her body tensed. She let out a loud sigh and walked to the door. "It's okay Connie, I'll handle this." She waited for Connie to leave before facing Paul. "What do you want, Paul?"

"I thought that would be obvious." Paul replied.

"No it isn't, enlighten me." Millie folded her arms defensively.

"I want you to come home Mil."

Millie didn't reply, she simply shook her head and started to close the door. She had expected an apology at the very least, but it was typical of Paul. Act like nothing had happened and everything would be fine. Until the next time.

"Mil, Ronnie's dead." Paul called.

"So?"

"A man's dead and that's all you've got to say. He was my friend."

"And how many men have you killed, or Ronnie? You know I bet they had friends and family too. Like you say he was your friend, so you deal with it." Millie closed the door and walked towards the front room, until the rattle of the letter box stopped her. She could see Paul's eyes through the gap.

"Millie, I'm sorry, it was all my fault. Please talk to me, let me explain." Paul called. "I'm not going anywhere until we've sorted this out. I mean it, I'll sleep on the step if I have to...... I love you."

Millie tiptoed up the stairs, she could see Paul's outline through the door, he had gone quiet. She pushed the window open and peered out. He sat on the step, his shoulders slumped. Millie stepped back and rubbed her forehead.

"Are you okay?" Connie asked.

Millie felt irritated by the question. No she wasn't okay. Her life had been one big fuck up since she had been born. "I'm fine." She lied. Millie sat back on the bed and stared at the sky. "It's starting to get dark."

"I'll do us some dinner." Connie replied. "I've got some sausages in the fridge."

"I'm not hungry." How could she eat with her stomach in knots? Millie massaged her temple, attempting to ease the pain that was building. "What's he doing now?"

"He's sleeping. On the step. Bloody hell, he must love you!" Connie stuck her head out one more time. "And he got you flowers."

"Well, we'll see how much he loves me by how long he stays there." Millie slumped back onto the bed, more confused than ever. She was having trouble shaking away the anger in Paul's voice. The accusations. The disappointment. "I'm going to get some sleep, close the door behind you, and thanks Connie."

"Don't you think we should talk?" Connie asked.

"About?" Millie replied. She knew what was coming and she wanted to avoid it.

"About? Millie I've just found my daughter.... I want to get to know you, know about your past. Be a part of your future...." Connie trailed off.

"I don't know what I want or how I feel." Millie replied sharply.

"You came here when you needed help, which must mean something." Connie reasoned.

Millie couldn't argue with that. She did come here. She wasn't sure why though. Was it because she wanted to get to know Connie? She had always wanted a mum, dreamed and wished for one, and now she had one, she didn't know what to do. "It's hard...." Millie replied.

"I know." Connie agreed. "It's hard for us all, especially Duke and Paul."

"Why Paul?" Millie frowned. "How is it hard for him?"

"He hates Travellers, especially Duke and now Duke's his father-in-law. I mean that's got to hurt." Connie reasoned.

Millie felt the bed move and looked up to see Connie sitting at the end. She had a gentle smile on her face. "I guess." Millie replied with a smile. "Look, I really need to get some sleep. We can talk tomorrow." Millie lay her head on the pillow and listened for the door to close. She had a lot to think about. If she took Paul back, would he still want her when she admits to Ronnie's murder?

Chapter Sixty-Five

Millie opened her eyes as the sound of chirping birds filled her head. She hadn't slept much, maybe a couple of hours on and off. She rubbed her eyes. Her life had become one big mess. Every time she thought she had it under control, boom, another bomb exploded and left a trail of destruction in its path. The latest being her marriage. Her mind flicked towards Paul. She threw the covers off and scrambled to the window. And there he was. He sat on the step with his elbows on his knees and his hands clasped under his chin. He had been there all night, waiting for her. She made her way downstairs, wearing only a cotton nightie. Which reminded her of something a granny would wear, Connie too, as she had lent it to her last night. She filled the kettle then placed it on the hob.

The house was deadly quiet, the only sound was the kettle as it started to boil. Millie filled the teapot, wondering if she was doing the right thing. She knew she had to face him, and she decided she would rather do it while Connie was asleep. When she had finished Millie then grabbed the cups and made her way to the front door. Placing one cup on the telephone table so she had a hand free to open it.

As she pulled the door open Paul's head turned and he reached for the tea, while Millie reached back for hers. Then she pulled the front door shut.

She sat on the step; Paul sat next to her and sipped the tea. "You always make a good cuppa Mil."

"I'm sure you haven't come here to talk about my tea making skills, so what do you want?" Millie asked sarcastically. She turned towards him. His shoulders were slumped, and he stared at the ground.

"I want my wife to come home, where she belongs." He replied as he rubbed the back of his neck.

"That's just it Paul, I don't belong there, in fact I don't belong anywhere." Millie placed her cup down and studied Paul. He looked rough, he had black circles under his eyes and stubble on his chin.

"Millie, you're my wife, you belong with me."

"There you go again. Dictating.... You demand I don't go out; you demand I keep my nose out of your businesses, which by the way I thought were 'our businesses'... I'm not a possession Paul, I'm your equal."

"It's my job to protect you Mil, I'm not gonna apologise for that." Paul replied sharply.

"It's my job to protect you too.... That's why I did what had to be done." Millie took a deep breath before she continued. "You said Ronnie had been acting strange. Well, I know why."

"Would you care to enlighten me then?" Paul asked.

"He was setting you up, with that fake company T Royal, which incidentally is an anagram of Taylor. Christ he must have thought you were stupid. I mean to dangle that so blatantly under your nose." Millie laughed. "Anyway, that's why you were the only one to sign any paperwork relating to it. Money was being syphoned into it, to make it look illegal and because you trusted Ronnie, you couldn't see it.... When you was in hospital I took my chance at finding as much out as I could, Ronnie obviously didn't like it and came moaning to you. You know it hurt me to see you run after him and take his side, that's when I realised, we weren't a partnership, but I was merely a possession."

"That's not true Mil, I did some digging after you said things weren't right. I had to keep Ron on side, so he didn't suspect.... There were anomalies with the accounts. But I hadn't finished investigating, and now he's dead...."

"I killed him." Millie blurted out. She watched the emotions flash across Paul's face. Disbelief, hurt, anger and then denial.

"What? Don't be ridiculous. Who are you covering for?" Paul demanded as he stood and loomed over Millie.

Millie stood and glared back at Paul, this time she wouldn't flinch or run. "And there you go again. Dismissing me. Well just for the record, I did, and before he met his end I asked him why, why was he setting you up and do ya know what he said...You were getting too successful, he had to take you down a peg or two."

Millie watched as Paul's scar started to raise, she wasn't sure if it was herself, he was angry with or Ronnie.

"I can't deal with this now." Paul turned and walked away.

Millie watched as she wiped her eyes, He couldn't even stand to look at her. She made her way inside and stopped. Connie was sitting on the bottom step. "How much of that did you hear?"

"All of it." Connie answered.

"I suppose you think I'm evil, killing someone?" Millie asked.

"Sit down Millie." Connie patted the step next to her.

Millie sat down and sighed. Of course Paul would side with Ronnie, he always had.

"Do you remember in the pub; you told me you didn't kill Billy?"

Millie nodded and kept her eyes on Connie. She seemed a little too calm. It's not every day you find out your daughter is a murderer.

"Duke killed him because I asked him to." Connie replied calmly.

"Why?" Millie asked.

"Because he would have come after you, and I couldn't have that, I lied to Duke, told him he had threatened me. So, you see Millie, we are the same. We will both do what we have to do, to keep our family safe. Paul will see that, just give him time." Connie patted Millie's knee. "I'll put the kettle on."

As Millie went to stand a frantic knock came from the front door. "I'll get it." As she opened it, she saw Paul standing with his hands in his pockets. "I'm not gonna lie Mil, I'm angry."

"So why have you come back?" Millie noticed the vein in his neck twitch.

"Because I love you and I want to save my marriage. But first I need to know what happened with Ronnie."

"Fine. I found out Ronnie was setting you up. So, I had the safe taken out and put somewhere no one would find it, and then I confronted Ronnie, Killed him, set fire to the office, and that's it. Nothing more to add...... I can see you're angry Paul. So, if you want revenge for your mate's death then you need to take it out on me."

"How did you kill him?"

"Does it matter how?" Millie wrapped her arms around herself and looked at the floor. There was no way she would involve Duke or her brothers. This was on her.

"Well you have been busy.... There's only one thing that don't make sense, there's no way you could have lifted that safe out on your own, but I guess you'll tell me who helped you when you're ready..... Do you still love me Mil?"

"Yes but loves not enough.... If you want to save this marriage you will treat me as an equal. I want to be involved in all the businesses, which by the way I think I've proven myself beyond reasonable doubt that I can handle, and I am going to learn to drive."

Millie watched Paul as he thought it over. "Okay, if that's what you want, but it's still my job to protect you and I will never apologise for that."

"We protect each other Paul, that's the point I'm getting at. Now, shall we go and see what's in that safe?"

Chapter Sixty-Six

Paul watched as Duke and his sons put the tyres back onto an old truck, which looked like it had been abandoned at the back of Duke's ground. "You turning this place into a fucking scrapyard now?"

"Paul, please." Millie held up her hand to stop Paul from speaking. "There's a good reason why this is here. Just watch."

"Ya know Millie, of all the men you could have married you pick him." Duke replied.

"Yeah she picked me, she didn't pick you to be her dad though, did she, she got lumbered with you." Paul took a step towards Duke as Duke turned to face him.

"Right, that's it. I've had enough of the pair of you." Millie glared between Paul and Duke. "Don't you think it's time you both try to get along.... For my sake?"

"Fine. I'll keep my thoughts to myself. Now can we go and get the safe Mil, I don't know why you've dragged me here." Paul replied with a huff.

"We are getting the safe Paul if you would kindly watch. Carry on Duke." Millie ordered.

Paul continued to watch as Duke moved the truck back and then jumped out and picked up a spade. He started to dig until he hit something hard. Paul walked towards the hole and saw the top of the safe. He grabbed one side of the safe while Duke grabbed the other. After lifting it out Paul thought about Ronnie changing the code. "I'll have to get someone to crack it open."

"How long will that take?" Millie asked as she looked at her watch.

"It shouldn't take long once he's here, I'll go and phone him now. Have you got something to cover this up with?" Paul asked Duke.

"I'll put some old tyres around it, no-one will see it." Duke called over his shoulder.

* * *

An hour later they stood around the safe as a close contact of Paul's cracked it open. As the door opened an inch the man stood up and looked at Paul. "I won't look, and I was never here."

Paul handed him an envelope of money with a nod and watched him walk away. "Right, let's see what Ronnie Taylor was up to." Pulling the door open Paul reached for a large bag and opened it. Tipping the contents onto the ground, Paul, Millie, and Duke stared in disbelief. "What the fuck?"

Duke bent down and picked the T-shirt up. It was blood stained and had two holes in it. "This is Rueben's, he used to wear this all the time."

Paul looked in the safe and reached for a gun that was placed at the back. He held it up to the others. "Well, this is definitely the murder weapon."

"So, Ronnie was fitting you up with murder as well as fraud." Millie replied. "So much for honour amongst thieves."

"There is no honour amongst thieves Mil." Paul shook his head. "Each one of them would turn you over for money or power." He added.

Duke looked at Paul then Millie. "Family is the only thing you can trust in this world, never forget that."

Millie thought of everything Duke and her brothers had done for her and then her thoughts turned to Connie. Connie had kept her safe from Billy. Maybe they could be a family "And on that note, don't you think you should go and get your wife back?" Millie asked Duke. "Because I think I'd like to get to know mine."

The End

About the Author

Carol Hellier was born in Oldchurch Hospital, Essex, in the mid sixty's. When she was in her mid-twenties she discovered her parents were in fact her grandparents, and her eldest sister was her mum.

She married a Romany and started her married life off living in a caravan/trailer. This has given her a useful insight into the Romany world which shows in her writing.

Now residing back in Essex, she spends her time working, writing and with family.

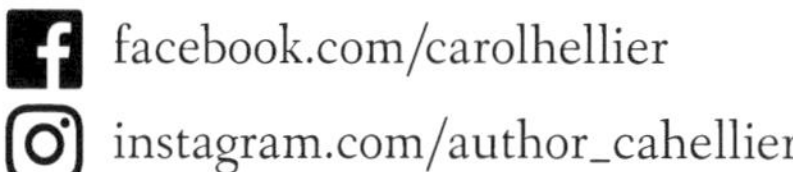

Printed in Great Britain
by Amazon